Monica La Porta

MARIE'S JOURNEY

Book 1.5 of the Ginecean Chronicles

To keep up to date with Monica's new releases and promotions
scan the QR code with your smartphone or mobile device.

To my husband, Roberto. Always.

TABLE OF CONTENTS

CHAPTER 1

Marie was happy. Only fifteen years old and she had been able to snatch one of the best jobs on the market. For being a fathered woman, she had done well. She had kissed her girlfriend good-bye. The moment had been uncomfortable for Marie, but judging from the amount of tears Idra had shed, it had been downright painful for her. Now, she was finally alone in her dorm—everybody was out to work at the farm. She looked around at the big room she had shared with thirty girls since her birth. It was a strange feeling to be finally leaving the Institute.

"I can't get away from here fast enough." She had said that so many times the other girls had started repeating the words to her as a joke. "I *really* can't get away from here soon enough." She walked to the end of the room and looked at herself in the long mirror precariously hanging on the wall. A pale, blond, big blue-eyed, freckled-skinned girl looked back at her. "Why so gloomy?" She went back to her bunk bed and jumped on, her shoeless feet dangling toward Idra's bed. Idra hated when she did that. *"Move those dirty feet away from my face."* Marie did that on purpose. She liked when Idra got all mad at her, her dark eyes staring up, her mouth pouting. It was worth the trouble because Idra couldn't stay mad long. Her laugh was what had attracted Marie to her. Now, someone else was going to sleep over Idra's bed. *But this is what I want, a chance to better my life.*

"Ready?" Madame Carla entered the room in that way of hers—without making a sound to announce her presence. More than once, Marie and Idra had been caught where they weren't supposed to be and paid for it. But Madame Carla wasn't a bad rector; she cared for her girls. *"You're my kids,"* she used to say anytime she had to dole out punishments, and inevitably, the guilty party felt even guiltier to have disappointed her so.

"I am." Marie looked at the satchel on her bed. All of her possessions had fit inside that small bag. She pulled the strings, tied them in a loose knot, and slung the satchel across her back.

"We're so proud of you." Madame Carla looked at her, eyes liquid already. One hand reached out to caress Marie's face in a maternal gesture.

"Thank you, Madame." She curtsied and lowered her head.

"It saddens me to lose you, but you must know how happy I am for you. Your accomplishment means a lot to this institution."

"Thank you, Madame," she repeated as she posed down in her curtsy and bow.

"Oh, dear child, enough of these formalities!" Madame Carla surprised Marie by hugging her in a fierce embrace.

Marie stood there, frozen, not sure of what to do.

"I can't believe you're an adult already." Madame Carla sniffed and released Marie. She then turned her back to her to clean her tears. "Well, it seems you've packed everything."

Marie smiled. It had taken less than five minutes to gather all her belongings and stuff them inside the satchel now lying almost weightlessly on her back.

"The bus has just arrived and they're in a hurry."

She followed Madame Carla outside of the dorm. The moment the crimson door slammed behind her, a feeling akin to panic possessed Marie. "I haven't said good-bye to the room." She looked at the rector, who nodded. She ran back inside, went to her ex-bunk bed, rummaged inside the satchel, and found what she was looking for, a hair barrette she had carved out of a piece of soft wood. She laid it on Idra's pillow, blew a kiss on it, and finally left.

On the bus, Marie walked toward the end and chose a free seat in the last row. She sat facing the window, her back to the two women talking to each other in the row next to hers. Her eyes snapped to something shiny protruding from her satchel. She hadn't noticed it back at the dorm. The room was always dark, only two windows to let the light in. It was the reason why they had moved the mirror from its original place and haphazardly hung it next to one of the windows.

"What is it?" She knew what it was the moment the small circle of glass beads came into view, and her eyes filled with unshed tears. *Idra...* A safety pin secured the bracelet to one of the satchel's strings. A small, red heart made of transparent glass dangled from the center of the bracelet. Two charms hung from it, an *I* and an *M*. Idra had written *Forever Together* on a round opal and Marie had helped her to attach it along with the rest of the charms. The bracelet produced a pleasant sound with every movement Idra made. Marie liked how she could hear Idra coming from far away. Now she would no more. She raised her wrist and let the bracelet sing for her. It wasn't the same. Sadness became a tangible pain, a sharp poke between her ribs just under her heart. She finally curled in a ball and sobbed. Thankfully, the two women didn't ask if she was okay.

Seven hours later, the cityscape of Samara loomed into view, and after another hour, the bus stopped before a big, old-looking building. She stared at the red bricks, slanted roof made of a dark metal rusted green in several places, and large, jutting windows. A sign read, "Redfarm," and a bell dangled at the end of a rope by a dark-red, wooden door. The bus had traveled all the way from Trin and the Maritime region to the inland in the very heart of the Mountainous region, but Marie had hardly seen anything beyond the glass she was staring at. She looked at her new home and immediately felt she didn't belong. She couldn't belong.

"Are you the new help?" A redhead waved at her from the entrance stairs.

She hadn't seen anybody coming out of the door. "Yes, I'm Marie from Madame—"

"You can tell me the whole story later, but hurry up now. You're late. Chef got sick and the staff needs help right away." The girl held the door for her and Marie followed inside, wondering if she had rushed through things and gotten everything wrong in the process.

Welcome to Samara, Marie thought, hurrying after the nameless woman whose majestic red mane undulated with every step she took. They went deep inside the building without leaving the same floor. They walked the whole length of a hallway that stretched forever. Sober décor and pale colors dominated the place. Marie had time to think, and her previous doubts became a certainty when, after five minutes of complete silence, the woman led her through an arch and inside a humongous kitchen. *What am I doing here?* She wanted to ask, but she was pushed past the threshold without as much as a please. The place was lit by four windows that took the whole back wall. A dozen women scurried about, the silence extending to the kitchen as well. Marie was unnerved by the lack of human interaction. She saw a thin woman walk toward her with a purposeful stride, only to stop a few feet away.

"Finally!" The thin woman, holding herself straight, her glasses pinched to the arch of her small nose by a long slim finger, gave her a judging look. "How old are you?" She turned toward the woman who had just brought Marie there. "How old is she?"

Marie felt she hadn't passed the test. "I'm fifteen years old, ma'am."

"You don't look fifteen. You look twelve." The thin woman straightened her back and looked down at Marie. "We'll make do for now." She went to a linen cabinet, took out an apron, and double-checked the size by opening it before Marie, then shook her head. She repeated the action twice and finally gave Marie an apron.

It's just an apron. Marie managed to keep her mouth shut and thank the thin woman without commenting.

"Carnia, you can leave." The thin woman dismissed the other. "Now, you'll start peeling potatoes—"

"Peeling potatoes? No, there must be some confusion... I'm Marie and I come from the Institute. Madame Carla talked to Redfarm's rector and she said I was going to start as an apprentice at the infirmary."

"I know what I told Carla." The thin woman pointed at the corner where a pile of potatoes lay on the floor by what looked like an ancient cauldron from some twisted fairytale.

Marie raised her eyes to meet Madame Lana, a person she had thought would be completely different and way more pleasant. "Madame Lana." She curtsied low. "I thought—"

"You thought what? That I would put you to work in the infirmary without a minimum of training? Is that what you thought?"

4

"No, of course not. I thought I was going to be trained in the infirmary."

"You must prove to be infirmary material, and then maybe I'll send you there. I can't believe my ears. The silliness coming out from your mouth. From now on, remember to talk only if asked to. Are we clear?"

"Yes, Madame Lana."

"Now go and peel that pile." The rector left the room, talking to herself. "We've important guests tonight. And Chef got sick! Of all days, Chef decided to get sick today. Can you believe my bad luck?"

If I were Chef, I'd have gotten sick myself. Marie looked at the corner Madame Lana was pointing at, the huge cauldron still there with the pile of potatoes, and dragged her feet toward it. The shock was such she couldn't cry. Not before Madame Lana, who was looking at her, waiting for her to break. Not before the dozen people who were busying themselves while listening to the conversation. She tied the apron, doubling the string on the front, sat on the three-legged stool, and began peeling potatoes. She was still wearing Idra's bracelet and every time she flicked away a peel, the charms hit each other and sang for her. She was sure Madame Carla didn't know about her new arrangement. Madame Carla would have never tricked one of her kids to accept a job under false pretenses. Two hours passed and she was still peeling potatoes. And so was she two hours later. Her hands were covered in blisters, her back was killing her, her butt had lost sensitivity along with her legs, but Marie didn't say a thing.

"I think that's enough potatoes for tonight," a girl, probably two or three years older than her, said. She had walked quietly and Marie hadn't heard her approaching. "I'm sorry I scared you. I didn't mean to."

"Don't worry. I was lost in thought." Marie saw the girl smiling at her, and she relaxed her shoulders.

"Yes, I can see how peeling vegetables can lead to hard thinking." The girl laughed, a genuine laugh, not something artificial. "I'm Verena, your roommate."

Verena was tall and curvy with long, brown hair left unbraided, big brown eyes, and tan skin. Madame Carla had mentioned a roommate. "Oh, you're Verena. I'm Marie. Nice meeting you." Marie reached out to shake hands with her, but her fingers refused to open from the curled position they had assumed. She bumped knuckles instead.

"Come, your turn was done an hour ago."

"But nobody told me—" Marie looked at the potato peelings lying by the cauldron, worried she would get in trouble if she didn't clean up. She saw a broom and a dustbin by the other corner, but Verena was faster than she was.

"I'll do it."

"Thanks."

"No worries. Every girl went through a similar period of assessment when she arrived at Redfarm. Madame Lana thinks it's good for character."

"Good for character? How?" Marie sat on the stool again. She was too tired to stand and she hadn't eaten since morning. Her head spun the moment she stood.

"She thinks it's easier to separate good people from the bad under duress. You normally show your true colors when put in trying situations."

"Do I have to expect more of this?"

"You'll remember peeling potatoes as the highlight of your time at Redfarm."

Marie heard Verena's tone, but she had the feeling the truth wasn't far from her attempt at a joke. "Where to?"

"Four floors up. The apprentices' wing. You'll like your new room. You'll see. We've a partial view of the lake, and on clear days, the Crystal Mountain peak is visible above the clouds."

"Yeah." Marie tried to raise a fist in the air to show her enthusiasm, but the gesture didn't come out as planned. She tried a smile instead.

"You don't have to try so hard." Verena laughed and walked ahead.

Four floors up. Somehow, the partial view of the lake didn't seem worth the trouble. Marie dragged her tired feet up the four flights of stairs. She had the distinct feeling every step was really four.

"Here it is, your new room." Verena opened a plain door and gestured for Marie to enter.

"Thank you." Marie peered inside, her lack of enthusiasm starting to get on her own nerves. "It's actually nice." She directed her tired body toward the one bed without personal items on it. "I didn't expect it to be so big."

"This is big?" Verena sat on one of the two chairs sitting by the small desk under the window.

"It is for me. I've been sleeping with thirty girls for fifteen years. Sharing this whole room with only one person is wonderful." Marie looked around, taking in the details. "You did a great job with this place."

"Thank you, but there wasn't a lot of space to work with, so it was easy."

"Love these curtains." Marie walked to the desk and took a closer look at the fabric. "It looks like Madame Carla's Sunday dress."

"It's just linen." Verena smiled.

"You think I'm an overly simplistic girl, don't you? That I've never seen anything." Marie pinched the fabric between her fingers. *I'd love to wear something made from linen.*

"No… I'm sorry. I didn't mean it that way. I—" Verena was at her side, one hand on Marie's arm.

"It's okay. I haven't seen anything." Marie laughed. The first laugh of the day, and it felt good. "I lived all my life within Madame Carla's institute. She's kind of protective and she didn't let us out without a proper chaperone."

"You had a chaperone? Why?"

Marie opened the curtain to get a look at the famous view. "The Institute is in a dangerous part of Trin. Between firework farms."

"And… Oh, I got it."

"Not a lot to look at today, is there?" Marie squinted. The low sunrays were reflected in hundreds of miniature rainbows by the droplets of rain on the glass panel.

"Too many clouds today."

Something caught Marie's attention. Four floors below, there was hurried activity that looked at odds with the forced quiet of the place. "Are they who I think they are?" She knew who they were. She could see them well enough.

"Yes, Redfarm uses workers for the harder tasks." Verena came closer and looked down.

"Aren't you scared?" Marie gave another look. Two men were carrying a heavy-looking plank of wood. She could see their strained muscles and the sweat glistening on their naked arms.

"They're confined in their quarters in a separate wing and normally never work so close to the main building, but at the carpentry. Madame Lana has everybody on pins and needles because of tonight's dinner. She ordered a gazebo built in one day and that's why the workers are here. There." Verena pointed at a white structure at the other end of the courtyard. "See? The place must be cleared before the dinner starts. Captain Callista imported guards from a nearby farm to help keep the men under control."

Marie shivered. "You never know with workers. That's why Madame Carla's so protective. The Institute is sandwiched between the two firework factories and they are always full of men." Another shiver ran down her spine, yet she kept looking. The two workers were almost out of her line of sight when one of them, the one with the lighter skin, looked up. For a moment, despite the physical distance separating the ground floor from her window, she thought their eyes locked.

"Come. I'll show you where the bathrooms are."

Marie was startled by Verena's words. She hadn't realized the girl had moved to the other side of the room. She was about to move, but on impulse, looked down. The men were gone.

"Coming?"

"Yes, right away." Marie closed the curtain, her eyes fleetingly going to the courtyard one last time. She shook her head.

"Something wrong?"

"No, just tired." Marie followed Verena into the hallway and soon realized she better memorize the route to the bathrooms. The apprentices' wing was a giant indoor maze. There were so many twists and turns it was impossible to remember which way to go.

"Don't worry. You won't get lost."

"Am I that transparent?"

"I probably wore the same expression on my face the first time I was shown around." Verena finally slowed down. "Those are our bathrooms." She turned around and indicated a second door. "And those are the elders' bathrooms. Never, ever, use the elders' bathrooms. They can be mean."

"Noted. Elders are mean everywhere. But back at the Institute, we didn't have enough space to separate dormitories and bathrooms, so the elders had to share the place with us. At least here, we have our bathrooms. There, we had to ask permission for every single thing."

"You had to ask permission to use the bathroom?"

"Of course." Marie shrugged at the recent memories. Idra had saved her from the ire of an elder more than once. "When I'm an elder, I'll never be like them." A promise she had worded every time Idra had to rescue her. Idra. *What are you doing now?* Dinnertime at the Institute had already come and gone. *Are you singing by the fire with Joanna and Marcia?* They had sung every time one of their friends had left the Institute to work or to learn a profession somewhere else. *Are you singing for me? Do you miss me already?* Marie had been so excited to leave the Institute she hadn't realized she was indeed leaving it for good.

"I never thought bathrooms could get people so emotional." Verena laughed.

Marie got a glimpse of herself in the mirror and saw her eyes were liquid and a tear hung to her eyelashes. "The separate stalls undid me."

"Do you want to refresh a bit? We still have time to eat."

Marie nodded, already longing for the big shower at the end of the room. A low growl coming from her stomach forced her to reassess her priorities. "It sounds great, but I'm too hungry. I need to eat something or I'll faint."

"Washing is overrated, anyway." Verena led the way down to the kitchens.

Marie noticed the big windows opening onto the stairs and illuminating the whitewashed walls with the calming tones of the early evening colors. She risked a look outside without daring to lean closer. Samara's dark rooftops filled the frames. The urge of looking down at the backyard was strong, but one sideways glance from Verena and she steered away from the windows.

"Samara is a nice city. I'll show you around as soon as we've the first day free."

"Looking forward to that." Roaming without adult supervision was one of the reasons she had wanted this job, but now the thought was bittersweet. They had reached the first floor when a sudden commotion commanded her attention to the world outside the immaculate panes of the windows. A whirl of colors went from one corner to the other of the glass frame. The sound of an angry whistle reached inside along with the sharp crack of a whip hitting the concrete floor. Marie was startled when a moment later, several women passed them and went outside through a door at the end of the stairs. One of them pushed Marie out of the way without as much as a "pardon me."

"Hey!"

"Don't mind those Elders. They're training to impress Captain Callista and get a shot at entering the Priestess's Army."

"Oh, they are? But they aren't pure breeds, are they?" As far as she remembered, only the captain would be a pure breed.

"No, of course not. They wouldn't be here otherwise."

"So how does it work?"

"The Army is only served by women."

"So they aspire to be the soldiers' maids?"

"Yes, but between you and me, none of them are good enough. Most likely, they'll end up serving farm guards as their maids. But they like to pose as if they're big shots."

"Where're they going?" Marie flattened against the wall as two latecomers ran down the stairs to reach the other army wannabes.

"To help outside with the men. But everything is already under control." Verena went to the window and pointed out.

Marie came close and tried to look uninterested.

"See? As I told you, no need for those idiots to make such a fuss." Verena turned and descended the last three steps, leaving Marie behind.

Marie lingered a moment and felt slightly disappointed there wasn't anything to see—just an empty courtyard and a lovely gazebo where several girls were now hanging delicate flower garlands. She followed Verena to the kitchen and remembered she was ravenous only when the smell of roasted meat wafted into the hallway and her stomach ached.

Later that night, she went to sleep with the unsettling feeling she didn't want to spend any time in a room with only one other person. It was wrong. She fell asleep and woke in the first hours of the morning, the sun slowly rising over Samara, its rays glinting off the sleek dark tiles covering the roofs in symmetric rows. It had rained again during the night and the city looked cleaner from her vantage point. She tiptoed to the bathroom, had the shower she hadn't taken earlier, then headed downstairs to eat breakfast. She was surprised to see nobody around. At the Institute, Madame Carla had taught the girls that sleeping late denoted lack of morals. Evidently, as stern as Madame Lana looked, her vision of what made a young girl a better human being didn't encompass her sleeping habits. *Maybe I'll like it here after all.*

Alone, she took the luxury of looking outside the windows on the stairs as long as she wanted. The men were cleaning the courtyard. The dinner must have ended late because the decorative lanterns hanging from the gazebo's posts were still burning. She stood, unable to move. She was both repulsed and attracted by the sight of so many men gathered in such a close space. One of them turned and looked in her direction. Theirs eyes met and she had the unsettling feeling he was the same man she had seen the day before. Marie was shocked she might have looked at a man long enough to recognize him, and even more shocked he didn't attempt to lower his head. Even though she was inside the building and he outside, the worker should've shown more respect and averted his green eyes as soon as she had looked at him. She raised her chin and stared down at him, but the man didn't seem affected by her display of power. Steps echoed in the deserted staircase, and she looked away for a moment, her heart beating loudly against her ribcage. When the person stopped at the second floor instead of descending toward her, Marie dared to look outside one more time, only to find the man staring back at her with a grin on his face. She ran away, reaching the kitchen in no time.

She knew a day of menial tasks awaited her, but when Carnia entered the kitchen a full two hours later to give her the chores list, Marie almost smiled. She was craving human contact.

"Did you sleep well?" Carnia asked, waving the list like a flag.

"Never better." She took the already crumpled piece of paper from Carnia's outstretched hand and gave a look at the items written in neat handwriting. "More potatoes in my future. Great."

"And don't forget to replenish the pantry when you're done peeling the ones inside the barrel."

At least I get to walk a bit, Marie thought after Carnia explained where the fresh vegetables where kept. Not that going back and forth from the cellars was worth celebrating, but it sure beat sitting the whole day on a three-legged stool. She gave the list another look and sighed. *This is not what I thought it would be.* She busied herself with her second meal of the day. She had woken so early she was hungry again, but it was a nervous hunger, an ache that didn't start from her stomach, but from her chest and left her lightheaded. She wolfed down two pancakes, then went to take her place by the corner where the potatoes were waiting for her.

When a pile of potato peelings reached as high as the now-empty bucket, she was grateful for the opportunity to leave the kitchen if only to run an errand. "Where are the cellars?" she asked the first person she saw. The room had populated while she was going through the whole barrel. She had noticed the hustle, but the helpers were so quiet it was unnatural. Not a laugh, not a word of gossip to be heard, just the clicking of the copper potteries and the stirring of spoons against ceramic surfaces. And the pleasant smell of fresh-baked bread and pastries.

"First door on the right, two floors down, follow the corridor." A small girl, no older than Marie, answered her question, barely raising her head from the stove where she was preparing what looked like egg cream custard. "Remember, two floors down, not one or you'll risk interrupting Captain Callista's training sessions. And you don't want that."

"I don't want that," Marie repeated, bringing her index and middle finger together to her forehead to give the girl a mock salute. "Thanks." She left the kitchen in a breeze and descended the flight of stairs, taking longer than necessary, anything to delay going back to that room. She reached the corridor with a heavy heart, thinking she felt less alone down there, where there was nobody, than in that kitchen full of silent, busy people. The cellar door was an imposing, scary piece of dark wood carved with a décor that must have at one time been nice, but was now faded and mutilated. She pushed the wood and it creaked on its hinges. Darkness engulfed her, and a slight sense of panic pressed on her chest. "I am not afraid of dark." Following the usual mantra, she breathed in and out while her right hand probed the wall by the door, looking for a switch. Muffled voices filtered through the walls and echoed inside the place. Her heart jumped.

"Who's there?" The voices—male voices, she realized—didn't stop talking. Her fingers touched the switch and the cellar was illuminated in a crude, too-bright, white light. She shielded her eyes for a moment, then looked around. The place was empty. The workers were in the adjacent room.

She should've run away anyway. Instead, she followed the sound and walked toward the farthest wall at the end of the cellar, but lost them somewhere in the middle of the walk. The opulent sight of the cellar's bounty stole her attention. Shelves full of fruits and vegetables, cheeses, meat in various stages of being cured, and bottles of wine lined the walls. The place was stocked with food, more than she'd ever seen in one place. At the Institute, girls never went hungry, but portions were rationed and desserts were reserved for special occasions. Madame Carla ate the same diet as her pupils, which had probably contributed to her slender figure. For a moment, Marie was tempted to hide a piece of marzipan under her shirt and feast on it later. She reached out to the closer shelf where she had spotted the treat, thrilled by her daring, when a sudden noise startled her. Her outstretched fingers froze in midair.

"Don't do it!" a deep, male voice commanded.

"I bet your dinner you won't do it," a second voice said. A younger man.

"And what if I do?" Another male voice, as young as the first.

Marie's head snapped to the right where the voices sounded clearer and closer. The men were on the other side of the cellar's wall. She thought she should've run back to the safety of the silent kitchen and yet again, she didn't move.

"I'll do it." A soft, scratching noise accompanied the statement.

Marie looked at the spot in the wall, and a breath caught in her chest. A few moments later, a brick was removed and it disappeared on the other side. Before a second brick could follow the first, she lunged toward one of the shelves standing in the middle of the room and crouched behind two big sacks packed with flour. Several bricks were dislodged until a rectangle opened on the darkness of the other side.

"Told you. You owe me your meal tonight." A head covered in dark-blond hair pushed through the opening, but didn't make it far. "Still too small." The head moved back and other bricks were removed. Not a minute later, a young man entered the room by lifting his body up and away from the freshly made window. He reached the floor with a small jump, both feet firmly on the ground, knees slightly bent.

It's him! Marie couldn't believe her eyes. The green-eyed man who had been staring at her had just trespassed into the cellar.

"Don't waste time. Take what you can and come back here." An older man appeared at the window, his face and shoulders leaning inside the cellar while he took a good look at the place. "Take this and move."

"God above! This place is stocked." The blond took the bag the man offered him and went to the shelf by the opening. "We starve to death and here there's enough food to feed the whole Priestess's Army." He grabbed fruits and vegetables and stuffed the bag with them. "Another one," he said to the man, passing him the bag.

"I think we got enough—"

"Another one. Hurry." The young man snatched a second bag from the man's hands and went to steal some more food. "What do you want to eat for dinner tonight?"

"I haven't had meat in three months," the man said with a grimace.

Someone from the other side, the third voice Marie had heard, spoke. "Please, Grant, let me have a steak tonight."

"Sure thing." The young man, Grant, looked purposefully around.

Marie saw him coming closer. She raised her eyes to look at the same thing he was looking at and saw the quartered chunks of what had been a big cow hanging from hooks over her hiding spot. He had already taken hold of the biggest piece when steps resonated from far away and Marie's name was called several times. He started running, but one of the loose sandals he was wearing slipped away and he stumbled. He reached the floor, but to break the fall and save his face from being smashed, he had to use both hands and he let the meat fall. It landed with a big thud only an inch shy of hitting Marie. He followed his prized, stolen possession and found her as well.

"Where are you, girl?" Verena called from the corridor.

Marie heard her friend, but she wouldn't answer. The man brought one finger to his mouth, silently asking her to keep quiet. His familiar green eyes were staring at her and he was slowly shaking his head.

"You didn't see me," he whispered and, piece of butchered animal on his shoulders, left, retracing the same route he had come from.

"Marie? Are you there?" Verena entered the cellar.

Without thinking, Marie stood and ran to meet the girl before Verena could see the hole in the wall.

"What are you doing?" Verena eyed her suspiciously.

Marie shrugged and walked out of the cellars. "I couldn't find the potatoes."

CHAPTER 2

The rest of the day passed in a blur. Marie knew she had to confess what she had seen. She thought about it and even came close to telling everything to Verena, but she didn't. At lunch, when everybody sat at the big communal table for the midday break, she stood silent. For dinner, she acted from the same script. She felt guilty for not talking to an adult and was terrified somebody could read it on her face, so she kept to herself.

He's called Grant. Somehow, the fact she knew the man's name made her feel even guiltier. *Grant.* Thinking about his name felt too intimate. She tried to divert her thoughts to safer topics. *What are they doing at the Institute? Are they already asleep?*

"Are you all right?" Verena asked once they were back in their room later that night.

Marie looked at her, once again debating if it was a good idea to spill her secret, then shook her head and answered, "Peeling potatoes all the day long isn't conducive to extreme euphoria."

"Humph…"

"Take my place tomorrow and see if you look better at the end of the day."

Verena didn't press the subject and went to take a shower. Marie followed her a few minutes later, but when she saw the long line of girls waiting for their turn to wash after a long day of working, she retraced her steps before Verena saw her. At the end of the long hallway, pale-blue moonlight illuminated the floor and the walls in a floral pattern cast by the light coming through the intricate latticework decorating the window. She walked toward it, attracted to the cold glass like a moth to the flame. She stopped before the window and leaned against it, her nose and forehead resting lightly on the dewy surface to cool her thoughts. Four floors below in the walled backyard, the men were still at work. She automatically searched the crowd for one blond head.

"Don't tell me you're the sleepwalker kind."

Marie spun around at Verena's words, her heart beating at double speed. "What…? No—"

"You're awake, good. Let's go down for the fire pit stories."

"I'm tired and I need to wash." Marie yawned and made to go back to their room.

"Nonsense. Sleeping can wait. We only have fire pit stories once per season. You don't want to miss them." Verena's expression didn't allow any other answer than yes.

"Maybe… I'll stay for a little while."

"Oh, you'll see. Once the elders start telling the stories, you won't leave until the last word is said." Verena took Marie by the elbow and redirected her toward their room. "Wear something warmer. It gets chillier later at night."

"Later? How late are we talking about?" Marie went to grab her only sweater.

"Don't you have anything, let's say, heavier, like made of wool or something?" Verena took one of the dangling sleeves from the sweater Marie was donning. She tested it between her fingers. "What's this made of, anyway?"

Marie freed her head from the sweater's neck—it had belonged to Idra and was two sizes too large for her. "Bamboo."

"You got to be kidding. Bamboo? Really?"

"Yep, bamboo. In the Maritime region, temperatures reach smoldering levels. Bamboo keeps your body cool. We also make sheets and duvets with bamboo fibers."

"But does it keep you warm?" Verena arched one eyebrow.

"Well, I don't have anything else to wear, so I guess I'll find out tonight." Marie was actually looking forward to being cold to have an excuse to bail out of socializing.

A few minutes later in the hallway, they joined a river of girls happily walking down the stairs. Laughs and sensible conversations all around her, Marie felt like a fish out of water. *Idra, I miss you.* Verena introduced her to several apprentices, but Marie didn't make an effort to memorize all their names. They looked nice, but she wasn't interested in getting to know anyone new that night. Despite her long face, two girls decided to hang around: Laila, a small blonde, and Cina, a tall and lanky brunette. Marie answered the ordinary questions about how she liked it so far and if she thought working in the kitchen sucked with monosyllabic grunts. Laila and Cina didn't seem to be put off by her reaction and so she let them do all the talking until something the blonde said made her pay attention.

"They're going to announce the donors tomorrow. Aren't you worried?" the girl asked Verena. "You've been here long enough and you have a sturdy build."

"Of course I'm worried, but what can I do if they choose me? It's not like I can say no."

Marie shivered.

"Oh, no. Marie, you're going to be fine. You're just fifteen." Laila smiled at her. "Captain Callista has never picked a girl younger than eighteen. I think there must be some kind of rule."

"And you're so slim. Donors are never thin. So maybe you'll never be chosen." Cina took Marie's hand in hers to give her some comfort. "Look at Verena. She's the perfect donor."

"And I've just turned eighteen. Lucky me."

"Maybe you're going to be lucky this time." It was Marie's turn to console the girl.

"Chances I can escape it forever are slim. I'll be eligible for seven years, and with my physique, it's almost a given I'll be a donor sooner or later."

"But I heard it's not as terrible as it was for our grandmothers. Now you won't come in contact with the sementals at all." Marie blushed as soon as she said the word semental.

"Still…"

"We won't treat you differently if you got picked tomorrow. I promise I'll be your friend no matter what happens." The brunette, Cina, hugged Verena and Laila joined her.

Marie looked at the group of friends and felt out of place when one of the girls sniffed, maybe Verena—but the sound came from within the human block of intertwined teens and it could've been any of them. She'd never met a donor. Madame Carla was protective of her girls to the extreme. There was a rumor that the Institute rector starved her children to prevent them from becoming donors. Marie had never believed it. Food was scarce in general. But it was true nobody was allowed to gain weight through a daily routine of physical activities that nobody was excused from. Rain or shine, the girls had to run, squat, and lift weights for two hours every day of the week. Madame Carla explained her fixation with the reasoning the chances a fathered woman being employed by a pure breed family were strictly related to her looking good. Why a woman would look better when she was a stick on legs was beyond Marie's comprehension. She was instinctively attracted by fuller figures. Idra. Beautiful, curvaceous Idra, who had never lost a pound despite the harsh dietary regimen of the Institute.

"You won't be chosen." Marie reached out one hand to touch Verena's head.

Verena disentangled herself from the communal hug and tried to smile. "We're going to be late. You know the elders don't like it when they are interrupted mid-story."

Cina and Laila nodded. They hurried outside, running down the last flight of stairs and heading toward the walled courtyard Marie had spied upon earlier. "But—" For a moment she worried they would see men up close and personal. Then she remembered the workers weren't usually employed inside Redfarm. At ground level, the courtyard looked bigger and emptier without the frenzy of activities the white gazebo had required. The structure was now towering in its brightness against the dark canvas of the night sky. Verena took her by the elbow and broke in a sprint, only to stop before the structure.

"It's so pretty." Marie couldn't help but feel like a little kid, a big smile on her face and wide eyes. "A fairytale house." The shimmer from countless candles waved with every gust of playful wind, giving it an undulating quality that added to the atmosphere. "Like being underwater." The low murmur from a crowd of happy girls came to an end when one elder stood and took the floor, raising her hand over her head. Marie joined Verena, Cina, and Laila on the wooden floor along the rest of the crowd.

"Apprentices!" the elder intoned. "We've gathered tonight to celebrate another great quarter for this farm. Let's ask the Goddess for another fruitful season. Let's have—"

Marie stopped listening; she was more interested in looking at the older girl, the way her long, fair hair almost brushed the floor, moving in sync with the wavering lights. Everybody applauded something the elder had just said and she did the same, looking right and left to get an idea of what they were doing. Madame Carla wasn't big on formalities and the elders at the Institute never had any propensity for them, either. The intensity in this elder's voice and her regal appearance intimidated Marie. A priestess-in-training syndrome it was called. A joke, a cruel, cheap expression used by pure breeds when they wanted to put a fathered woman back in her rightful place: way beneath them. But the expression did come to Marie's mind in regard of the long-haired beauty talking to the apprentices as if they were garbage. *You aren't better than us, just older,* she thought and then, with a hint of malice on her mind, added, *You'll never be anything else. Just a fathered woman like me.* Apparently, she was the only one who wasn't focused on the elder's words. Four or five more bursts of applause and another elder, a slightly less exalted copy of the first, took her spot to tell the first story of the night.

Marie liked to hear a good tale like anybody else and her eyes and focus zeroed in on the newcomer.

"Darlene is one of the best storytellers. You'll see." Cina elbowed Marie. "I'm sure you've never heard anybody so good."

Cina wasn't exaggerating. Darlene had a gift. The whole time the elder spoke, not a single breath was heard. Darlene's voice was pleasant enough, but the quality of the narration was what kept everybody glued to the story she slowly unraveled. "What a complicated plot, and with so many characters." Marie shook her head in awe, unable to shush her inner thoughts. "She sure has a great imagination."

"It's said she's *friends* with the captain..."

"Oh, do you mean...?" Marie lowered her voice to a whisper.

"I mean what you're thinking. Darlene has special permission to watch TV with her pure breed friend."

"I'd give anything to watch a TV show again." Marie had a glimpse of a television show once and sighed at the memory. Madame Carla installed the television for the pure breeds who occasionally visited the Institute to snatch promising fathered girls. Although usually locked, during one of those visits, someone left the television room open and she snuck in and turned on the big screen. She had reverently taken the remote control in her hands and flickered through channels until she had found the program she was looking for. She had loved every one of the four minutes the wondrous experience had lasted before a pure breed caught her and sent her away. In her mind, she still played the photograms over and over, adding parts to the story she imagined happened right before and after those four minutes. It was a historical show. The actresses wore beautiful dresses and there was a duel being fought over a wife's stained honor. The pure breed had showed up at the exact moment the pistols shot. Marie had begged the woman to let her see the end. Still to this day, she didn't know who had died because of the gunshot. Marie's malcontent toward pure breeds and what they stood for probably took form that day.

"Me too," both Cina and Laila commented, bringing Marie back to the present.

Verena was silent. Marie noticed how the girl watched Darlene as if she were the last drop of water in the desert and felt sympathy for her. She knew exactly how that story was going to end, with Verena's heart broken. It wasn't uncommon that fathered girls, especially if beautiful, chose to elevate their lives by attracting pure breeds' attentions. It normally meant a job inside that pure breed's family and a series of privileges that lasted as long as the fathered girl's beauty stayed fresh. Not the life Marie would have wanted for herself, but good enough for many other fathered women. When you were born on the wrong side of the woman race, there weren't a lot of choices. Still, she wouldn't have condemned herself to a loveless life just to eat or dress better. She nudged Verena's shoulder with hers and when the girl turned, she smiled at her.

Verena lowered her eyes and blushed. "Am I that easy to read?"

Marie shrugged but tilted her head slightly and widened her smile.

"She deserves a better life." For the briefest of moments, Verena's gaze went back to Darlene. "I know I'll never be able to give her what she wants." She slowly uncurled from her sitting position. "I need to loosen up my legs."

"I'll come with you." Marie would have preferred to stay and listen to some more stories, but it was clear Verena could use some company and neither Cina nor Laila were looking in their direction, their faces rapt by the narration. "You too deserve a better life, you know?" Marie said, unable to contain her frustration at Verena's fatalism. "I know I deserve better than peeling potatoes."

"You must come from a nice place."

"I suppose I do." Once again, sadness invaded her heart at the consideration she wasn't at the Institute anymore. They moved silently, exiting the gazebo without disturbing the other girls.

Verena led her to a darker corner. "They can't see us from there."

"Does she know your feelings?" Marie looked around, letting her eyes get used to the dim light surrounding them. Only a flickering sconce illuminated the archway at the end of a small courtyard created by the recessing walls of the building. She looked up, wondering which wing the walls belonged to.

"I was stupid enough to declare my love." Verena laughed.

Marie lowered her eyes to the herringbone-patterned cobblestones. "I'm sorry." What else could she say? It wasn't that she had any experience in unrequited love. She had kissed Idra and Idra had kissed her back. And before Idra, there had been nobody else. She was only fifteen, not old enough to have her heart broken.

"Well, I should've known better." Verena walked slowly, kicking a pebble that skidded on the stone pavement with a pleasant metallic sound. She stopped under the sconce and removed a small box from one of the pocket on her pants. "Mint?"

"No, thanks—" Something moved under the archway and Marie jumped.

"What is it?" Verena put her body before Marie's in a protective, bigger-sister way. "Is anybody there?" She walked closer to the archway where the sound had originated. "I don't have time for stupid pranks. Come out."

"People do this kind of thing here?"

"Pranks?"

Marie nodded. "Yes, pranks."

"All the time."

Marie shivered at the idea. She hated pranks. Especially if they were aimed to scare the unfortunate recipient.

"Maybe it was a rat." Verena made sign to go farther inside.

"A rat?" Marie didn't follow her. Darkness and scurrying rodents weren't a combination she liked.

"Probably. That's another entry to the cellars." Verena disappeared, wrapped by the shadows.

Marie stood, certain she didn't want to go any closer to the archway, but not happy to be left there outside all by herself. A few seconds later, she heard the distinct click of an opening locket and Verena's disembodied voice calling her.

"Why are we going there?" Marie asked to the archway.

"Got a surprise for you." Verena reemerged from the shadows, empty hand outstretched, a big smile on her face.

"Are we going to get in trouble?" Marie couldn't believe that sentence had escaped her mouth. Until a day ago, she would've been the one looking for trouble. She cursed, appalled at her own thoughts, and took Verena's hand. *I've been here less than three days for the Goddess's sake.*

"If we're caught."

Marie felt the dare in Verena's words and stepped into the darkness, angry with herself for looking like a coward.

"Thought so."

Marie felt overly pleased by Verena's approval, but when the door was closed behind her and not a single ray of flickering light illuminated her steps, she gasped. The humidity pressed against her skin like a wet cloth.

"Are you nyctophobic by any chance?"

"Am I a nycto… what?" Marie had never heard the word. She wasn't even sure she could repeat it. Verena's status grew in her mind. *She's one smart cookie.*

"Are you afraid of the dark?"

Marie appreciated that Verena didn't make her feel an idiot by repeating the question in words she could understand. "No, I'm not," she lied. *So that's what it is.*

"Nyctophobia is a common fear."

"Which I don't have." Marie reached to the side with her palm outstretched, looking for the safety of the wall to guide her. "How do you even know that word?"

"Redfarm has a well-stocked medical library and I like to read in my spare time." Verena shrugged. "Be careful now. We're going two floors down. Give me your hand and follow me."

Is all of this really necessary? And what happened to, "You don't want to miss the stories...?" Marie was regretting coming. *She needs a straightjacket. Smart, but still crazy. What fun is it to blindly break your neck while falling down a flight of stairs?* She slipped once or twice on the dew-coated steps. Although the temperature steadily decreased as they descended, she was feeling warmer. Or maybe it was her heart beating so fast. She couldn't be sure.

"Almost there."

"There, where?" The flat sole of her leather sandal slipped once more, unbalancing her.

"Easy." Verena's strong arms caught her before she could fall. "Behind the cellars is the Apothecary."

Marie knew that word. They had an apothecary at the Institute where Madame Carla prepared the concoctions to treat the small ailments plaguing the girls monthly. The rector never gave them medicines unless necessary. *More side effects than benefits,* the stern woman used to say. "I like apothecaries."

"Oh, you'll love this one." Verena stopped and released her hand. "Just a sec."

Marie didn't move. She kept her body at an angle so she was still touching Verena, if only by the hem of her shirt. She didn't want the girl to think less of her, but she couldn't stand the darkness and the humidity anymore.

"The Redfarm Apothecary," Verena announced as a room appeared behind the door she had opened.

The light inside wasn't bright, but compared to the obscurity, it was a relief. Marie entered the room and looked around, eyes wide in wonder. This apothecary was different than she had expected. It had the same good smell of lavender and roses she associated with that kind of place, but here, the bouquet was richer. Her nose high in the air, and she walked around, sniffing the scents. "What kind of medicines do you make here?" She lingered close to a table where petals of flowers she didn't recognize had been laid to dry. The perfume was sweet with a hint of citrus. Her fingers traveled to the table to grab a handful.

"No medicines. We make perfumes at Redfarm."

"But what about the name?" She crushed the fragrant petal between index and thumb and then brought the powder to her nose. "Love this smell."

"Jasmine." Verena mimed what Marie had just done, and at her puzzled look, Verena explained, "Jasmine is the name of the flower. This place is called the Apothecary because it was one a long time ago. Nobody needs homemade medicines anymore, but the room was already here. Why not use it? The name remained. They tried to call it the Perfumery, but it didn't stick."

Marie wandered toward the end of the room, only to see the Apothecary was bigger than she had thought; branching from the main room were several smaller rooms opening to a narrow hallway that curved, hiding what lay beyond its cream wall. Curiosity won and she was attracted by the fragrant smell coming from around the corner. Soft murmurs caught her attention. She turned toward the noise and almost stumbled at the unexpected sight. She brought a hand to her mouth and backed against the wall, unable to leave. There was a woman and a man hugging in the darkness of one of the small rooms. Marie kept her body at an angle, confident they couldn't see her, busy as they were kissing. She was horrified the woman wasn't struggling to free herself from the man's clutches. Instead, she leaned against him, gluing her body to his.

A hand gently tapped on her shoulder and Marie turned to face Verena, who brought a finger to her lips and shot Marie a warning look. "Let's get out of here," Verena whispered in her ear and took her by the elbow.

Marie stepped back and turned to face the hallway when the couple moved. The woman's head was under the light for a moment. A glimpse of deep red. "But, it's—"

"Don't say it." Verena pulled her away.

Marie freed herself from Verena's grip but followed her. *I can't believe Carnia is a man lover.* She turned at the last moment and saw the man looking at her. A flash of green eyes. *Grant?* After an impatient tug from Verena, she unfroze. They were back into the main room in no time. Marie's heart was beating as if she had run a marathon. She felt dizzy and her mind kept playing the scene she had witnessed, making it impossible for her to concentrate on what Verena was saying.

"You aren't going to say anything to anybody. Do you understand?" Verena shook Marie with both hands on her shoulders. "Are you listening to me?"

"Yes, I'm not to say anything to any living soul." Marie looked at Verena, but didn't see her. "Why?"

"Because I say so." Verena accompanied her to the door and out of the Apothecary. They ascended the dark staircase fast, not speaking a word.

"Carnia—" Marie started, unable to let the argument go without an explanation. She needed to talk about it.

"Carnia nothing." Verena led them back to the courtyard, her voice betraying how upset she was.

"But don't we have to report her to Madame Lana?" Marie couldn't help but look back at the dark archway, but nobody came after them.

"Carnia's dead if you report her. Do you understand?" Verena stopped several steps away from the gazebo and kept her voice low. Applause drowned out her voice.

"Dead?" Marie looked at the crowd cheering for an encore.

"Worse than dead. If Madame Lana gets wind of it, Carnia will be sent to a waste plant." Verena's eyes were imploring Marie and she felt horrible.

"A waste plant?" She couldn't believe her ears.

"Yes, she would become a wasted woman."

Marie felt sick at the mere idea of condemning someone to that fate. Women sent to waste plants were called *wasted*, marked with serial numbers on their arms like the men, and forced to live away from civilization. They lost contact with the rest of the world and died there, forgotten. Even their families gave them up for dead once sentenced to serve in a waste plant. "I won't say anything."

Verena nodded at her words.

"What are you doing there? Come here!" Cina called them from under the gazebo, bright eyes and a big smile on her face. "You missed the best already. Come on."

"Don't worry," Marie said to Verena and then went to join the rest of the crowd.

Cina and Laila moved out of the way to make space for the two of them and Marie resigned herself to stay until the very end of the night, although the only desire she had was to climb four flights of stairs and jump in her bed. She laughed, gasped, and cried with everybody else, but her mind wasn't there. Verena kept sending her glances, but Marie couldn't meet her eyes.

Once back in her room, Marie undressed facing the wall, avoiding Verena. She wanted to ask if those kinds of things happened often at Redfarm and if she knew of anybody who'd been caught and sent to a waste plant. But she didn't. Somehow, just asking seemed inappropriate and Madame Carla had raised her right. She wasn't that kind of girl. "I need a shower."

"Now? Weren't you just too tired to hang with the girls after the stories?" Verena repeated what she had just told Cina and Laila when they had asked if they wanted to join them for a late snack down in the kitchen. Apparently, it was something they did often after those celebrations.

Marie understood why. *Tomorrow could be the last day at Redfarm for some of them. Tomorrow could be the last day here for Verena.* "You should've gone without me."

"I'm not in the mood." Verena was at the desk, looking outside at the dark night. The roofs glinted under the moonlight.

Marie saw a tear glide down Verena's cheek, but the girl didn't seem to notice it and let it fall on the desk where it landed heavily. Marie decided to follow Verena's clue and pretended to have seen nothing. "You won't be picked tomorrow. You'll see." She didn't know why she felt the urge to say something she couldn't possibly know, but the words were out already.

"Thank you." Verena turned to face her. "Go take your shower."

"Are you sure...?" Marie had always been clumsy with words and feelings. Now she felt useless and wanted nothing more than leave. Still, she had a conscience.

"Sure. If you don't mind, I'd like to be alone for a few minutes." Verena's eyes were already looking for a faraway place outside of the window.

Marie exited the room in silence and went directly to the bathroom, her mind a chaos of discorded thoughts. She wondered what her roommate was thinking. She had never worried about the chance of being a donor. At the Institute, they never talked of such things. The mere topic was considered inappropriate conversation. But here, in the real world, fathered women were used to procreate men—the idea made her shiver, and by association, the recent memory of the intertwined couple popped in uninvited. Or maybe it had been there all along, eager to be acknowledged. She tried to push it away under a jet of cold water, but her body didn't seem to cool down. She stayed there, blue extremities and racing heart. The way Carnia had leaned against Grant. The man's bright green eyes. The surprise he showed at seeing her looking at them.

What did you see, Grant? Did you recognize me? A strange fluttering broke havoc in her stomach. Marie couldn't understand why she was asking herself such questions. She couldn't understand why she recognized him so easily when he should've been just a nameless man to her. But as hard as she tried to divert her mind somewhere else, the image of Carnia cradled by Grant's arms stood before her eyes long after her shower was done. She lay in bed, sleepless for hours. Flustered by the erratic directions her thoughts were heading without her consent, she finally decided to go downstairs and see if anyone was still around. Verena had left while Marie tried to wash away the day's grime and hadn't come back. Hoping to find her in the kitchen, Marie put on the first thing she found in the dim illumination provided by the small night-light by the door and went out again.

The stairs were silent. Not a sound echoed from downstairs. *Maybe they're being quiet.* Madame Lana couldn't be aware of those impromptu parties. Madame Carla would have never authorized late-hour celebrations. The elders enforced curfew hours with great zeal. Unnerving silence accompanied Marie until she reached the kitchen and she knew before entering that the place was deserted. A single, forgotten lamp barely lit the large room. It scarcely illuminated the corner of the sink and the small area where someone had left a few dishes and mugs to dry. Not sure of what to do, she walked toward it and hit the leg of one of the tables in the middle of the room. The sudden, sharp pain made her curse out loud. Angry tears filled her eyes, but she refused to cry. Instead, she pulled a chair out and sat, head lowered on the unpleasantly cold surface of the table. She had never liked marble. The pure breed cemetery in Trin was filled with rows and rows of marble headstones. It didn't matter that the different colors or the veins crisscrossing every slate made them different; marble always reminded her of death.

The next morning, the girl on cleaning duty woke her by unceremoniously poking her folded arms with the tip of the broom. "Partying the whole night, useless the day after. Don't think for a moment you'll be exempt from your duty."

"What…?" Marie could barely open her eyes, a series of images still playing in her mind. The girl poked her again viciously and Marie yelped. "No need for that." She stood up and wobbled on unsteady legs.

"How drunk are you?" The girl looked around, her expression disappointed when she couldn't find the proof of her suspicion. "I got sorted to clean and *I* miss Donor Day when this idiot gets lucky," she muttered under her breath.

"I didn't drink at all." *Do they also get drunk here?* Marie steadied herself, planting her hands on the back of the chair. "I'm only tired." *Thank the Goddess I got to sleep some.*

"I don't believe you." The girl's eye narrowed and Marie could almost see what she was thinking.

I'm not going to convince you, am I? Marie waited patiently, knowing what was going to happen next.

"I'll go tell Madame Lana I found you hung over and out of your room."

Just say it and get it over with. Marie maintained her gaze on the girl, her mouth closed in a straight line.

"Aren't you worried about Madame Lana knowing what you've done?" The girl didn't like Marie not cowering before her suggested threat.

"I've done nothing." Marie moved her weight to the balls of her feet, rocking back and forth to reestablish blood circulation in her legs.

"Madame Lana won't see it that way once I tell her." The girl was getting angry at Marie's attitude.

Legs working again and the painful tingling gone, she looked at the girl. "What do you want?"

"I won't tell if you volunteer for me."

Of course. "I'll do it." She didn't want to go to Donor Day in the first place, and what better excuse than being blackmailed for cleaning duty? She didn't want to be present at the ceremony and face Verena if she got picked.

The girl eyed her suspiciously but passed Marie the broom and instructed her on what to say if somebody asked. Marie memorized the message, repeated it for the girl, and then took possession of the broom. She started sweeping the floor, unable to hide the small smile tugging at her lips, but lowered her face before the girl could see her.

Two hours later, she was far from finishing all the chores the girl had seen fit to bestow upon her, but the kitchen was still empty. A few minutes earlier, she had heard the bell calling everybody outside to gather in the courtyard to participate in the ceremony. *Oh, Verena...* A feeling of hollowness possessed her at the idea of losing her newly acquired friend to a terrible fate. *What's going to happen to you?* Idra once had said that she would've killed herself before being touched by a man. Marie had nervously laughed at her words and told her not to be daft. The memory made her shiver. One look at the board where all her chores were appointed in neat writing and she groaned out loud. *I won't ever get done.* Out of the blue, she felt a sudden craving for that piece of marzipan she had meant to smuggle the day before. *I shouldn't go back to the cellars.* The more she said no to herself the more the aromatic sweetness called her until she was salivating at the mere idea of placing a piece of marzipan on her tongue.

A last gaze at the board and the sheer magnitude of the chores waiting for her left Marie thinking ten minutes wouldn't make any difference. "Nobody will notice I'm gone anyway." She reassured herself with a nod. She entered the cellars a moment later, having run the steps three at a time. She walked straight to the shelf where the sweets were stored and grabbed a big chunk of almond paste from a rectangular mold. The marzipan was in her mouth and she was already going for a second helping.

"You're not going to betray another woman, are you?"

She spun around, mouth hanging open, marzipan spilling from her lips. Grant was a few steps behind her, staring unblinkingly at her. Shocked she hadn't heard him coming, her heart started racing in fear.

"You won't, right?" He closed the gap between them, forcing Marie to step back, only to be stopped by the hard edge of the shelf behind her. Grant towered over her and his proximity was menacing.

"Are you going to hurt me?" One look at him and she was already shaking.

"Hurt you?" His eyes finally registered a glimpse of a feeling. *He's angry.* Marie nodded to answer his question.

"I'm not a woman." His voice was low and carried such contempt that Marie wished she had never thought of stealing the marzipan. "Are you going to betray your friend?" he repeated.

"She's no friend of mine." *Wrong answer.* The fury in his eyes flared and she closed hers, waiting for him to beat her or do something worse. Every time some of the younger girls tried to escape the strict rules of the Institute, the elders told horrific tales of women killed by men. They didn't spare details. Marie instinctively brought her arms over her chest, closing the lapels of her shirt with her crossed hands.

"What are you doing?"

Marie opened one eye and saw Grant looking at her with a strange expression. He could've been shocked for all she knew. Unable to read his thoughts, she said, "Please, let me go. Carnia is not my friend, but I won't say a word to anybody. Promise." She felt her knees shaking to the point she could barely stand. Grant moved away a few steps, still looking down at Marie with eyes she could only describe as bewildered. "I won't say a thing," she repeated.

He seemed mollified at her statement. "Thank you." His facial muscles relaxed and he let out his breath as if he had been holding it, then turned and left.

Marie watched as he disappeared through the window opening at the end of the cellar. She stood still several minutes, not knowing what to make of the whole episode. *He's protecting Carnia,* she finally realized and the thought surprised her more than the fact he hadn't beaten her. *A man protecting a woman.*

CHAPTER 3

The taste of marzipan lingering on her tongue became sour and she had to spit it out. Once the shaking of her legs abated, she ran back to the kitchen where a group of somber girls was comforting a crying brunette. The girl had her face hidden under her hair, but Marie recognized the shirt and her heart lurched down to her stomach in less than a second.

"Verena?" Marie walked straight through the circle of girls and went to hug Verena. "Were you…?" She was desperate for better words, but there wasn't a lot she could say.

Verena's weeping became so loud that when she answered, Marie didn't understand a word. "I'm so sorry."

"I wasn't chosen! Marie, I wasn't chosen—" Verena managed to utter between heartbreaking sobs.

Marie's reaction was to start laughing. "Oh, my Goddess! You just killed me." Happiness replaced the dread that had squeezed her heart to the size of a walnut.

"I was sure this was it." Verena finally raised her face and Marie saw she was smiling. "I'd already prepared my bag." Another round of heartbreaking sobs replaced the smile and Verena buried her head against Marie's chest.

The scene was almost comical, big and tall Verena leaning down, looking for comfort in Marie's embrace. "It's fine. Everything's fine." She let Verena cry for a few seconds, then disentangled herself from the embrace and looked at her. "You weren't chosen. You can breathe now."

"You weren't at the ceremony. Why?" Verena sniffled once or twice, but the worst seemed to have passed.

"Got blackmailed to kitchen duty."

"How?" Verena went to sit at the table and one of the girls promptly brought her something to drink.

"Wrong place at the wrong time." Marie joined her at the table. "Not important." But it was, and her mind, now that Verena turned out to be safe, went immediately back to the cellars. The memory of Grant's piercing, unblinking stare assailed her. She despised him for looking at her as if she were a vile creature ready to betray her own race. She didn't want to be looked at that way. *You, a man, disrespecting me.* She was getting upset and didn't like it.

"Poor Carnia, I feel so bad for her."

Marie was abruptly snapped out of her thoughts by Verena's comment. "Carnia was chosen?"

"Yes, Captain Callista called her name—" one of the girls answered, but then her voice broke and she couldn't finish the sentence.

"She ran off after the announcement. The elders gave order to leave her alone." Verena said the last words looking directly at Marie.

What's up with all of you and this obsession of looking after Carnia? What's so special about her?

"I barely know Carnia." Marie felt an ugly tinge coloring her words, but nobody seemed to notice and she hurried to add, "She needs close friends now, I imagine." *Oh, she has plenty of those, doesn't she?* And there it was, unbidden, the image of the redhead being consoled by Grant.

"I'd want to be alone in a moment like this," one of the girls surrounding Verena said, her voice almost broken.

Yeah, right. Alone my butt. Marie snorted and tried to cover it as a sneeze. "Something in the air…"

"When is Carnia going to leave?" the same girl asked, seemingly too upset by Carnia's fate to notice Marie's flounders.

"I guess the elders are giving her a few hours to compose herself and then she'll be shipped to—" Verena blushed and everybody nodded, filling the blank.

A good fathered woman would have problems even thinking about the place Carnia was going to, let alone saying it out loud. Semental farms were the place fathered women dreaded the most. Madame Carla had taught everyone that a waste plant was a better option for a fathered woman. *She didn't get caught for being a man lover, but she got her comeuppance anyway.* The ugly tug had come back with a vengeance. Marie was troubled by her own thoughts. *What's up with me?*

"So soon?" several voices commented the same.

"Why prolong her agony?" Verena shrugged, her eyes liquid again.

"Okay, stop. It doesn't help Carnia anyway." Marie felt she was being childish and unfair, but words had left her mouth and there was no going back. "Let's focus on the positive. You're here and are going to stay here, and that's all that matters. Right?"

A few of the girls nodded. Others didn't dare say anything one way or the other.

In the afternoon, the elders gave the order to look for Carnia. Nobody could find her and the bus was waiting. Madame Lana made an appearance in the kitchen and icily asked if anybody knew where Carnia was. Nobody dared breathe a word. The rector stormed away, threating to punish the whole farm. A few of the younger girls, barely floor sweepers, started crying. Marie had the feeling they knew firsthand the kind of punishment of which the woman was capable.

"I'll go find her." Verena removed her apron and sailed off soon after Madame Lana left.

Marie was checking off items from her interminable list. "I'll come with you." She couldn't pass the opportunity to leave the kitchen if even for a moment.

"Don't judge her," Verena warned her with a whisper, but didn't say she couldn't come. She left without checking if Marie was following.

Marie ran after her. "Of course not." She was happy Verena had reached that conclusion about her reaction. It was the appropriate reaction given the circumstances. "But, do the elders know about her…?" *Perversion.* She shivered at the thought.

"Don't know, but probably."

"But why has nobody denounced her?"

"We stick together no matter what. We fathered women protect each other, always." Verena slowed her stride to look at her as if she were from another planet. "Didn't they teach you that at the Institute?"

"We never had cases... like Carnia."

Verena stopped altogether and laughed. "You're so young."

"I'm fifteen already." Marie hated when people assumed she was a child just because she didn't look like a woman yet. "And I would've known if we had *cases* at the Institute." She wasn't surprised they went directly to the Apothecary. It was the first place she would've gone and wasn't sure if Verena knew anything about the window in the cellars. For some reason, she didn't want to divulge that information. Maybe because it felt exciting to be the only one privy to a secret.

This time, Verena had thought beforehand and brought a flashlight. Without breaking stride, they walked through the main room to reach the dim-lit, smaller hallway. The faint noise of whispered words stopped immediately when Verena called, "Carnia? Are you here?"

Silence stretched for a few seconds before Carnia emerged from the safety of the darkest corner at the end of the hallway. As Marie had imagined, the redhead wasn't alone. Grant, who kept his arm around her waist, followed Carnia. He looked at Marie and she felt judged once again.

"Verena, please, don't tell anybody you saw me." Carnia's eyes were red and swollen, her face streaked from hours of crying.

Marie pitied her, but she couldn't understand why Carnia was taking it so hard. Clearly, she didn't have a problem being around men.

"I can't. You know that." Verena sounded even more heartbroken than Carnia.

"I won't leave." Carnia's statement had a finality Marie didn't like.

"Don't say it like that." Marie was getting scared. It was an unfamiliar situation for her and she wasn't sure what they were dealing with exactly. The presence of a man among them unnerved her. It was wrong. "They'll treat you with respect. I've been told you aren't forced to—" She didn't know how to say the words without being crude.

"I won't leave him."

"What?" *What the heck is she talking about?* "Verena?" Marie looked at her roommate, hoping she could confirm she had heard wrong.

"I'll kill myself." Carnia raised one hand and showed a pair of open scissors before directing the sharp edge against her wrist.

"Wow! You can't be serious." Marie's head went back and forth from Verena to Carnia. Once, she intercepted Grant looking at her, desperation in his eyes. *This is not happening.* "Verena, do something!"

"Carnia, please, think." Verena walked slowly toward the couple. "You don't want to harm yourself." She reached out her hand and took Carnia's, carefully putting distance between the razor edge of the scissors and her wrist. "It's not the end of the world. You'll serve seven years and then you'll retire somewhere nice."

"I'll wait for you," Grant said, surprising everybody.

"Will you?" Carnia turned to face him, her arms flying to his shoulders.

"I will." He took her in his arms, then bent to kiss her as if they were alone.

Marie gasped, her senses confused by a barrage of feelings fighting for supremacy. One, stronger than the others, begged to be recognized and Marie gasped again. A longing to be held like Carnia was being held by Grant. Wanting to see the possessiveness in his eyes while he was looking at her. Marie wanted that. *Idra?* She thought that conjuring her soft lips would realign her emotional chaos, but it didn't. Thinking of all the stolen embraces in the dark corridors of the Institute didn't douse the flames of the fire consuming her. She finally averted her eyes, ashamed of looking longer than was proper. Ashamed for much more than that.

The couple stood silent and still for a while, neither Verena nor Marie saying anything to break the spell, but eventually, Carnia stepped away from Grant and went straight to Verena's open arms.

"You'll see. Seven years will fly away." Verena contained her voice until the last word, and then she started crying along Carnia. "It won't be long until I'm chosen. We'll be together soon. Don't worry."

Marie felt bad for Verena, who was so sure she was destined to bear fathered kids and couldn't envision anything better.

"Can you give us ten more minutes?" Carnia had gone to Grant again.

"Sure." Verena gave Marie a look and they both retraced their steps and exited the Apothecary in complete silence. Once outside, Verena led a meaningless chase through the main building and courtyard, letting everybody know she was still looking for Carnia. Close to an hour later, they went back to the Apothecary to retrieve Carnia.

"I'm sorry, but you must come with me now." Verena offered her hand to the redhead.

Marie saw how Grant's arms tightened around Carnia for the briefest moment before he relaxed them, but at the last moment, he bent and murmured something in her ear. Carnia threw her arms around his neck and kissed him fiercely, sobs wracking her slim frame.

"Please." Verena pried Carnia from Grant by gently grabbing her shoulders. "Please, don't make me call the elders."

At her plead, Grant helped by stepping back as he pushed Carnia forward.

"I don't want anybody else but you." Carnia refused to let him go, freeing herself from Verena's hold to seek his embrace once more.

Only this time, he slowly shook his head and kept her away from him. "You'll be treated with respect."

"Carnia, I'm begging you. I can't stall people forever. You must come with me now."

Voices and steps echoed from the outside. "I found her!" Verena yelled, then added at a softer volume, "Go away," looking at Grant.

He nodded, gave Carnia one last kiss, and disappeared into the shadows. One moment later, the three of them met the elders who had come looking for Carnia. Not a single question was asked, which Marie found peculiar, and Carnia was escorted to the bus, her belongings already packed in one big sack.

When the bus left, Marie finally felt something akin to sympathy for the girl who had stared at them by the window, eyes bloodshot.

"I'm next." She heard Verena whisper.

"No, you aren't," she shot back, angry at the whole world. Angry she was only fifteen. Angry she was born a fathered woman. Just angry.

A whole week passed; nothing new happened. Carnia's departure had touched everybody. Even Marie felt her mood darkening. The kitchen, normally a silent place, became sepulchral. Girls cried at every small remark from the chef, who had finally come back. People got sick to their stomachs from Madame Lana's cold stares, literally. One girl had to be sent to the infirmary after an unfortunate accident involving the rector and a salty salad. Verena escaped into hard work and went to sleep every night exhausted, only to exchange no more than two words with Marie, who at the end of the week was starving for human contact. Any human contact.

Anytime the chef looked for volunteers to go fetch something from the cellars, Marie found herself raising her hands with barely hidden enthusiasm. She was never alone though; one or more scullery maids were sent along to help her carry the heavier burdens.

"Forget something?" the girl running errands with her asked, looking toward the dark spot Marie had been staring at for the last minute.

"Do you know where they keep the marzipan?" Marie immediately made up a question.

"Over there." The girl's chin pointed at the aisle where the sweets were kept.

Marie nodded. "Do you think I can take some?"

"I saw nothing." The girl smiled and turned the other way, not before giving her a wink, then hopping toward the exit.

Marie went along with the charade and took a small piece of marzipan from the big square. Then she changed her mind and took a second piece for the girl. One last look at the corner, where she expected a rectangular opening into the men's world, and a big sigh escaped her mouth. The wall looked untouched and perfectly sound. She backed up slowly and joined the girl waiting for her at the end of the stairs with an expectant look on her face.

"Thank you." The girl's eyes widened at the sight of the sweet morsel. The marzipan disappeared in her mouth and she moaned loudly.

Marie laughed at the girl's reaction to her small gift. "For what?" She winked.

"Nothing at all." The girl laughed back, wiping her mouth with her small hand.

Marie walked to the kitchen, her mood worsening again after the temporary reprieve. Normally, the sight of the cavernous room devoid of happiness wasn't conducive to happiness, but she felt even more despondent than usual. Hours passed, tedious chore after tedious chore, and finally, dinnertime arrived. She didn't feel like eating or talking, and so, after grabbing a half loaf of fresh bread and a few olives from a jar, she opted for a walk in the courtyard. She headed toward a big mulberry tree with its limbs shaped by the gardeners to resemble a big umbrella and sat under it. Someone had put a soft cushion on the tree's roots and Marie's thoughts went to the sweet embraces she had shared so many times with Idra. She hadn't expected to miss Idra with such heartache.

"Do you mind if I join you?" Verena was looking at her, peeking between the carefully laced limbs of the tree.

Marie blinked once and tried to smile. "Come inside." She moved on the cushion to free some space.

"Sorry I haven't been great company lately." Verena sat, graciously folding her long legs beneath her.

Marie liked that trait in her. Verena managed to be elegant despite her statuesque size and she was a nice person. "Don't worry about it. I understand."

"I wonder how she's doing." Verena shifted on the cushion, her hand curling up one of her long locks, her fingers rolling her dark hair in a tight coil.

"Can you talk to her?" Marie didn't want to talk about Carnia, but the look in her friend's eyes said she needed to.

"Not the first three months. They're kept in isolation and tested."

"Tested?" Marie felt uncomfortable.

Verena nodded, her eyes suddenly distant. "If she's lucky, she'll prove to be difficult."

"What do you mean?" The uneasiness evolved into fear of hearing the answer. She had heard rumors.

"At the factories, they don't have time to waste with girls who don't prove to be fertile right away."

"What happen to those girls?"

"It's said they're discarded."

"Waste plants?" A sudden gust of wind reached them under the safety of the tree's branches and Marie shivered.

Verena shrugged. "I guess."

Although Marie had been taught that ending in a waste plant was a better fate than serving as a *mother*, she wasn't sure Carnia would be happy. "She'll be fine. Don't worry." She didn't have a clue of what she was talking about, but she felt the need to reassure Verena once more. The wind shook the branches with more strength and the whole green umbrella swayed under the assault. Something darted at the corner of Marie's eye and she automatically turned right, only to see Grant stepping back into the shadows of the corner. *He was listening.* Her heart skipped a beat.

"What was it?" Verena tilted her head and Marie rearranged her body in a useless attempt at hiding Grant's presence when he was probably already gone.

"Nothing."

"A cat, probably."

Marie wished she were alone. "Yes, a cat." *He wants to know about Carnia.* She felt her stomach contract.

"Are you okay?" Verena had already forgotten the cat, worriedly staring at Marie.

"I must've eaten too fast." With a swift touch of her fingers, she pushed the untouched bread and olives behind her. "It's getting cold." She massaged her arms to reinforce her statement. "Let's go inside."

Verena followed her back to their room. Much to Marie's disappointment, it was soon evident Verena was in a chatty mood, whereas Marie would've preferred silence and solitude. She sat on the desk, her body uncomfortably angled toward the window, her eyes trying to locate the mulberry tree four floors below. Darkness had already claimed the courtyard, but she kept looking downward, hoping against hope to see Grant. A sudden shift in light made her glue her face to the windowpane.

"You're acting strange." Verena stopped folding the pile of clothes on the bed and walked to the desk, leaning to peer over Marie's shoulders. "The moon's so pretty tonight."

Marie raised her eyes to the sky, saw the full moon illuminating the roofs, and wished the light could reach the dark courtyard, but the buildings facing Redfarm were tall and stole the moonlight for themselves. The flickering light she had seen a moment ago was already lost under the canopy of the tall trees Madame Lana was proud of. She squinted, hoping to see the light reemerge between one swaying branch and another, but the wind had simmered to a gentle breeze and nothing moved.

Suddenly, a gnawing longing to be needed assailed Marie. It must have shown on her face because Verena hugged her.

"You still miss her." Verena released her to look into her eyes. "Idra," she explained when Marie looked back, puzzled by her statement.

"How do you know about her?" But Marie had an idea of how her roommate would know Idra's name.

"You talk in your sleep. A lot."

Marie flushed.

"Don't be ashamed. I had a sweetheart before coming here. Had to leave her behind too." Verena tilted her head to mimic Marie's position. "I liked her, but I was young and she was young."

"What about her?"

"Haven't heard from her in years. She's pretty. I'm sure she found someone who makes her happy."

"Do you ever think that if you hadn't left, you'd be together now?" Marie walked to the bed to put some personal space between her and Verena, sat on the edge, and hugged herself.

"Of course I do. I wouldn't be crying after a girl who'll never look at me twice. I think I'd be happy." Verena sighed and sat on the bed, back to back with Marie "I know I'd be happier."

Marie couldn't see the girl's face, but she heard the sadness in her voice. Her hand traveled on the duvet, looking for Verena's.

Verena squeezed back. "I'm telling you this so you know life goes on. A month from now, or maybe two, this pain you're feeling when you think of her will lessen and it will disappear altogether."

Marie changed position to take Verena in her arms and cradled her. *You're lying. It doesn't get any better, does it?* She caressed her friend's head, following the cascade of hair down to the bed. "You'll be happy."

"Thank you." Verena sniffed again, and from the tone of her voice, Marie understood she didn't believe her.

They stayed silent for a while and then retired for the night in their respective beds. Marie closed her eyes, and the last thing she thought before finally falling asleep was that someone was still pining over Carnia. And she didn't like it. *A man shouldn't even dare thinking about a woman.* She rationalized her distress over the situation. *It isn't natural.*

CHAPTER 4

Two months later, Marie had found a boring, although not completely unpleasant, rhythm in her daily chores. She still was nothing more than a scullery maid, but a growing familiarity with the other girls helped a great deal in making her judge Redfarm with different eyes—with the exception of those situations where the farm rector was involved.

"When you're done with your kitchen duty, come up to the infirmary." Madame Lana had graced the kitchen with one of her unexpected and unwelcomed visits. Now, she was staring at a dumbfounded Marie, who should've known better by now and acted smart before the rector. Instead, Marie was silently praying to have understood the order correctly. "Are you deaf?"

"I apologize, madam." Marie bowed her head low. "I'm just too happy for—"

Madame Lana raised her bony hand to stop her in midsentence. "There's no opportunity yet. First, you must prove I need you out of the kitchen."

"Thank you, thank you—"

Madame Lana's fingers came dangerously close to Marie's moving lips, but thankfully stopped before making contact. Marie inadvertently stepped back to avoid being touched by the rector's cold hand and realized she had probably offended her. Something flickered behind the woman's eyes, something as cold as her skin. "Finish what you're doing and go upstairs." She barked several orders and then left the kitchen followed by two unlucky girls who were responsible for having poured one teaspoon of sugar too many in her coffee.

The chef smiled a sad smile Marie's way and she shivered. Chef had just treated the two crying girls with the same show of affection.

"I'm going to train as a nurse," Marie said out loud to test how the idea sounded once worded.

"The doctor needs a replacement for Carnia, but so far nobody has passed the first two weeks." Chef shrugged as if she didn't like to be the bearer of bad news. "Two full months have passed already since Carnia left and the infirmary doesn't have a full staff yet. Madame Lana—"

"But *she*'s not there often, is she?" Marie had the presence of mind of lowering her voice and avoided mentioning Madame Lana directly.

Chef covered her mouth with her beefy hand to muffle her words. "She's everywhere at Redfarm. Lately, she's driving everybody crazy." Everybody in the kitchen had heard, judging from the coughing and the unnecessary stirring of wooden ladles inside empty pots. "Don't worry with peeling the rest of the potatoes. Go wash yourself clean."

Marie thanked the chef but hesitated. All of a sudden, the idea of leaving the kitchen—the place she had despised wholeheartedly until a minute ago—didn't sound as promising as she had fantasized so many times in the last three months.

"Go, don't make her wait."

"But she was adamant about me finishing my chores…" Marie felt like a child digging her heels on the ground.

"You don't know her like I do. Go scrub your skin until it's squeaky clean and don't forget to wear a pinafore over your dress." Chef walked her out, gently pushing her along. "Remember, listen to her, nod, and never contradict Madame Lana."

"Yes, ma'am. Thanks, ma'am." Marie found herself unwillingly thrown out of the kitchen.

"Don't waste time, child." Chef's words echoed in the hallway and several elders passing by raised their collective brows to stare at Marie. She was on the second floor when running steps reached her.

"Is it true? You got out of potato duty?" Verena jumped on the step before Marie, forcing her to stop. "It's true, then. How did you manage?" Something resembling a mix of awe and mischievousness colored the girl's face.

"You're pretty when you think the worst about friends." Marie couldn't help but smile. "From what I understand, I didn't exactly win a prize."

"You hate the kitchen." Verena moved out of the way and they both resumed climbing toward the fourth floor.

"Not sure I'm going to like the infirmary any better." Once again, she felt childish.

"Madame Lana's been particularly a pain in the—"

"Nothing better to do, apprentice?" An elder appeared from behind.

"I was sent to retrieve a sweater for Darlene."

Marie was proud of her friend. Verena didn't lower her eyes when she talked back to the haughty elder.

"Well, don't be wasting time. Go."

As the elder passed them, Verena raised her fingers in an obscene gesture while whispering, "Hope Captain Callista makes your day hell."

Marie almost choked but managed to keep quiet.

Verena winked at her. "Remember, nod to Madame—"

Marie stopped her. "I know the drill. Now run before *you* get in trouble." She saw Verena hurrying upstairs, wondering if she had told the truth about fetching stuff for Darlene. Verena's sentiments for the harpy hadn't dimmed. If nothing else, she hadn't missed a single occasion to be within an earshot from the elder. Marie didn't like to see her friend suffering for someone so vain and shallow. On one of those endless Samarian nights, she even joked about them getting together if nobody else would have them in five years. Verena had smiled and said it was a good plan.

She entered the infirmary a good hour later—she had wasted time on a long shower and precious minutes she hadn't had to comb her hair. After long, wistful looks in the mirror, she opted to tie her wispy mane out of the way in a long, elaborate braid.

"How long does it take to peel a bag of potatoes?" Madame Lana gestured for her to close the door and approach a long table full of numbered packages. "Take one and go to the men's infirmary to help the nurses."

Marie forgot both Chef's and Verena's suggestions and she did exactly what she had been told to avoid doing. "But… but I thought I was needed here. I thought I was going to finally start training as a nurse—"

"You must be kidding! Would you believe this one?" Madame Lana asked three nurses who hurried to scamper out of the way. "Tora!" The rector stormed outside as was her habit. Her minions normally ended what she started.

One of the three women came forth and gave Marie a pitiful look. "At Redfarm we never allow nurses to start training on women first. You must prove useful."

For the second time, Marie couldn't believe her ears. The first shock she had received once Carnia had told her she was expected in the kitchen, and now this. "But—you can't be serious… I mean, no disrespect, but is it truly necessary I train on men?" She was so upset she had forgotten her place.

"You better thank the Heavens we're understaffed. Otherwise I'd kick you back to the kitchen." Tora gave her a cold stare.

Marie knew there was no way to change the situation, so she took the package the woman was not so gently pushing into her arms.

Tora rotated her index finger to let Marie know she was to turn on her heels and leave. "Three floors down, under the cellars."

Marie did as she was told, dragging her feet down the stairs and dreading the moment she had to enter the men's infirmary. *If only Madame Carla knew… She would be so mad that one of her girls is being sent to work on men.* Her mind heavy with clouded thoughts, she descended toward her destination, noticing how darker, more humid, and narrower the flight of stairs became. She could barely contain her rage when she knocked on the door, fist trembling. *Madame Carla would've never, ever allowed this… this…* Tears stinging in her eyes, she knocked a second time when nobody answered.

"Come in!" a voice called, muffled by the walls.

Marie gingerly opened the door and peered inside, not sure what to expect. The men's infirmary looked like any other and that surprised her greatly. The space was large, illuminated by artificial light, and seemingly clean in stark contrast with the dampness of the stairs. Three rows of narrow beds lined the room, each numbered with a rectangular plaque at the foot. Several were occupied by workers either sleeping or waiting to be checked by the only woman present, who was busily moving from one bed to the other. Overall, a sense of calm pervaded the place, and that surprised Marie even more. Her attention was directed toward the thirty-something brunette with short tresses and a curvaceous body, who made a summoning sound without looking at her. Expecting directions, she walked closer to the woman who exuded an air of command.

"Don scrubs. Wear gloves. Start changing the dressings on bed one." The brunette was busy stitching a large gash on a man's forearm. She raised her dark eyes from the wound to give an immobile Marie a puzzled look. "You know how to do that, right?"

Marie, dazzled by the sight, shook her head slowly. The man was in pain and his face was white, but he was stoically suffering the treatment. Blood gushed from the jarred wound and the brunette swiftly cleaned it with a white cloth she immediately discarded inside a bin at her feet.

"What are you doing here, then?" The brunette's mood was changing before Marie's eyes.

"I thought I was going to train as a nurse?" She automatically stepped back, almost eager to be sent back to peeling potatoes.

The man under the brunette's care moaned in pain as she threaded the needle in and out of his skin. "I'm sorry, but it's better this way. The longer it takes the more painful it is for you." She patted his arm in a display of tenderness Marie found out of place. "The rector sent me another useless, snotty girl," the brunette said under her breath, but loud enough to be heard. The man smiled through thin, bloodless lips.

Marie had already reached the door and was, for once, looking longingly at the darkness of the stairs when the brunette called her back. "Where do you think you're going?"

"I thought—" Sweat freezing on her forehead, Marie understood she wasn't getting away from that job.

"Do you want to start training or not?" The brunette gave a good look at her handiwork and applied two more stiches. "Better?" she asked the man, who nodded in response. "Good."

"I'd like to train." Marie couldn't believe her eyes and her ears. The woman was so attentive to the man's needs and he wasn't afraid of her.

"Then you'll train all right." The brunette showed her the cubicle where the scrubs and the gloves were stacked in two neat piles. "You'll learn more here than anywhere else." She had finished with the man and gently helped him to sit on a nearby bed. "I'm Doctor Rane. But you can call me by my name. No need for formality around here. It's going to be just you and me, anyway. What's your name?"

"Marie."

"Nice meeting you, Marie." Rane removed her gloves, discarded them, and offered Marie her hand. "Today, you'll help me with some chores to get you accustomed to what we do here. In a day or two, you'll know if it's for you or not." Rane smiled a beautiful, all white-teeth smile.

Marie wondered if the doctor was temperamental or menstrual. Either way, she wasn't sure she was going to like working with her in such a confined space.

"Come here. I'll show you how to properly dress a wound." Rane made a sign to join her at bed number one, where a man was soundly sleeping. "Time for your medication," she whispered, leaning toward the blond head.

The head whispered back, "Okay."

"What do you need me to do?" Marie saw the cart with medicines parked by the bed and remembered the bulgy envelope Tora had given her four floors up and an entire universe apart. She proffered the package to Rane, hoping she knew what to do with it.

"Thanks, we go through more first-aid kits than I can count." She took the package from Marie and tore the seal. "Good, I needed some penicillin and I can always use the tincture of iodine. You wouldn't believe the condition these men arrive in. Sometimes, I don't understand the way pure breeds use them."

Marie didn't understand where Rane's speech was going and didn't want to know. She didn't find her words appropriate, but she was smart enough to keep her thoughts to herself.

"The patient needs his wound cleaned and dressed with clean gauzes." Rane put together what was needed for the task and then passed the tray to Marie. "You must come close if you want to learn anything."

Marie felt Rane's disapproving look and hurried to join her at the head of the bed where a blond mane was slowly moving as if its owner were waking from deep sleep, although he had answered Rane a few seconds ago.

"He's heavily sedated. Don't worry. He isn't going to bite." Rane beckoned her closer still and Marie obliged fearfully, worrying she was never going to please the woman.

"What happened to him?" Marie could see bandages on his naked arms and shoulders. Someone had carefully tucked linens around the rest of his body.

Rane answered her question by gently peeling the linen down to the man's abdomen. Then with equal gentleness, she raised the hem of his undershirt and uncovered his torso. She moved him to his right side where a bloodied bandage covered a big portion of the upper body. She removed the dressing to show what lay beneath. Two wide, angry-red marks marred his already-ruined skin. "They treat them like animals and then pretend they work again the morning after."

Again, Marie didn't ask who "they" were. She had already decided it was safer to let the woman mumble her heretic thoughts and pretend she hadn't heard or understood. The aftermath of the recent whipping sickened Marie and she had to avert her gaze. She remembered how a slap she had once received on her face had stung and wondered how much a whipping that had cut the skin in two long gashes would hurt.

"Pass me the peroxide. I'm worried it's going to get infected." Rane pointed to a small plastic bottle on the tray she had given Marie, which she promptly opened and handed to her.

Marie didn't expect the reaction of the transparent disinfectant once poured on the wounds. The peroxide sizzled on contact, forming white foam that engulfed the red wounds. "Good," Rane said and Marie shivered at the same time the blond head thrashed side to side.

"Keep him in place," Rane ordered, filling the gashes with the peroxide and dabbing at the liquid as she poured with a steady hand.

Marie applied all her weight on the man's shoulders to stop his frenzied rocking and ended with her face close to his. She heard him swearing softly, and when his eyes fluttered open for one brief moment, she was surprised by two bright-green lights staring back at her. *Dear Goddess, it's Grant!* She recoiled from the shock. The wounded back, his deep gashes… The whole picture seemed uglier than a moment earlier and she had to repress a gasp.

"Keep him down, would you?" Rane muttered something else Marie didn't understand.

Rane shoved Marie out of the way as the doctor calmed Grant and finished dressing his wounds by herself. "What's the problem with you? Didn't you want to be a nurse? What do you think it means? Redecorating the patients' rooms?" The woman was furious and her eyes shone dark and bright.

Marie felt small and useless as Rane towered over her and pushed her toward the wall by poking at her chest with a finger. "Change your attitude or get out of here and nev—" Grant moved on the bed and emitted a haunting sound that stopped Rane midsentence. Both Rane and Marie ran back to him.

"Why is he screaming?" Marie couldn't bear to hear the piercing laments. "Can't we do something?" *Please make it stop.*

"He turned on his back. That's why he's screaming. And yes, we can do something to help him. It's called a strong opiate." Rane showed her how to keep Grant on his side and then went to a cabinet where there several small bottles stood behind glass. The brunette fished a key out of one of the pockets on her vest and opened the cabinet. "Here, take one. You'll feel better." She placed a small blue pill between Grant's lips and gave him some water from a plastic cup. Grant gulped down the pill the first try.

Marie waited, her breath caught somewhere in her throat. "How long does it take for the medicine to work?"

Rane shrugged. "It must dissolve in the stomach. Not soon enough."

"Isn't there something faster?" Marie didn't want to look at Grant, but she couldn't resist the urge. His face was covered in sweat and his already fair complexion had paled to a ghostly white. "There must be something."

"Of course there is." Rane gave her a look as if she had asked a stupid question.

"Then why didn't you give it to him?"

"Because."

Marie was going to ask what she had meant with that answer, but Rane made a face and then exclaimed, "You really are naïve, aren't you?"

Marie was offended by her remark. "I'm fifteen—"

"The better, faster, safer medicines aren't to be wasted on workers," Rane recited. "I work with expired antibiotics and barely enough painkillers to keep them alive." She started to caress Grant's shoulders. "Do the same to his arms."

"Do you want me to touch *him*?" Marie choked at the end.

"Yes, I want you to touch him."

Marie mustered some courage, timidly took one of Grant's arms in her hand, and slowly stroked it. All the while, she couldn't stop shivering.

"The touch calms sick patients." The woman gestured to use both hands to give the massage. "Don't you feel better when you're caressed?"

Marie blushed. *Of course I feel better when someone caresses me! What a silly question.*

"Well, you'd be surprised, but men feel better too when treated like human beings." Rane gave her a pointed look.

Maybe she's testing me. Marie redoubled her effort, and trying her best to ignore the way she reacted to his proximity, starting with Grant's right hand, she massaged it with an upward motion. "Is this good?"

"Yes, it feels good," Grant replied, surprising her. The result was that Marie dropped his arm as if it weighted a ton and jumped back at the same time. Rane rebuked her. To add insult to the injury,

Grant gave her an amused look, despite the fact he was ridden with pain. "Thank you," he said, keeping his focus on Marie.

"Try to relax now," Rane said to Grant, and after passing a hand through his hair in a tender gesture, she moved away from his bed to check on a man two beds on the right who had just called her.

"Hi, Marie." Grant hadn't lowered his eyes. He was still looking at her.

Marie felt a strange tingle at his words. She hadn't seen him since Carnia had left Redfarm, and her thoughts were scattered several directions at once. "What happened to you?"

"I got whipped." He turned slightly on his side and grimaced in pain.

She closed the distance between them in a second, her hands reaching for him by their own volition. "Don't move. Let me help you."

"I can't stay in this position for long. I think I've a broken rib or something." His voice was a rattle now.

At closer scrutiny, his eyes looked red and feverish and dark circles sat under them. "Don't talk." She could see every word he spoke forced him to expand his thorax, pushing on the broken rib. She brought a wheeled stool closer and sat by him. "I'll massage your shoulders. Is that okay?"

He nodded and let his head slip farther down the pillow. "Tell me something about yourself." He sounded sleepy already.

"Me?" The question took Marie by surprise. A worker asking about a woman's life. She saw the sickly sheen on his skin and how much it hurt him to keep talking. "I don't like the color yellow," she blathered, not knowing what else to say.

"You don't like the color yellow?" His eyes, on the verge of closing a moment ago, now flashed wide open and focused on her mouth.

Or so it seemed to Marie. "I hate the color yellow."

"But, why?" He moved his head on the pillow to better look at her.

She moved accordingly to help him avoid unnecessary movements. "My hair is yellow and I truly wish it was darker."

"I like it." His hand reached for one of her long locks before she understood what he intended. "It's silky." His fingers slid through her hair in long strokes before she had the wits to stop him.

She shivered, then realized his hand was still under hers and she wanted to let it go, but couldn't move. "What are you doing?"

"Wanted to touch your hair." His voice was blurred, but the hurt was unmistakable.

She was shocked, and at the same time, she felt bad for him. "You shouldn't take these kinds of liberties with a woman," she murmured under her breath. As if she wanted to explain her words, she added, "I could report you." But deep inside, she knew she wouldn't have. As she hadn't reported him when she had seen him for the first time stealing food from the cellars.

He surprised Marie by throwing another compliment at her. "You have pretty eyes." His owns eyes were closing and he was trying his best to keep them open, but it was a lost battle. "You're nice." And with that, he finally went to sleep, leaving her angry and flustered.

Angry because she was flustered by his words. She shouldn't have been flustered by a man's words.

"Under opiates, they say the darnedest things. Don't mind the boy. He's been having the worst luck lately. In and out of this place three times already in the last two weeks." Rane was back at Grant's side and Marie hadn't heard her coming. "Didn't mean to startle you."

"You didn't." Marie lied through her teeth because she needed to feel in control again. "What happened to him?"

Rane let her have her small victory and answered her question. "He got caught, not once, but three different times, trying to escape."

"Escaping?" Marie left the stool for Rane, who thanked her and went to check Grant's vitals. "But to go where?" Where would a worker go once outside the farm's walls?

"Somewhere nicer for him." Rane was holding his right wrist between thumb and index. "Do you know how to take the pulse?"

Marie shook her head. She had seen Madame Carla check one of the girls who had fainted once, but she didn't know what to do.

"Come here and take his other wrist." Rane waited for Marie to take position by her and reach for Grant's left wrist. "Yes, like that, good." She helped Marie to find his pulse. "Gently press your finger on the bigger vein and count his heartbeats."

Marie didn't feel anything at first, but then she registered a soft thump under her fingertip and her heart thumped in unison with his. It felt too intimate, but she didn't move. Rane was looking at her and she didn't want to disappoint the woman.

"He's okay for now. Let's hope he doesn't wake up soon." Rane let down the wrist she was holding tenderly.

"Where would he go?" Marie mimed her and gently laid Grant's hand on the sheet. The skin on the back of his hand was splashed with dark freckles and amidst them, there were old scars. She caressed his marred knuckles without realizing she was doing it and blushed when Rane gave her a pointed look. "If he were to escape, where could he possibly go?"

"How would I know?" Rane's eyes were inscrutable. "This isn't suitable conversation for a fathered woman."

"But you started—" Marie regretted having opened her big mouth the moment she said the first word. "I apologize." Still, she wanted to tell Rane what she thought of her choice of suitable conversations. *Do as I say, not as I do. Fine by me.*

"Help me with the patient on bed four. Bad concussion." Rane was already past the lecture.

"How did he hit his head?" Marie followed the brunette to the fourth bed and took a look at the man's head. A big bump was visible under plastered hair.

"Do you want to know?" Rane raised an eyebrow.

Marie couldn't fathom the woman. Was she playing with her? Was she testing her somehow? Was she just emotionally unstable? "I don't need details."

"His head collided with a piece of wood." The brunette waited for her to ask more, the corner of her lips slightly turned up.

"I see." Several images ran through Marie's mind and her face must've shown her inner turmoil.

Rane's expression sweetened. "We must keep him awake and check if his pupils are dilating."

Did I pass the test? Marie followed instructions as Rane doled them out and she didn't give the woman any reason to complain for the rest of the day. She was asked to check on Grant twice, but didn't approach his bed if not asked to, although her eyes wandered several times toward it. He didn't stir from the long sleep the opiate had induced.

"He needs to reenergize his batteries," Rane commented when she caught Marie looking at Grant's unmoving shape under the white sheets.

Marie nodded, not knowing what to say. Soon after, Rane declared she could retire for the day.

"You've done better than I expected." And with those words, she looked at the exit and then went back to her patient.

Marie left the men's infirmary without looking back, although she wanted to go see Grant one last time. But she had the feeling Rane hadn't stopped watching her and felt the doctor's dark eyes on her as she opened the door and closed it behind her. Once in the dark hallway, she leaned against the damp brick walls and let her heart slow for a moment before facing the upper floors' population. She was worried her face showed how upside-down she felt and wasn't in a mood to give explanations. After several long minutes, she decided to start the ascension back to the women's world. She would've lingered in the hallway, but the certainty that Rane could leave at any moment made her move. And sure enough, Marie's feet had touched the last flight of steps around the corner when the unmistakable sound of a door swinging on its hinges reached her ears. The door closed immediately and nobody followed her.

Chapter 5

"So, how was it?" Verena was filling her plate with everything in sight.

Marie had found her in the kitchen and waited for Verena's shift to end so they could eat together. The cafeteria was blissfully empty this early in the evening and they could talk without worries; the ladies behind the counter weren't paying attention to them and there were only a handful of girls sitting at the tables. Marie steered Verena toward the most isolated table, the one in the darker corner not reached by the windows' light. Nobody wanted it for that reason and it was perfect if you didn't want to share your space with anybody else. Marie had found out about it soon enough. As one of the last arrivals to Redfarm, she'd been forced to sit at the unwanted table several times when her turn hadn't coincided with her new friends. She didn't mind though.

"So?" Verena reluctantly followed her to the dark corner, made an eloquent face as her eyes darted toward better-illuminated spots, and finally sat on the proffered chair.

"Dreadful." Marie wasn't sure she wanted to share what she had felt while working under Rane, but she needed to talk to someone. "I was sent to tend to the men." She had lowered her voice, even though the closest person was several tables away and engaging in a conversation with the lunch ladies.

"Hmm…" Verena dropped the spoon with the soup on the plate, splashing vegetables and little chunks of meat on the tablecloth. "So you worked at the men's infirmary, ah?"

"Not that I had a choice." She felt her cheeks redden. "Madame Lana sent me there. I didn't go because I wanted to."

"Of course not." Verena gave her a puzzled look, and Marie realized her vehement comments had been unnecessary. "What did you do the whole day?"

"Mostly I dressed wounds." She fought for a moment with the idea of not saying anything else, but then she always felt safe in Verena's presence and she added, "Grant was there."

"Grant?" Verena scooped up the pieces of soup from the table and put them on the edge of her tray.

"Carnia's... Grant." Marie couldn't help but lower her voice even more.

"I know who you were talking about. What about him?" Verena was eating her soup with great pleasure.

Watching her friend enjoying her dinner, Marie realized her stomach didn't seem to be open for business. Actually, the idea of eating made her feel queasy. "He'd been whipped. Badly."

Verena shrugged. "It happens." Done with the soup, she was already attacking the heap of mashed potatoes.

"It does." Marie didn't want to appear unsophisticated and didn't confess how much seeing Grant's marred flesh had affected her.

"It's the way things go..." Verena waved her fork in the air.

"I know—" Marie bit her tongue.

"But?" Verena had lowered her voice and looked behind Marie.

Apprentices and elders were slowly filling the cafeteria and voices echoed around the big room. Verena composed her face in a smile and saluted someone. Marie turned to face Cina and Laila. "Hi, girls." She followed Verena's example and plastered a smile on her face.

The two girls took two chairs from a nearby empty table and joined them. "I heard you lucked out on peeling duty." Cina deposited her tray on the table.

"Not the way I see it." Marie mindlessly moved pieces of broccoli and chicken all around her plate. A swirly pattern took shape and she erased it with her fork.

"She got the men's infirmary," Verena supplied, licking the sticky sweetness of a small pastry cake from her fingers.

"I see." Laila didn't seem surprised.

"Well, why do you think they can't find a substitute for Carnia? There aren't enough girls willing to pass the first part of the training under Rane." Cina looked at Marie as if she were an idiot.

She felt like one at the moment. "Everyone knows about this except me, huh?" She gave Verena a piercing look; her friend had the decency to lower her eyes to her empty plate. "Well, I had no idea when I left the Institute that training to be a nurse meant working with men." She sounded childish even to herself, but couldn't stop from adding, "And I'm pretty sure Madame Carla would be furious to know I've been forced to do just that."

"You weren't forced." Verena looked at her from over the cup of steaming tea she was drinking.

"Feels the same to me." Marie grabbed her own cup of tea to have something to do with her hands instead of punching the trio in front of her.

"She didn't know about the training-on-the-workers-first deal." Laila was playing with the metallic beads on her bracelet, letting them clink against each other.

The gesture reminded Marie of the bracelet she had once given Idra, now lying under her pillow. Instantaneous guilt trip. She had thought of the girl she had professed undying love to not once in several days. Maybe weeks.

"Marie?" Cina waved one hand before Marie's face to make her come back to Ginecea.

They had kept talking while guilt ripped through her about not having thought of Idra. "Sorry—"

"It's okay. I'd be out of it too if I had to touch a man." Laila shivered.

"Did you?" Cina looked particularly interested in what Marie had to say on the topic.

"Did I what?" She knew what she had been asked, but wanted to play coy.

"Did you touch Grant?" Verena surprised everybody with the question.

"You mean Carnia's...?" Laila's eyes became big as saucers.

"I didn't," Marie lied without thinking. "Rane didn't let me do anything." The words came out of her mouth before she could stop them.

"Sounds strange. Doctor Rane's famous for her hands-on teaching." Verena looked Marie in the eyes and didn't lower her gaze for several unblinking moments. "And... didn't you just say you dressed wounds?" She had lowered her voice to a whisper to be heard only by Marie.

A plate fell on the floor not far from they were sitting and the whole table jumped. Laila and Cina started laughing and Verena and Marie followed a moment later. The rest of the dinner was pleasantly spent in recanting old and new gossip. The questions about the infirmary seemingly forgotten by everybody.

Once back in their room though, Verena asked, "Are we friends?"

Marie spun around, surprised by her question. She took a moment to collect herself by methodically closing the door behind her, then sat on her bed and removed her shoes. Once she started slowly massaging her feet, she thought she was ready to talk. "Why would you ask that?"

"Are you going to tell me the truth about Grant?" Verena hadn't moved. She finally turned and gave her back to Marie when she hesitated to answer. "Fine."

"Why do you want to know?" Marie wanted to come clean about the mixed feelings she had regarding the day spent at the infirmary, but she felt ashamed of not having clear thoughts about the whole situation.

"I need to know where you stand." Verena had resumed her earlier position, a wall towering over Marie, her arms crossed under her breasts.

"I don't understand." Marie gulped down the knot that had formed in her throat.

"Are you attracted to men?" Apart from the lips, not a single muscle moved on Verena's stony face.

Marie chocked on air and sputtered, "How...? What...?" She felt hot and wiped sweat from her forehead. "Someone could hear you asking me... that. Are you crazy?" She was angry at her friend and couldn't repress the shaking in her hands.

"You wouldn't be so mad at me if my question didn't make *you* mad." Verena's voice was now sympathetic, which enraged Marie even more. "You wouldn't be the first one to like men—"

"I'd never like a man. I could never, ever like a man. How dare you say anything like that?" But the more she said it, the more it sounded hollow to her own ears. Unwanted memories of her fingers caressing Grant's hand came back to her. "I'd never…" Tears stung her eyes and she angrily wiped them away. She was at the mercy of feelings she didn't have a use for and a friend who could read her mind. "Never say anything like that again."

"I won't. Promise." Verena reached her and sat on the bed. "I didn't mean to upset you. I'm sorry." She drew a sobbing Marie closer and hugged her. "But remember, if you ever need a friend to confide in, I'll be here for you. Understand?"

Marie sniffed, grateful for Verena's warmth, but uncertain about her words.

"Sometimes, I forget how young you are," Verena murmured, and for once, Marie didn't rebuke her.

She had no strength left to feel angry at the slight to her age and felt even less at the moment. The maturity she always claimed to have temporarily took a leave of absence. "I'm no men lover."

"You shouldn't use that phrasing." It was Verena instead who rebuked her. "It isn't nice."

Marie didn't know what to think anymore. The whole day had been one shock after another and she was mentally and physically exhausted. Her eyes felt heavy, but she was too unnerved to relax. "I'll go take a shower." Marie left the room with the unsettling certainty that she and Verena had reached a new level in their friendship, but she wasn't sure she liked it. It felt too intimate.

In the shower stall, under a stream of hot water, she released all her encaged rage and screamed. She didn't say anything, only a guttural sound that would've scared her any other time.

Someone asked her if she was okay. "I'm fine," she grunted toward the glass door. The shadow outside lingered a moment. "Don't need anything," Marie said, and the girl walked away. Alone again, she started laughing.

"Marie?" Verena was outside the shower stall.

"Yes?" She wondered how long she had been under the water. The shower wasn't as hot as before, but she couldn't see past the fog covering everything from her body to the glass door.

"Are you okay?" Verena unsuccessfully tried to clear the glass by wiping it with her hand. "Why don't you come out?"

"Was just about to." Marie turned off the water and let the showerhead sprinkle her with the last lukewarm drops. Then she opened the door and grabbed the oversized bath towel hanging from a hook. "Brrr." The temperature outside was cold and drafty. She doubled the towel over her chest and ran to the drying station where hairdryers were aligned in neat rows.

Verena handed her a comb and said, "You forgot it in your hurry to escape."

Her tone was teasing, but Marie knew her friend was telling the truth and thanked her.

"Also, someone told me you were acting weird in here." Verena gently took one of Marie's limp, wet tresses and disentangled it with her fingers. "You've the prettiest hair when dry, but it's a mess to take care of when it's not."

Marie smiled, but Verena's statement evoked another compliment paid to her mane just the same day. Her smile was immediately replaced by an expression that prompted Verena to apologize. "I was trying to lighten the mood." She raised her hands in the air in mock surrender.

"I know... My hair's so fine it's impossible to comb after I wash it. Once, when I was little, Madame Carla had to cut this much because it got so tangled after a bath that it hurt too much to brush." Marie accompanied the tale by raising her palm to show Verena the length of the cut and then layered her hand on top of the other. "At least ten fingers, if not more. I cried for days."

"I would've cried too." Verena resumed the untangling. "You could use an oil mask."

"I'll keep that in mind." She dried her hair so it wasn't dripping anymore, combed it with hurried strokes, then decided it was enough. She was even more restless than before the shower. "Have you ever felt as if your thoughts don't belong to you?" She turned to look straight at Verena's eyes, as if her image reflected in the mirror wasn't good enough to talk to.

Verena took a moment before answering, but when she did her lips were curved in an enigmatic smile. "Lately? Always."

"What happens when you can't follow rules?" Marie couldn't be more precise; she thought she had already said enough to incriminate her.

"Sometimes, nothing happens. Sometimes, life happens." Verena leaned to take Marie in her arms. "Don't worry about nothing. The confusion you're feeling will clear soon enough."

Marie relaxed in her friend's warmth. Verena made her feel better even when she forced her to confront unwanted thoughts. "Don't leave me," she murmured in her friend's shirt.

"Not planning on it." Verena's soft laugh reverberated through the fabric. "Unless they make me."

The ghost of the next Donor Day was always present at the farm. Nobody wanted to talk about that day, but it was the foremost thought in everybody's mind. Unless they had something even more disconcerting to think about. *Maybe, that's why workers are kept close to fathered women's places. To let them become familiarized with them*, she thought but didn't dare voice her ideas. *And when they're chosen to be donors, it doesn't seem as terrible.* But it sounded so farfetched that she shook her head.

"What is it?" Verena asked from over her head.

"Silly thoughts." *Maybe they are right. I'm still too young.*

"They're good for you." Verena laid a soft kiss on her head.

"If you say so." Marie burrowed farther in her friend's embrace, breathing her calming scent. "You make me feel good."

"Anytime." Verena playfully ruffled her still wet mane. "You didn't do a great job with your hay straws."

"But I thought you said my hair was pretty." Marie disentangled her limbs from the bear hug she kept Verena locked in and stuck her tongue out.

"You're even prettier when you smile." Verena smiled one of her all-white-teeth smiles and Marie reciprocated but couldn't help a yawn. "Time to go nighty night, sleepy head."

Marie woke the next morning, energized and with the hope she could survive another shift in the men's infirmary if Verena was there at the end of the day to patch her wounds. After a good breakfast, she hopped down to face what Rane had in mind for her today.

"Good morning," she greeted the doctor as soon as she entered the men's infirmary.

"It must be for you." Rane was hands-deep in what looked like a bucket of blood resting over a table; she was standing by a bed occupied by a man who didn't seem to be breathing.

"Is he...?" Marie's heart was racing against her ribcage. She had never seen a dead person and didn't want to start today.

"No, he's alive. The human body shuts down when in shock to preserve much-needed energy." Rane pulled her hands out. "Wear some gloves and then pass me that cloth, please." She indicated the transparent gloves sitting by a pile of white cotton squares on the tray on the cart by the bed.

Marie hurried to give her the cloth, which Rane used to dab the man's forehead where blood oozed from a neat cut.

"The report says it was *accidental*." Rane cleaned the blood and then reached toward the tray for gauze. "Hold here with two fingers, but be careful not to put too much pressure."

Marie put her hand over the wound and then gingerly lowered it to keep the cloth in place. "Like this?"

"Yes, like that." Rane gave her a reassuring nod without looking at her, her eyes on the tray. "Must ask Madame Lana to give me more first aid supplies." She cut a piece of skin-colored tape. "Thank you, now you can remove the cloth. Throw it in the garbage can that says 'hazardous materials' and then come back here."

"Hazardous material?" Marie didn't like the sound of it and looked at the gloves she was wearing.

"Anything that touches a man is considered potentially infective. Higher directives. We must follow protocol. You're safe. The only thing those men carry is their unlucky genes."

Marie disposed of the bloodied cloth in the special bin and then returned to Rane's side, waiting for instruction. Her eyes darted right and left when she thought the doctor wasn't minding her.

"Looking for something?" Rane hadn't moved from her position, bent over the unconscious man, closely checking that the wound was cleaned. "Someone?"

"I see there're fewer patients today." Marie hoped the doctor didn't turn and see the crimson rapidly coloring her fair skin.

Sometimes, like now, she wished to have the same dark complexion as Rane or Verena.

"A good day. We have some of them once in a while. But they're rare. Don't get used to this peace. It normally doesn't last long." Rane showed her a needle and a thread. "Come closer and look. You need to learn fast here. As you can see, we're kind of short on personnel."

Marie observed as the woman closed the wound on the man's forehead by putting together the edges of the slash between the fingers of her left hand and passing the thread in and out of his skin with her right hand. The doctor worked with slow and methodic gestures, breathing evenly through the process. When the gash was completely sutured, she finally turned and smiled at Marie.

"Good job," Rane said to her.

"Well, thanks, but for what?" Marie cleaned the tray and threw the used material away.

"You just passed an important test." Rane went to the closed cabinet by the entry door and retrieved something from it.

"Did I?"

"Congrats, you're officially my new training nurse." The doctor offered her the folded green scrub she was holding. "Unless you aren't interested anymore. Then you're free to leave now," she added when Marie didn't make a move to accept her gift.

"No second thoughts, I want to do this." Marie just realized that she had passed a test indeed. Until a few minutes ago, she had always fantasized about becoming a doctor someday, and as a fathered woman, her chances were slim. But thanks to Rane, she now knew she wanted to help people, and it didn't matter if she would ever be a doctor as long as she was working in a medical facility. And the part she would've never imagined was that the gender of the patient didn't matter to her. She hadn't thought for a moment that Rane was working on a man while the doctor carefully stitched his wound. It hadn't mattered in the least. She had focused on the part to be treated and forgot the rest of the world existed. "I can do this."

"I can see that." Rane's eyes shone bright and Marie felt proud of herself.

The rest of the day passed in relative tranquility. She wondered how Grant was, and her eyes darted once or twice to the bed where he had lain the day before, but she was careful not to let the doctor see her. Two workers were brought in at the end of Marie's shift and she offered to stay. Both men had light injuries on their arms and torsos. When asked what had happened, they refused to say a word. Dinnertime came and went, but she helped Rane until none of the men were left to tend to.

"All in all, it was a great day." The doctor stretched her arms and tilted her head first toward her right shoulder and then the left, finally forward and backward with a big, contented sigh. "Tonight I can go to bed in my room."

"Do you sleep here sometimes?" Marie massaged her arms up and down. Now that they had stopped working, she felt cold.

"Most of the time. It's so early in the morning when I finish with my patients that I'm too tired to haul my butt five floors up, so I just lie on one of the beds and nap before morning comes and everything starts again." Rane went to restock the first aid packages and lined them up on one of carts. "Go, get some rest. Tomorrow could be a different day."

"Have a good night's sleep, Doctor." Marie doffed and folded the scrubs, then put it in the small cubicle Rane had freed for her. She was already opening the door to leave, when the doctor called her. "Yes?"

"You didn't ask about your patient from yesterday." Rane's dark eyes held a mischievous light.

Marie felt the urge to lower hers. "Is he okay?"

"Yes, I released him early in the morning. He was feeling much better and the guards needed him to finish some maintenance job." Rane kept looking at her.

"Good… See you tomorrow, then." Marie wanted to run away, but the doctor's stare was pinning her to the spot.

"See you tomorrow, Marie." A smile curved Rane's mouth.

After a solitary dinner, Marie went straight to shower and then to her room. Verena was out and she was happy to have the place for herself. One of the few things she had come to appreciate at Redfarm was the privacy one could have. She put on her nightgown, softly combed her hair, and then went to lie on her bed only to have her routine disturbed by an intermittent light illuminating the room. "What…?" When the phenomenon didn't cease, she went to the window to see what was causing it. After a moment of blindly staring at the glass panel without being able to see anything, she noticed a pattern in the length of the light and following darkness. It kept repeating in a loop, until she understood someone was sending a message of sort in Morse code. "What is it?"

When nothing more than little girls, Marie and Idra had spent whole afternoons playing spies with the other girls, happily dreaming of adventures and exotic places they had read about in the magazines they stole from Madame Carla's closet. The rector had a penchant for gossip tableaux, but must have been ashamed of it because she took great care in hiding the proof of her vice inside a box stashed under blankets in her closet. Discovering such treasure had been the pinnacle of their spying agency. Unfortunately, they had been eager to share their success and Madame Carla had shut down their operation with a stern rebuke before the whole Institute. The memory stole a smile from her, but Marie's knowledge of Morse code was rusty at best. Not enough mysteries to solve or exotic places to go if you were a fathered woman.

T… H… A… what else? Marie squinted at the window as if it helped deciphering the letters. *N… K… S…* Long pause. *M… A… R…I…*

"What are you doing?" Verena asked, tapping on Marie's back and making her jump out of her skin.

"What the heck, Verena!" One hand on her chest to silence her galloping heart, Marie sat on the edge of the desk. "At least make some noise."

"I called you." Verena stepped back and went to her bed.

"Did you?" Marie saw the intervals of light and darkness dancing on the walls, but refrained from looking at the window.

"I did. What's this, anyway?" Verena gestured toward the window and back to the display taking place.

"I have no clue." *Thanks, Marie.* She shrugged, feeling like the worst of liars. Then, thinking that she would've lied about this even to Idra, it made her feel terrible. *What on Ginecea is happening to me?*

"Is someone using Morse code?" Verena opened the window and the light flickering stopped right away. "Hmmm, strange." She turned to face Marie, who, at loss for words, shrugged again. "How long did it last?"

"Just started." Marie tucked herself in her bed and pulled the sheets and quilt up to her chin.

CHAPTER 6

"This was left for you." Rane pointed at a small package lying on one of the infirmary's carts. Marie had just entered the room. The doctor was taking a worker's temperature and writing down notes on a pad, slightly swirling on her wheeled chair. "Aren't you curious? I am." She raised her eyes from the pad.

Marie went to the cart and looked at the small package without daring to touch it; her name was on it, written in neat handwriting over a faded newspaper page used to wrap it, and a piece of rope closed it. "Who sent it?"

"It was outside the door when I opened the infirmary two hours ago."

Marie leaned toward it and then stopped.

"For Goddess's sake! It isn't going to bite you." Rane wheeled her chair to the cart, took the package, and threw it at Marie, who, taken by surprise, almost missed it. "Good catch."

Marie looked at the small item and passed it from one hand to the other, trying to understand what it could be.

"Open it." Rane sighed. "Or I'll do it for you." She reached out to take the package from Marie's hand.

"Gimme a second!" Marie tore the paper away before Rane could get hold of it. "Oh…"

"What is it?"

Marie stared at the gift she had just unwrapped. "A piece of marzipan." No point in hiding it.

"We have an admirer, don't we? How romantic." Rane smiled at her. "Do you know who could it be?"

"Not a clue." *Grant.* Her heart had a strange reaction at the thought he had sent her the gift.

"Well, she must know your tastes to send you marzipan of all things." The doctor was back to her patient, giving Marie her back.

"She must." She went to her cubicle to pick up her scrubs and leave the gift she had already carefully rewrapped. Without being asked, she started sweeping the floor and then dusted the counters. A peculiar sense of happiness spread through her.

During the day, the door of the infirmary opened several times for the guards escorting workers to be patched. Every time, Marie's heart sped up, leaving her utterly confused when disappointment struck at the realization it was just the guards and some random man. At lunch break, she asked to be excused and left with the intention to eat with her friends. As soon as the infirmary door closed behind her, her legs, acting on their own will, brought her to the cellars' entry. *What am I doing?* Her doubt was short lived because a moment later, she entered the cellars. Her eyes went to the far wall where she knew the little window was. From a distance, everything looked exactly as it should, but she walked directly to the wall and found the evidence the opening had been recently used and hastily closed. A fine dust had settled on the floor, and when she looked at the wall closely, it was possible to see light coming through cracks between the bricks. Whoever had used the passage hadn't had time to patch the gaps in the wall.

Acting on impulse, she tapped on one of the bricks. "Is there anybody there?" she asked in her smallest voice. When nobody answered, she pulled one of the corners of a brick toward her, repeated the question, obtained no answer, and finally removed the brick from the wall. She peeked at the other side and was disappointed with the view. The room seemed uninteresting, just a large storage closet with brooms and buckets. She stood before the opening she had just made, hoping for... She didn't even know what exactly, and then put the brick back where it belonged.

She was leaving when the sound of steps coming from the other side made her stop. As before, curiosity won and she stood still instead of walking back to the infirmary, or better yet, showing her face in the cafeteria where she was supposed to be eating.

"Do you reckon it's true, then?" A mature voice Marie recognized.

"It must be." Grant.

She felt that little whoosh in her stomach she was starting to associate with him.

"I think you risked too much…"

"I can't live what's left of my life without hope. It must be true. I need something to live for. I can't go through another day hoping the captain isn't going to look my way." Grant sounded sad, tired.

Marie was deeply touched by his words.

"And you think I like it? Of course not, but what would happen if we finally manage to escape and this City of Men doesn't exist? Assuming we leave and we're not caught by Callista's guards, like you were three times already. Assuming we don't die outside in the desert. Assuming we ever reach this place—"

"I don't want to think of all the things that could go wrong. I just want to leave this place and never come back."

Marie could imagine Grant's motions by the vehemence of his voice.

"I wish for all of us you're right and this fabled place exists. We sure could use some hope. Anyway, let's get some rice. We've lingered enough already." The older man finished his speech and the steps sounded closer to the wall.

Marie was at the end of the cellars before the brick was removed once again.

"Eat well?" Rane asked a few seconds after Marie silently entered the infirmary.

She looked at the doctor, confused by her question, the conversation between the older man and Grant still playing in her mind. She blurted out one barely audible "yes."

"Glad to hear that." Rane showed her a tray on the cart by her side. "I've been informed by her highness, Captain Callista herself, that there's some kind of virus spreading among the workers. Wear the mask and wash your hands frequently."

True to her words, not even an hour later, annoyed guards started bringing men to the infirmary. Almost every one of them presented the same symptoms. When the sixth man came down with severe dehydration due to a stomach bug, the doctor asked what they had to eat for breakfast. Then when the answers she obtained didn't convince her, she started uncovering them, looking for something.

Marie looked at her, Rane carefully passing her hands over some of the men's arms and backsides. Rane bared more than Marie was ready to look at and she busied herself with something else. Suddenly Marie's skin was too warm and she went to refresh herself in the bathroom.

Marie returned a few minutes later. "What kind of virus is it?" She affected a detachment she didn't feel and her whole front wet due to a vigorous encounter with the water.

"Virus my butt." Rane gestured for her to come close to one of the men she was sponging with a soft cloth. "Look. What do you see?"

That he's almost completely naked? Somehow, she knew that wasn't the correct answer. "His skin looks… reddish?" It was the only thing she had noticed.

"Yes, and what else?" Rane made space for her to step even closer and her eyes went to the man's arm.

Marie diligently followed her gaze and saw a small red dot at the center of a small swollen circle on his skin. "He got a shot?"

"They all got shots this morning." Rane's eyes encompassed the rest of the room, where some of her patients were still sick after hours of continuously emptying their stomachs.

"Are they vaccinating them or what?" Marie looked too. They'd had to ask for additional buckets. The ones they had were not enough.

"Who knows?" Rane looked like a person who indeed would know, but Marie didn't press the matter.

She realized something. "None of them were here in the past three days."

"What?" It was Rane's turn to look surprised.

"None of these men, not even one, have visited the infirmary since I started working here."

"You're right." Rane smacked her forehead, then looked at her with renewed respect. "You're absolutely right. This means the women are experimenting with healthy specimens."

"Experimenting?" Marie looked at the workers and shivered at the notion of experimenting on human beings. Yes, they were men.

But still. They felt pain as women did. She had plenty of evidence before her eyes. "What kind of experiments?"

"New vaccines and experimental drugs are tested on workers…" Rane's voice faded as her eyes seemed to focus on something that eluded Marie. Then the doctor's attention was snatched back into the room and she gave Marie a startling look. "I don't understand… There're sementals among these men. Normally sementals are left alone."

Marie winced. "Do they have… those here? Why?" Although she wanted to become a nurse and she had accepted that she had to train on men first, the mention of sementals still stirred her sensibility. She wasn't as offended as she would have been a few weeks ago, but years of Madame Carla's teaching had shaped her to be the fathered woman she was and talking of sementals was improper. "Redfarm isn't a—"

"Redfarm isn't a semen factory, but we still keep track of good specimens that could be better *employed*. We test them before sending them to their final destination," Rane answered, oblivious to Marie's embarrassment. "But what kind of drugs could they be testing?" She paused a moment, as if collecting her thoughts, then sighed. "They must be playing with the semen enhancers again. Can't believe after they lost so many workers last time, they're still pushing—"

Marie had reached her limit. "Who are *they*, exactly?"

"The Temple's doctors." Rane started pacing back and forth from one wall of the infirmary to the other.

"What temple's doctors?" Marie saw Rane's raised eyebrow and gasped. "The Priestess's Temple?"

"What else? The Temple's doctors go from facility to facility, looking for fresh subjects to experiment on."

"But—" Marie was confused. The Temple was the holy place where pure breeds went to have their daughters. Fathered women held the place in high esteem—probably higher than the pure breeds themselves did—because they rarely put foot inside of it. In fact, the few of them who had were treated like royalty. Hearing Rane talking about the Temple in association with sementals and what they were bred for was blasphemy. She was so shocked she couldn't say all the things a good fathered woman should've said in such circumstance.

Rane came closer and lowered her voice to a whisper. "Mark my words, sooner or later those men will rise against us."

Marie couldn't suppress her shock and several men turned toward her. She put both hands over her mouth and shook her head.

"Remember what I said." Rane gave her one last look and then, as if she had said nothing at all, she turned and went to work on one of her patients. "Help me with this one." She kicked a wheeled stool toward Marie and motioned her to approach the bed.

Marie obeyed the command and did what was asked of her, but she didn't know how to act around the doctor anymore. She had heard her make risky statements before, but Rane had never reached such level of profanity. The idea of asking Madame Lana to be excused from duty crossed her mind. The man under their combined care emitted a sound, part rattle, part pained moan.

"They have nobody who's willing to defend them." The doctor didn't turn, but stopped Maria's hand with hers over the man's chest. "Their heart beats like ours."

Maria cried in surprise. "What?"

Rane released her hold on Marie's hand. "Your shift just ended. Go back upstairs to finally have your lunch."

Heart beating fast, stomach upset, and sweat covering her forehead, Marie ran away from the infirmary, only to be stopped at the door, as it seemed to be the doctor's habit.

"And next time, don't bother lying to me again." Rane gave her one final, cold stare. "Decide if you really want to save lives and come back only if your answer is yes."

Back in her room, several floors between them, she thought of what the doctor said and didn't know what to think. If training under Rane meant being exposed to her ideas, she wasn't sure she could do it anymore. Maybe she could write Madame Carla and ask her to take her back. She could offer to work at the Institute and never leave again. She would be such a good elder for the little girls. *Yes, I'll explain to Madame Carla I can't stay here anymore. She won't deny my request once I tell her what's going on at Redfarm.* Then, in the middle of her furious reasoning, she remembered she had left

Grant's gift at the infirmary. And for same reason, she knew without a doubt she wouldn't say anything about Rane and her perverted ideas. She then realized Idra hadn't crossed her mind the whole day, again, and sadness engulfed her. Big tears swelled in her eyes and she sobbed against the pillow, trying to smother the sound of her misery. Longing for some solace, she probed under the pillow, looking for the bracelet she had hidden there, and when her fingers found the cold charms, she seized it like a lifeline. From far away, she heard the door opening and closing, but was beyond caring.

"It's that time of the month again?" Verena approached the bed and playfully ruffled Marie's hair.

"You'd think." She smiled between sobs and eventually started laughing. *That's it. I'm hormonal. It's the only explanation.* At the Institute the older girls always talked about that and how they were mean to each other because hormones made them say awful things. She had never believed it, but lately she had been changing moods more times she could count.

"What did Rane make you do?" Verena stopped playing with her hair and slowly combed it in multiple small braids. "By the way, I came looking for you at lunch break."

Of course. "The doctor wasn't in a good mood today." She relaxed under her friend's therapeutic hands.

Verena's fingers gently massaged her scalp and she purred like a contented kitten. "I heard you had the infirmary full for some virus."

"It was no virus." She closed her mouth four words too late. She wasn't sure Rane wanted the truth to be paraded outside of the infirmary.

"Then what was it?" Verena stopped massaging her, Marie complained, and she resumed her controlled gestures.

"Not sure." She took her bottom lip between her teeth.

"You don't want to say." Verena didn't even sound disappointed, which made her feel worse for lying.

"Rane thinks they're experimenting on the workers." She was tired of not saying things.

Verena must have been surprised by Marie's willingness to talk because her fingers hesitated for the briefest moment. "Why? And who are they?"

"That's exactly what I asked." She was satisfied her friend reaction was the same. "As for the who, it seems the Temple's doctors are involved—"

"The Priestess's Temple?" Verena couldn't contain her surprise and stood without warning, sending Marie down on the bed.

Marie managed not to roll off the bed and started laughing, rocking her body back and forth and almost falling again. She laughed until she cried.

Verena patiently waited until she was done and then when Marie raised her eyes to her, she gave her a stern look. "I don't see how what I said could be so funny."

"You repeated my question, word for word." She cleaned the tears with her sleeve. The idea that none of this was funny at all did pass her mind, but it only made her want to laugh again. "Hormones." She breathed in and out and finally answered her friend's question. "Yes, the Priestess's Temple."

"Are you sure the Temple's doctors are involved with workers…?" Verena looked outraged.

"Rane thinks so. I don't know." She shrugged.

"And why?" Verena sat back on the edge of the bed, looking directly at Marie.

"As for the why, according to Rane, they're experimenting with fertility drugs to increment—" She couldn't bring herself to say the last words, but Verena understood and blushed.

"No!" Verena mirroring Marie's reaction to the letter brought her hands to her mouth and stifled a cry. "That can't be! The Temple is the holiest of places."

"Could you work for Rane?" Marie abruptly asked. The question burned a trail from her heart to her stomach.

"Is she talking about this kind of thing all the time?" Verena inched closer to her.

"Not all the time." Marie wanted to be fair. "I thought you knew what kind of person she is." Since everybody had known about

Redfarm's habit of sending trainees to work on men first, why not knowing about Rane's unorthodox agenda?

"Obviously, only a few people know about that. No wonder Carnia didn't want to leave the infirmary…" Verena moved on the bed and went to sit with her back against the wall, mirroring Maria.

"Would you work with her?" She shifted uncomfortably, averting her friend's eyes.

"You're asking because?"

In moments like these, Marie was reminded that Verena was older than she was and she felt silly. "Because I still want to work there."

"Then you shouldn't mind what Rane says." Verena pulled her close and let Marie's head rest on her arm, both of them with their backs to the wall.

Marie, who had gone from laughing hysterically to worried and sad in the span of a sentence, breathed in relief. "Do you think people will think I'm a… men lover?" She whispered the last part.

"People will think what they want to think." It was Verena's turn to shrug. "I wouldn't judge you for it."

Marie had thought about that. Verena was as normal as they get, but had defended Carnia's blasphemous relationship. "But I would never, ever be one of them."

"Sometimes, you don't decide whom you want to be with." Verena hugged her closer and kissed her head in that sisterly way of hers.

Marie was relieved by her words, but Verena still remained a mystery to her. She wouldn't get caught thinking about a man, but she was the most tolerant person she knew. "Why are you like this?"

Verena distanced herself from Marie and smiled. "Like what?" But from the smirk she couldn't hide, she knew what Marie had asked.

"So good to people, even people like Carnia." She didn't want to know why, but it was important to her Verena answered with the truth.

"It's easier to be nice." She gave Marie a smile. "Come here." Verena pulled her back to her side and they stood still, silently looking at the wall in front of them. "We should hang something there. I didn't know it was so depressing to look at."

They both started laughing and kept laughing for a while.

The morning after, Marie entered the infirmary with a new resolution and didn't waste time waiting for the right moment to communicate it to Rane. "I won't be intimidated by your talk, but I would appreciate you minding your words." She spoke slowly, deliberately enunciating the letters.

"Are you done?" Rane, who hadn't even had time to acknowledge her presence, looked at her from the medicinal cabinet she was restocking and then pointed at one cart topped with a big piece of meat and surgical instruments.

"Yes—" Marie was taken aback by the doctor's reaction. She had expected to have to work it out longer.

"You'll practice stitches on the roast beef." Rane moved items on the shelf level to her eyes.

Marie went to look at the piece of bloody meat and wore the gloves, but didn't know what to do next.

"Make a deep incision with the scalpel." Rane opened a box at her feet and extracted a few books from it. "What are you waiting for?"

Marie was gingerly holding the scalpel, but she hadn't reached for the meat and was startled by the doctor's abruptness. She didn't want to be told off twice though and focused on the task ahead. "Like this?" A large, deep gap now marred the meat.

Rane gave one brief look and nodded. "Now, start closing it again like you saw me doing the other day."

Marie washed the scalpel and then came back to grab needle and thread. Forehead wrinkled in deep concentration, her fingers carefully went back and forth, threading in and out of the two ridges of separated tissue. Some time later, she gave one final stitch and raised her head to find Rane not two feet away from the cart, intently looking first at her handiwork and then at her.

"You're a natural, of that I'm sure." She sighed. "You could be invaluable to me." Arms folded on her back, she paced a few steps. "I'd hate to lose you."

Marie wanted to reply she didn't have to, but the infirmary door opened and two guards escorted in two men: Grant and another man Grant supported through the door.

"Same stomach virus the workers had yesterday," one of the two guards said when Rane asked what symptoms the man had.

The other guard made sure Grant was at her side as soon as he left the worker on one of the beds.

Marie had her eyes on him the whole time, hoping she could say something to him, but the guard had him to the door in no time. He was almost out when he tripped and almost fell.

He turned to face Marie, and while regaining his balance, he mouthed, "Thank you," a second before the guard shouted how clumsy and useless he was. The door closed behind him and she heard a thump followed by a muffled cry. Breath coming in shallow bouts, she fought the urge to run after them and see if he was all right.

"He's strong and still very useful. They wouldn't hurt him badly." Rane was at the worker's bedside already administering fluids and asking questions. "I see. Another victim of the *virus*." She lowered the hem of the shirt she had lifted to check his back.

Marie wasn't sure if the first part of what she had said was directed at her. Maybe she wasn't as discreet as she had thought in showing her emotions and Rane had seen right through her. Or maybe it was a coincidence and she had read too much in the doctor's words. *She'll drive me crazy. I'm driving myself crazy.* This wasn't the first time she wondered about her sentiments and how people would react to them. Finally, her worries over Grant won over the rest of her rational thinking. "Young workers are treated differently than the older?" Still, she couldn't bring herself to be direct.

"As long as they're needed, they're fine." Rane shook her head and then added, "Well, fine isn't the right word, but you get what I mean. They aren't treated as bad as the ones that are no longer useful." She raised one eyebrow. "You asked."

Marie nodded. She had asked knowing the answer already. Partially reassured Grant would be okay for the time being, she redoubled her efforts to get on Rane's good side. The day at the infirmary went better than she had expected, and she finished her shift having learned how to stitch almost to perfection. Rane had her practicing the whole day by cutting the same piece of meat everywhere until there was no whole tissue left to slash.

Once out of the infirmary, instead of going to the cafeteria, she ran outside to the courtyard, the piece of marzipan retrieved from her cubicle when Rane was too busy with a patient and secured inside her dress' front pockets. She'd been thinking about the small square the whole time and now she wanted to savor it alone. Safely hidden by the mulberry trees' foliage, she sat inside the natural gazebo and slowly unwrapped her gift, her mouth salivating at the thought. She bit the smallest piece out of it and let it melt on her tongue, the sweetness and smoothness of the almond paste making her moan.

"I knew it was the right gift for you." Grant stood a few feet from her hiding spot, just outside the trees' canopy but sheltered by its shadow and the safety of the building wall.

She saw his smile and the way his eyes shone bright and made her smile back. "Love marzipan."

"I'm glad I could get some for you." He stepped under the canopy and went to sit by her side, his legs close to hers but not touching.

"I'm glad you stole some for me." She couldn't help to rectify his statement, but her tone was light and he laughed. She was happy about that. *I like his smell,* she caught herself thinking and almost said it out loud. "Would you like a bite?" She offered the tiny morsel on her outstretched palm.

He made to push her hand away, then shook his head without reaching for her. "It's just for you, but thank you."

Marie felt disappointment grow inside of her. "Have you had news from Carnia?" And there she had asked the only question she didn't want to hear the answer to. She normally wasn't so irrational.

Grant hesitated and then raked his hand through his hair. "No. I was hoping you'd have some…"

All of a sudden, the sweetness lingering in her mouth soured. Marie lowered the piece of marzipan on her lap, her temper rising, her eyes stinging. She was aware she started it, but it didn't lessen the dark coil from tightening inside her stomach. "Don't know anything about her. Already told you we weren't friends."

"Yes, I remember." He scooted away, as if her mood had created a rejecting wall. "It's not why I sent you the gift though."

She frowned, liking the sound of what he was saying, but afraid he would crush her hope with the next word. "Why did you?"

"Because you helped me even though you don't like Carnia or me. You didn't rat me out and you took care of me at the infirmary. I wanted to thank you for that." Grant slowly moved closer to her as if testing the waters. "Nothing more."

In the span of a moment, her mood had lifted again. "You're welcome." She didn't rectify him this time. She didn't like Carnia, and she was starting to understand why. It scared her.

"Must go…" He stood up but didn't leave, his mouth open and silent.

Marie wanted him to stay a moment longer, but noises from the farm brought her back to a reality where she was willingly having a conversation with a worker. "Go!" She watched as he disappeared behind the corner, the dark shadows safely wrapping his tall figure, and then she went back inside, uncertain steps leading her way.

CHAPTER 7

Later, back in her room, alone—Verena had left to run an errand for some elders—Marie lay on her bed and had time to think about her day while staring at the ceiling. Grant was the ever-present thought from which every other thought derived. She had let go of any pretense of not wanting to think of him. Finally, she had to accept she liked thinking of him. *Could I like him?* It was a blasphemous thought and it still made her feel dirty, but there was no way around it. Otherwise, why would she get so riled up when Carnia was mentioned? She had been so sure of Idra's affection. She had never felt the sting of jealousy. It was such an unpleasant, dark, diminishing feeling and she hated everything about it. '"What's happening to me?"

"I don't know. Something bothering you?" Verena was staring down at her.

"Not sure." Marie had vaguely heard her coming this time, but hadn't bothered silencing her voice. "How's Darlene?"

Verena blushed and retreated to go sit on her bed. "How do you know the errand was for her?"

Marie turned on her side to look at her. "Please." She raised one eyebrow and whirled her hand in the air. "Why are you still wasting your time with a girl like her?"

"I don't have a choice." Verena shrugged, sadness emanating from her in waves.

"We always have a choice." Marie's voice sounded harsh even to herself and one look at her friend confirmed it. She regretted her words but couldn't take them back.

In contrast, Verena's rebuke was soft. "Not when you're in love with someone."

"I think we've already talked about this." Marie dismissed her before they would delve into the anguish of unrequited affects.

"Changing subject, if I had any doubt the women knew there was no mysterious virus attacking healthy workers, I got proof now. Two guards came down to the infirmary escorting two men and they wore no masks or gloves to protect themselves from getting sick."

"Experimenting on men isn't right. I know they're men, but—" Verena was playing with her hair, coiling and uncoiling her luscious tresses.

"They're still human beings." Again, Marie's voice came out louder than the situation asked for.

A series of shots reverberated from outside. Both Marie and Verena hurried to the window. They didn't have time to see what was happening before a second round followed and then a third and fourth in rapid succession. Finally, the alarm siren came alive and covered every other sound.

"What?" Marie looked at Verena. The frightened look in her friend's eyes scared her.

They stood like that, frozen, for a long moment, then started firing questions at each other, shouting to be heard over the loud noise. Once in a while, Marie would look at the glass panel, hoping the darkness outside would lighten and show her what was happening on the ground. Meanwhile, the buildings in front of them had come alive. People appeared at the lit windows, anxious faces scanning the night for answers. A girl holding hands over her ears was rushed back inside by one of her mothers; the other remained to watch over the farm. The alarm was abruptly shut off, but it took several minutes before Marie's heart slowed down. One by one, the opposite buildings' lights were shut off as well, and she turned to face the normalcy of her room.

In the awkward silence that followed the blaring of the siren, a knock resonated from the hallway and startled Marie and Verena. Before they could answer, a girl flew into their room. "Rane wants you downstairs. Immediately."

Marie gave one look at Verena, who nodded at her and then followed the messenger. The girl didn't know anything. "I was just told by Madame Lana to get you there."

"Madame Lana?" Marie was surprised the command had come from the rector, but the girl was reluctant to talk. Either she didn't know anything or she had orders not to say more than necessary. Her ears still ringing, Marie was disoriented by the absence of life permeating the building. Normally, girly chatting would be heard reaching the stairs from the dormitories. The silence was eerie and she was scared by the stillness in the air. At the infirmary door, the girl without a name—she hadn't offered one and Marie hadn't asked—left her with a nod and a "good luck."

"Are you out there?" Rane's voice cut through the wall and there was a note of panic in it Marie couldn't ignore.

She entered the room to find a scene she couldn't understand. Everywhere she looked, there were wounded men. Some of them looked too broken and pale to be alive. Others were crying. One wailed, right there before her eyes. A sound she had never heard before. She froze. Rane ran to the man.

"Need help here." The doctor screamed to be heard and several workers stepped forward and hurried to her. "Keep him down." The men crowded around the doctor and bent over the worker who had let out that horrible cry a moment earlier.

Marie felt threatened by the army of men filling the room. Her legs didn't want to sustain her, and she was sweating.

"Marie! Come here!" Rane was hidden behind the wall of men, but her voice was loud and clear.

Marie tried to walk, but the trembling in her legs worsened. Someone approached her but stopped a few inches away from her. She turned and saw Grant.

"Don't be scared." He raised one hand as if to reach for her, but let it fall by his side as he had done earlier.

"I can't help it." She hated to admit that, but most of all she hated to admit the fact she had longed for his touch.

"It's okay. It's understandable." Although he looked tense, his voice was warm.

She focused on the calming quality of his voice. "I'm better."

Grant tilted his head toward the corner where the doctor was. "Are you going to be okay?"

Marie nodded.

"I'll be around if you need me." His hand hovered close to her arm, but once again, he lowered it and slowly walked away from her.

She went to don her scrubs and gloves, her eyes on him the whole time.

"Marie! I really need you here. Now!" Rane emerged, the men opening to give Marie space.

She looked down at the thrashing figure on the floor. "What's happening to him?" The man's eyes were wide, his mouth was open, and a foamy trickle ran from his bottom lip to his chin.

"Gas." Rane beckoned her to come closer to the man. "Take that belt and put it between his teeth."

"I heard shooting…" Helped by one of the workers who kept the man's mouth open for her, Marie inserted the belt as the doctor had asked. She removed her fingers a moment before the man closed his jaws around the leather strip and his head shot backward.

"He was one of the lucky ones who got gassed," the worker who had helped her said.

One brief look at the rest of the room and then at back at the worker, she saw he wasn't being sarcastic. "Why?"

"A small group of workers were caught trying to break free and the rest of them fought the women to give their mates time to clear the breach in the wall." Rane emptied the whole content of a syringe into the man's right arm and waited a few seconds for the thrashing to diminish. The man relaxed on her arms and she sighed in relief. "Thank the Goddess, I thought he was gone."

Memories of the conversation Marie had heard only recently came back to her. "Did any of them…?" She wasn't sure she should be asking those kinds of questions.

"None of the workers who were trying to escape survived." Another of the men surrounding the doctor raised his head to look at Marie.

"I'm sorry." She lowered her head, soaking in the sadness permeating the room. It was a palpable element, impossible to tune out. It wasn't just the cries or the moaning. The despair and the hopelessness hung heavily over her heart and darkly colored her thoughts.

"Triage all the new arrivals." Rane, followed by the same handful of workers, went to the next patient, a man who lay preternaturally still on a stretcher, blood dripping from a gun wound to his left leg. A small pool of dark-red, viscous fluid had formed on the tiled floor.

Marie averted her eyes. "We're expecting other patients?" She had thought the whole farm's male population was already there. She hadn't finished asking when the infirmary's door opened. Several men entered the room in haste, some showing wounds so severe she wondered how could they be walking, let alone carrying others. Pain etched in their faces, they were careful not to mishandle the unconscious in their care, but they left bloodied prints in their wake. The dreadful parade was closed by five guards ready to shoot anybody who disobeyed. Marie saw how the men at the back of the line trembled any time the women raised their guns or used them to better convey their orders. One of the improvised porters stumbled and almost dropped his cargo. She was at his side without thinking, helping him up by hoisting his weight with her whole body. She was taken aback by how heavy he was, but what surprised her the most was the terrified face the man made a moment before understanding she didn't mean to harm him.

"Why are you wasting time and effort on these animals?" the oldest guard asked Marie, her cold, blue eyes staring unblinkingly at her. The focus of her disgust seemingly limitless. "I can't believe you found another willing to help you," she said to Rane, but still looking at Marie, her patrician features expressing her feelings as well as her tone.

From the number of barrettes on the woman's grey-and-black, tightly fitting uniform, Marie knew she was the one in charge. The pure breed guard, captain, or lieutenant—Marie could never remember the order—coiled and uncoiled a whip around her hand in a sickening display of power. The man Marie was holding stepped back and tripped again, his body shaking in fear. She let him go, her own limbs slightly trembling. It wasn't the first time she'd been in the presence of a pure breed, but she had never interacted with one before. The kid-snatchers—as she called the pure breeds who visited the Institute—rarely exchanged words with the girls.

"Do you have an estimate of how many men you're sending here, Callista?" Rane, displaying an impressive calm given the way the pure breed had addressed her, gave the woman a brief nod in salute and then turned to face her patient once again.

So you're the famous Captain Callista. Marie had heard of her since the first day at Redfarm and wondered about the woman. Now, she was more interested in understanding what kind of relation there was between the doctor and the officer if Rane could use her given name with such familiarity.

"We should be done soon." The pure breed seemed annoyed by the doctor's lack of proper fear. "There aren't many left standing anyway." A malevolent glee illuminated her blue eyes.

Marie shivered even though she wasn't under the woman's stare anymore.

"Send them over once and for all, then. Haven't you had enough fun already?" Rane kept her body at an angle, her face hidden from the pure breed, but visible to Marie who saw how repulsed she was and how her words betrayed a history between the two.

Callista raised one meticulously trimmed eyebrow—probably to maximize the sharp angles of her high cheekbones—and shot back immediately. "At my own pace, mind you, dear Rane. And be thankful I've already taken care of the lame and old—"

"Have you? How considerate." She dragged her last words more than necessary and closed her right hand in a fist only Marie could see. "Have you informed the morgue already?"

"No need to waste your time in expensive and useless autopsies. I've sent orders to dig a mass grave outside in the desert. Much more practical, don't you think?" Callista waited for a response from Rane, and when the doctor remained silent, she turned on her heels, the clicking of her steel-reinforced boots accompanying her exit.

Marie watched as the pure breed was silently followed by her minions. A collective sigh of relief became audible when the door closed behind them. A loud clank made her jump out of her skin and she swung toward the point of origin of the noise. A tray of surgical instruments lay on the floor by Rane's feet and she looked distressed. Marie ran toward her. "Let me—"

Rane looked at Marie as if she had forgotten she was there too. "Thanks." Her voice shook and she couldn't keep still.

Marie picked up the instruments, placed them back on the tray, careful not to cut her fingers with the knives' sharp edges, then located the big pot Rane used as a sterilizer and dumped the contents of the tray in it. She tried to assess what she should do first, but after one gaze at the room, now overcrowded, she felt lost.

Rane had slowly composed herself and was now bent over a man who was holding the left side of his stomach with both hands. "I wish I could do more for you."

Marie felt sad at the doctor's statement. She met Grant's eyes for a moment and saw the rage burning in them. She understood him.

"Can you give this man something for the pain?" He looked down and she saw him carefully holding someone's hand in his.

"Yes—" She was going to ask Rane permission to give the man a painkiller, but then thought better of it and went for the cabinet where all the medicines were kept. From the cries escaping the man's mouth, his pain must have been excruciating. If she wanted to become a nurse, she had to also to become accustomed to making decisions. Better sooner than later. "Here." She brought the two innocuous-looking pills to the man's mouth.

"Are they strong enough?" Grant didn't seem impressed by the medication's appearance.

"Opiate," was all she said, wondering if maybe she had brought too much. The man gave a shout that pierced her ears and she felt better. "Enough, but the effect won't be immediate. The pills need to break down in his stomach."

Grant whispered something to the man and then looked at her. "How long?"

"Twenty, thirty minutes." She pulled the answer from what Rane had recently told her and her memory of the first time she had taken a painkiller for a strong headache. Madame Carla would have never permitted her to contaminate the holiness of her body with anything chemical. She had felt guilty at ingesting the medicine for a whole half an hour. Then the headache had lulled to nothing more than an afterthought and she had wondered why on Ginecea Madame Carla didn't believe in painkillers. "Nothing else we can do for him, but talk to him and try to distract him from his pain."

Grant whispered to the man, "Joe, you'll feel much better soon," and then raised his eyes to her. "Thank you."

"Just my job." Urgent cries called her to another corner of the infirmary. "Must go." She went to take care of the ones in more pain, meticulously assessing their wounds and what could be done for them. Once or twice she had to ask Rane about the best line of action, but for the most part, it only took a bit of common sense to be of help. Madame Carla's teaching came handy once or twice. Hours passed; more men arrived. Some of them showed signs of torture. Marie didn't rest the whole night. She kept moving from one bed to the other, and when the beds were all taken, she crouched on the floor from one thrashing form to the other. She crossed paths with Grant several times. He too had been moving from one man to the next, helping the two women. He wasn't the only worker doing so; others followed his example as soon as they got back on their feet.

Feeling rather worn out, Marie glanced at the clock on the wall and discovered breakfast had already passed. Her eyelids were heavy and she struggled to keep them open. Even her ears weren't properly working because all she could hear were muffled sounds. She scanned the room, looking for Rane. "Doctor?" She couldn't see her anywhere. "Rane?"

"You should sit." Grant was at her side, a worried look on his face.

Marie swayed and steadied herself by reaching for the back of a chair standing nearby. "Can you see where the doctor is?"

"She left a few minutes ago." He reached for the chair as well and turned it for her. "You should sit."

Losing her fight to keep upright, Marie fell back on it. "Where did she go? Why didn't she tell me she was leaving?" The questions were more for herself. She didn't expect him to answer.

"She went to talk to the captain."

"Why?"

"She needed to know which gas was used during the last attack." His eyes went to a corner of the room where several men curled in balls or held their chest in pain. They were still and gray looking; none of them cried out or even whimpered. At Marie's raised eyebrows, he added, "Nothing she's given them is working. She's worried it must be something lethal."

She tried to remember when those men had arrived, but the events of the previous hours had blurred together. At one point, there had been a constant stream of guards escorting workers, who in turn carried other workers on stretchers. She had heard Rane screaming orders and she had seen men running to help her. At the same time, Marie—per the doctor's direct order—was too busy washing wounds, calming patients, and looking for clean dressings to pay any attention to anything else. "Are they dying?"

"Yes, they are. If Rane doesn't find out what they used… They don't have much left." His voice was sad and his expression resigned.

Her head was light, and the rest of the room turned upside down, but she forced her tired body to respond and slowly stood on her legs. "Help me there." She pointed at the men. She couldn't bear to let them die alone.

Grant opened his arm and slightly bowed to her. "After you."

Rane must have thought the dying men couldn't stand the light because the corner where the men lay was dark. But Marie saw their puffy faces and the way their bodies seemed to be frozen in the most unnatural positions. She repressed a sob and sat on the floor by one of them, a young worker, maybe her age or slightly older, and without thinking, she took his hand in hers. "I'm sorry this happened to you. To any of you."

The young man's eyes misted and two fat tears rolled down his otherwise still face. Marie felt anger building at such sufferance and being unable to do anything. She instinctively turned toward the medicine cabinet, but Grant shook his head.

"The doctor has already given him three or four times the amount you gave Joe." He passed his hand through his hair and sighed. "She said it's too dangerous to give him more."

She wanted to scream. Any options she had to help these men had been stripped from her. Marie slouched against the wall. Her body was so tired it ached and her mind couldn't articulate a single thought anymore. The night had drained her. A loud noise echoed through the room and she opened her eyes, her heart pumping against her ribcage. A second later, she realized it was the infirmary door swinging on its hinges after Rane had kicked it.

"I thought she would listen to reason." Rane paced like a caged animal, back and forth on the same three tiles. "She doesn't even care the farm is under the minimum number of required workers—" She kept blathering, probably used to being alone in the infirmary and too distressed to realize she was talking out loud before an audience.

Everything appeared to move in fast-forward. Marie's ears and vision were adjusting to the new level of volume and activity. "Did the captain tell you what gas she used?" Marie saw a halo of dark spots around the edges of her sight when she tried to get to her feet.

"Callista said, 'Let them be an example.' She prefers to lose good workers." Rane had stopped pacing but was now tapping her clog on the floor.

Marie hoped she would stop soon but didn't dare ask her to settle down. "What can we do for them?" She checked on the young man; he had his eyes closed now and his breathing was shallower.

"Nothing. We can do nothing but watch them die." Rane finally stopped and Marie saw she had been crying. The doctor went to slump beside her and let her head fall backward against the wall. Eyes to the ceiling, tears falling down on her scrubs, she whispered, "I'm so tired of watching them die."

Marie couldn't say anything. There were no suitable words for a moment like that.

Grant left them and then came back with a few pillows and blankets he had probably taken from more fortunate patients. "We can make their last moments more comfortable."

"You're right." Rane left the infirmary before Marie could ask where she was going.

Grant gave Marie a puzzled look and then proceeded to rearrange the men so that their heads were pillowed and their bodies were covered with the blankets. Then he sat by the young man and took his hand as Marie had done, and he started talking to him.

Lulled by his voice, Marie closed her eyes and fell asleep. When she woke, she felt disoriented and slightly nauseous. Meanwhile, the doctor had come back with some medicine she was injecting the dying men with. "Something stronger to ease their passing," Rane answered Marie's silent question.

Almost immediately, they seemed to drift into a peaceful slumber. Grant silently thanked Rane and then resumed his tale. Marie listened as he told the boy about the last time they went to the cellars to steal food and the steak they ate that night. Rane didn't move the whole time Grant reminisced about their criminal endeavors. Marie noticed the doctor didn't seem surprised, and when Rane gave her a knowing look, Marie realized she hadn't acted surprised or shocked either. She was past caring though. The pain she was witnessing trumped every last bit of her propriety.

Grant talked for hours, his voice remaining even and soft while he recounted every single episode he had shared with those unfortunate men. Now and then, he even chuckled at something he had just said. "Remember when Rufus turned sixteen and we dared him to touch a guard's baton when she wasn't looking?"

There were lots of stories like that, and while Marie failed to see how most of those situations could be funny under any circumstance, she was grateful Grant could do something for those men. The young man had become completely unresponsive after the first hour and his eyes had rolled to white. She gently lowered his eyelids and couldn't help but hope he was beyond physical pain and misery.

Rane took his wrist between her fingers and sighed in relief. "He'll be gone soon."

Marie had never thought wishing someone's death would be an act of mercy and wondered if working in the men's infirmary meant mostly that. How could anyone maintain her sanity? No wonder the doctor appeared so unstable. What would be of her in a month or so?

A few hours later, the young man's body wilted on the floor, the last remnant of life slipping through him. She had the unsettling feeling she saw the moment he died and the realization chilled her to the bone. The young man's face relaxed before her eyes, and in death, he looked even younger, no more than thirteen.

Grant stopped his stream of words and for a moment was unable to tell the next story, his effort at not crying visible through his clenched jaw and red eyes. He breathed slowly, waited a moment, then resumed his talking for the other men until, one by one, they were gone. Only then did he howl to the ceiling, a sound so sad and so haunting, every movement in the infirmary ceased at once.

Marie realized through her stupor that the rest of the men had kept tending to the wounded, carrying on their job while she and Rane took care of the dying. The silence stretched as every standing man slowly walked to give their mates their last salutes. Nobody said a word, but each man placed his right hand over his heart. Grant was the last one; he stood up on uncertain legs and repeated the salute, his eyes moving from body to body, then dropped to his knees and covered them with their blankets.

A sound coming from outside invaded the sanctity of the moment. A loud voice was calling for Rane, but she didn't react. The doctor's eyes were fixed on the covered bodies, and her lips were moving. Marie didn't understand what she saying, but it sounded repetitive, like a prayer. The yelling became louder and closer. The door was unceremoniously opened by an irate Captain Callista, who was immediately followed by a handful of her women.

"I told you not to mettle with me." In a few strides, Callista had walked by Rane's side and was now pointing a manicured finger at her. "I told you before I wouldn't tolerate your interfering one more time." Despite her authoritative tone, her finger trembled, betraying how angry she was. "Didn't I tell you?" She moved closer to Rane, her body towering over the doctor, who hadn't yet acknowledged her presence. "Did you think you could get away with it?" Finally, she forced Rane to look at her by pulling her hair and tilting her face up. "I'll make you pay for this act of insubordination."

Rane kept silent and still. The only exception was her eyes that, for the briefest of moments, wandered toward the men being herded at the back of the room by the captain's guards.

Callista noticed though, and her free hand balled in a fist, but she didn't move it from its resting place on her hip. Instead, after a moment of awkward silence, she released the hold she had on the doctor and turned to face her guards. "Round them up and take them to the court. Then put them in a straight line. One every three will be flogged. The second in line will go without food for five days. The third will be sent to a waste plant tonight."

Marie dared a look at Grant, and she saw the fear in his face. The captain turned on her heels and Marie lowered her eyes to the tiles while the men were escorted out in complete silence. She raised her chin, but Grant had already exited the room. Her attention was diverted toward Callista, who made a scene to remove dust from her immaculate pants.

"Where were we?" Callista walked closer to Rane, until she was invading her personal space once again, but she kept her hands to herself this time. "Oh, yes. Now I remember." She smiled and spoke slowly and close to Rane's face, but Rane still didn't flinch.

Marie didn't understand how Rane could be so composed while she was on the verge of throwing up. She was worried for Grant, for the doctor, and for herself. There was something in the captain's maniacal calm that promised more unpleasantness to come.

Callista took Rane's face between her hands, and for a moment Marie thought she was going to kiss the doctor, but she didn't.

"When I realized what you had done, I thought of a way to repay you and decided a change of air would do you great. I'm sure you'll like it there. Won't you, Rane?" Callista lowered one hand to Rane's jaw and tilted her chin left and right. "Always the savior you were. But in reality, you are garbage and I think it's only fitting you should end your days amongst garbage."

Rane had the audacity to smile. Just her upper lip curved up, but a smile nevertheless. That simple gesture brought the captain over the brink and she slapped Rane with such strength her head lolled back and hit the wall behind her.

"You'll die there, you know that? But, at a waste plant, death is never fast or merciful. It's slow and shameful, and you deserve every painful bit of it," the woman spat with a low hiss, her demeanor altered by the confrontation, her eyes wild and cruel, her breathing ragged.

It took several seconds for Marie to fully understand what the captain had just said, but when she finally did, she cried out loud, "You can't send her to a waste plant!" Her plea managed to attract Callista's attention and she wished she could disappear under a rock when the woman's eyes focused on her. "Please—"

"Please what?" The Captain smiled at her, a cold show of perfect, white teeth.

Marie shivered, knowing Callista was playing with her. "Please, she's a good fathered woman."

Callista seemed to think about that for a moment. "A good fathered woman, you say."

Marie felt Rane's hand touching her arm, warning her to stop talking, but she went ahead anyway. "Yes, I'm begging you—"

"Don't—" Rane started saying, but Callista interrupted her.

"Yes, listen to her, child. Don't interfere in adults' business." Callista turned toward Rane once more, but kept talking to Marie in her haughty tone, as if imparting a moral lesson. "You see, a good fathered woman, as you erroneously called her, would have never ignored precise orders from a pure breed. She would've never gone behind my back and asked for medicine I didn't order. And I didn't order them because they're expensive and wasted on workers. And what did she need those medicines for?" She paused.

Marie didn't know if she was expected to respond.

Callista resumed before Marie could decide. "This fool needed the medicine to ease the passage of a few workers who were dying because of their stupidity. And she signed the order on my behalf. Did you not think I would discover your betrayal sooner or later?"

"They were in a lot of pain," Marie couldn't help but whisper.

"What did you just say?" Callista spun so rapidly, Marie didn't see the woman grabbing her by the shoulders and pulling her up, her feet dangling in midair.

Out of the blue, something possessed Marie. Without fully understanding what she was doing, she repeated her words and added, "She was only doing her job. Nobody should suffer so much." Fully conscious of what she had just done, she braced for the slap that didn't come. Eyes half-closed, she peeked and saw the captain was looking at her intently.

"Well, I was right in my first assessment. You did find a replacement for the other man-lover. I got rid of the redhead by sending her to a semen farm, but you look too young…" Callista slowly released Marie to the floor, where she stood on shaking legs. The captain held the pause longer than necessary, as if she were waiting for Marie to respond to her silent threat.

This time, Rane squeezed Marie's arm and intervened before she could say anything. "Don't take it out on her, Callista. She didn't mean it. We have worked through last night and today. She's clearly disoriented."

"How convenient to blame heresy on sleep deprivation." The woman kept looking at Marie with her predatory stare. "How old are you anyway?"

Rane stood up. "Please, leave her alone. She's just fifteen."

"It's settled, then. She's too young to be a donor, isn't she? Pity." The captain stepped back and gave Marie one last chilling smile before heading to the exit.

"You're angry with me—" Rane's voice broke and with that Marie's hope as well.

At the door, Callista slowed her stride to impart one final blow. "Pack light, child. At the waste plant, you won't need a lot of clothes."

Marie didn't react at first. She refused to believe what she had heard. It couldn't be true.

"I didn't mean for you to get in the middle of my mess." Rane held out her hands to hug her, but Marie collapsed on herself, a heap on the floor.

She felt hands touching her, but she couldn't see anything. Her eyes shut and her body felt too heavy. Thankfully, darkness came to her rescue and she drifted toward a soundless haven.

CHAPTER 8

Something, maybe someone, woke her. Other than the fact that she was still at the infirmary, Marie couldn't be sure of anything. She tried to climb off the narrow bed she didn't remember lying on, but didn't make it far. Her right wrist sported a handcuff. "What's that?"

"Callista gave orders to stop us from leaving this room." Rane appeared to be equally tied to the bed next to her.

"Why?" Marie needed only a second to remember why and then wished she hadn't. It was all true. The nightmare she thought she had was her new reality. "When?" she asked after a moment.

"I expect Callista to come any moment now. I let you sleep through the best part of yesterday afternoon and tonight. It's already five in the morning." Rane spoke slowly as if collecting her thoughts. "Marie, I'm so sorry—"

The door opened and several guards entered, followed by Callista. The woman had taken great care with her appearance. There wasn't a single detail out of place; even her boots were shined to perfection. The contrast with Rane's and Marie's slovenly appearances was evident.

"Callista, I'm begging you to reconsider. Marie has learned her lesson." Rane tried to stand upright, but she'd been handcuffed at an uncomfortable angle and didn't have the same range of motion Marie had.

"It's too late." Callista waved her elegant hand in the air.

Marie smelled an expensive scent wafting her way and automatically became conscious of her condition. She could smell her own fear emerging among the unpleasant aromas emanated by her unwashed body. The sheer magnitude of the disgrace Callista had called upon her made her stupid. She simply wasn't able to think beyond the immediate or maybe she didn't want to think what would happen one minute from now. She heard the conversation, understood everything, but felt as if she wasn't there.

"Spare her this humiliation. I'll do anything you ask." Rane grew more and more anxious, her voice betraying her fear.

"Yesterday, I made an example out of those miserable workers. Today, I'll make an example out of two stupid fathered women." Callista snapped her fingers and four guards flanked Marie's and Rane's beds. "Good-bye, Rane."

The guards removed their handcuffs and hastily hoisted them up. "Move and don't make a scene," the one who was holding Rane ordered and then accompanied her words with a sharp slap to the doctor's face.

Marie thought the punishment uncalled for, but she was still floating somewhere above the scene, not fully connected with what was happening. She followed instructions but still earned a baton poke by one of the guards. She cried out, but didn't recognize the sound as hers. Once out of the infirmary, silence swallowed her and that somehow managed to put a dent in her armor. They walked the stairs two at a time, only to slow when they reached the first floor. The guards brought them to a halt outside the kitchen. The silence became a suffocating presence, and she saw them. All the people she knew at Redfarm were there, staring at her, mouths agape in shock and judgment. Her friends were there, first in line, looking at her, eyes wide. Verena was there, face puffy. Her eyes were red, and long streaks of dried tears stained her beautiful skin.

"I don't believe what they're saying—" Verena said, at first her voice too broken to be fully understood. "I don't believe them!" she screamed and everybody turned from Marie to her. "It's a lie. You wouldn't do it!"

"I didn't do anything..." Marie didn't understand. Her head was clearing and she didn't like it. As the numbness was receding, a feeling of despair took its place. Not caring was better compared to the agony slowly working its way to her heart. "What did they say I did?" She looked at Verena, hoping for an answer, but Callista demanded the audience's full attention by hitting the floor with a whip lash that zinged through the air and produced a thunder-like noise.

"All of you take a good look at those two women. Have you?" Callista paused for effect. Some of the younger girls even nodded at her question. "This is what happens to men lovers who help workers escape. They are sentenced to life in a waste plant."

At the last statement, people reacted. Some of the apprentices gasped in shock, part of the elders who evidently had already helped spread the rumor stood silent, while others cried their disbelief. Finally, Callista's words dissipated with what was left of the fog in Marie's mind. Or maybe it was the way her name was called by her friends. Or the tears in Verena's eyes. Marie felt her legs giving out and sagged to the floor before she could reach for Rane's proffered hand. She looked at Callista, who was coldly staring at her, and she wished she had fainted.

"Here at Redfarm, we punish perversion with the maximum penalty. Do not ever forget that." Callista grabbed Marie by the collar of her shirt. "Do not feel sorry for her." She shook Marie, whose limbs swayed as if she were a ragdoll.

Cina, Laila, and some of the apprentices she had worked with in the kitchen sobbed. Verena was beyond crying, her face frozen in a silent scream.

"This is not your friend anymore. She committed blasphemy. She will be pay for her sins." Callista gave her another jerk.

Marie couldn't help but let her tears fall. When she thought her humiliation was complete, Madame Lana appeared. She hadn't seen the woman descending the stairs, but there she was to be testimony of her last moment at Redfarm. Marie started crying in earnest. None of the numbness she had felt before was left, only searing pain tearing through her body. She didn't grovel and beg; she knew it wouldn't help. The captain was power-angry and a pure breed, and she was nothing more than a fathered girl.

"Captain, I believe you proved your point eloquently." Madame Lana walked slowly toward them.

"Madame, these women are culpable of harboring and aiding workers. They are men lovers." Callista looked at the older woman in suspicion.

"I'm sure it was a misunderstanding." Madame Lana stepped closer and calmly reached for Marie and freed her from the captain's hold.

Marie stood still for a long moment, uncertain of what to do. Her body shook so hard it became difficult to stand still. She saw Madame Lana open her arms to receive her, but Marie couldn't move.

The woman closed the gap and embraced Marie, who, had she any sanity left, would've been shocked by the rector's demeanor. "This girl wouldn't hurt a mosquito and I've never heard a single complaint about Doctor Rane. Helping workers to escape… demonstrating unhealthy affections toward men… those are big accusations. Let the matter settle for a few days. We can open an official inquiry."

At the rector's last suggestion, Callista's eyes narrowed into two slits, her mouth serrated in a white line, and when she finally opened her mouth, her voice was calmer and colder than before. "The bus has just arrived and these two fathered women will be leaving. There won't be any delay in delivering their punishment, because today, tomorrow, or a week from now, the sentence will be the same. I'd leave things the way they are if I were you." She had come face-to-face with Madame Lana to whisper her warning.

"I'm not trying to hinder—" Madame Lana couldn't finish.

Callista snatched Marie from the older woman's arms and said out loud, "If you sin, you will be branded as a sinner."

Marie was thrown toward Rane, who caught her. She thought she heard Verena raising her voice and then a louder whiplash than the first.

"Escort them out." Captain Callista's order echoed in the absolute silence. "Vasura is waiting."

The collective gasp following the disclosure of the waste plant's name sounded deafening. Fathered women whose crimes were so heinous imprisonment wasn't punishment enough were sent to Vasura. For a moment, Marie looked at the people staring in shock. A feeling of disconnection swarmed over her yet again. Then, Verena's face stood out and she was painfully reminded of her reality.

Rane put one hand on the small of her back. "Start walking. The guards are hoping we make a scene so they can punish us in front of everybody."

Marie followed Rane's suggestion and slowly put one foot in front of the other, trying not to look back at Verena. The hallway only one step ahead, she had to turn to say good-bye to her friend. "Verena! I'll never forget you!" The baton hit her on her back with unexpected strength, and she breathlessly fumbled forward.

"This isn't necessary." Madame Lana hastily helped her to her feet. "Child, don't make them angrier. I won't be able to keep you safe once you're outside these walls."

Marie looked at the woman and nodded, dark spots dancing before her eyes. Rane took Madame Lana's place by her side and gently pushed her out of the big hall. She had only a brief moment to realize she was leaving Redfarm for good and was on the bus before anybody could say a word to her.

"Enjoy the view." One of the guards showed her and Rane the seats behind the driver.

Marie raised her eyes to look at the guard and realized the young woman was staring at her with genuine worry. "Thank you." She slid inside and took her place by the window.

The guard nodded, then tilted her head slightly, checking if she was being watched. "Madame Lana sends this." She reached inside her uniform and retrieved a brown envelope from an internal pocket.

Rane took the proffered item and hid it under her seat. "Tell her…" Her voice trailed, and tears silently washed her face.

"She knows." The guard took Rane's hand in hers and squeezed it. "She knows. You don't have to say anything."

"Tell her anyway." Rane's eyes turned to look outside the window and she shook her head. "What are you doing here?" she whispered to the glass. "I don't want you to see me like this."

Madame Lana was standing on the first step of the landing by the majestic dark-red door. She waved her slim hand, her lips moving.

Rane put one hand on her heart and leaned toward the window, almost sitting on Marie's lap, to put the other hand on the glass. "Me too."

Callista appeared at the door, a malevolent presence behind the rector, and Rane immediately dropped her hand. The captain called the young guard outside, and two armed guards hurried inside as she climbed down. The door closed, and the driver moved the bus in one single movement. In a few seconds, Redfarm disappeared behind a corner in the road.

Samara passed by, the clean streets and the elegant buildings resplendent in the morning sun. Marie watched as stores opened for business, clerks showed their wares in the best light, and café owners arranged tables behind stained glass. In a few days, the debutant season would begin and all the pure breed girls of age would make their official appearance in society. Not that she would ever have had a chance to be part of it, not even as hired help. Still, tears fell for all the conversations about silly, vain pure breeds she would never have with Verena. And then she sobbed because she would never make fun again of pure breeds who didn't know how to tie their shoes without the help of a fathered woman. Finally, she realized she'd never had the promised outing and never visited the city she was leaving to never return.

Samara was replaced by several towns. Marie kept her eyes glued to the glass and followed the guard's suggestion, although enjoying the scenery was the least of her thoughts. She couldn't face Rane, couldn't utter a single word. Not because she would cry if she tried to talk. She simply couldn't think of anything to say that wasn't an accusation toward the doctor, and she didn't want to unleash her anger on her. When Marie turned to see how she was faring, Rane resembled more a stone statue than a person. Grief emanated in waves from her and Marie couldn't bear the sight. She angled her body toward the window and let the hours pass, her mind mercifully blank. They were both so quiet the two armed guards busied themselves bickering about the long drive. After a while, Marie forgot they were there to make sure they wouldn't try to escape their fate. As if a fathered woman could ever do that.

After several hours, Rane gave signs of life. "Tirsa." She shook Marie from her torpor and Marie frowned in wonder at Rane's solitary word. The doctor reached over to tap on the glass with one shaky finger. "There."

Marie looked and saw the far away outline of a cityscape. Elongated spires stood out against the afternoon sky, the sun slowly descending toward the horizon. She took note of the fact that almost an entire day had gone already.

"I was born in Tirsa." Rane straightened and sat back on her seat but kept looking at the window. "I always thought I was going to see it again someday." Her hands nervously played with the hem of her sweater. "Never imagined it was going to be like this." She glanced behind her seat to see if the guards were looking at them, and when she saw the two women were napping, she bent and retrieved the envelope she had hidden under her seat. Marie made to turn to give her some privacy, but Rane smiled and laid one hand on her arm.

"These are only childhood memories." She opened the envelope and took out a few pictures from it. "Look at me…" She angled one of the pictures toward Marie. It was a yellowed image of a small girl hugging a smiling woman, in the distance a fountain and several buildings with terraced ceilings. "I was such a scrawny kid." She chuckled and then let out a sob.

Marie couldn't comment. She had questions about that woman smiling at the young Rane, about her childhood, but couldn't think of anything to say that wouldn't pry in on the doctor's sorrow. She gave one last glance at the image before Rane brought it to her chest, and couldn't help but feel a pang of sadness. After that exchange, the doctor took out six more pictures one by one and silently looked at them for a long time. Only when the guards behind them stirred, Rane put the pictures back inside the envelope and then hid it under her shirt.

The bus never traveled any closer to Tirsa's city limits, but skirted along the mountain road at a steady, lulling pace. Fast enough to make it impossible to focus on details one might want to take a second look at, but at the same time maddeningly slow. Marie wanted to reach her final destination in a flash; she didn't need the cruise through the Ginecean landscape. She didn't need a reminder of how heartbreakingly beautiful her land was.

"In a few hours, we're going to stop in the capital." The driver, who had been silent the whole time, turned to face them.

"We're passing through Ginecea?" Marie was surprised.

"We're spending the night in Ginecea." Eyebrow raised, the driver gave her a look as if she had asked a silly question.

"But why?" Marie had never paid attention during geography class, but she was confident the infamous Vasura wasn't anywhere near Ginecea.

"It's an act of kindness to you." The driver kept her eyes on Marie a moment longer, then focused on the road again. "To let you see the city before you're retired at the plant."

"That's what they say…" Rane's voice was a whisper, but the guards behind them must have heard because one pushed hard against Rane's seat, making her double against the rail.

"Quiet!" Another blow and the whole seat rattled.

Marie exchanged a meaningful look with the doctor and then relaxed against the glass, not wanting to unleash the ire of the two guards. From Rane's unfinished sentence, Marie doubted showing future wasted women a glimpse of Ginecea was an act of kindness. It sounded more like giving the thirsty a jar full of marine water.

The landscape changed several times, from the Mountainous region's rocky badlands to the more gentle hills of the Ginecean Federal District, then passing through the Lake region, a holiday destination for the pure breeds. Marie had seen pictures of those places in the glossy magazine that keep track of the latest gossip regarding the rich and the famous. Once she had been mildly curious about visiting there herself. Now she only wanted the ride to be over. She watched as the sun finally disappeared behind the Great Pass beyond which the Desertica Region started and wondered only for a moment if it was true that wild men lived out there. She had heard the rumor back at the Institute, but never believed it. The thought of Grant followed and with it, a different kind of pain she didn't want to analyze. Soon, the moon owned the sky and she only saw her reflection staring back at her from the glass. Although she hadn't been focusing on what she was looking at, not having that choice made her feel desperate.

Rane's hand rested on her arm. "I won't leave you alone out there."

Marie put her hand on top of hers and murmured a thanks. "Will it be long before we arrive in Ginecea?"

"We're almost there." The driver must have had excellent hearing because Marie had made sure to lower her voice.

Rane nodded. "One or two hours tops."

Marie didn't think she could stand after the hours she sat in that seat, but asked the guards permission to use the bathroom at the end of the bus and splashed her face with the lukewarm water dripping from the minuscule faucet. She went back, dragging her feet in a vain attempt to waste time and even tried to close her eyes and sleep once on her seat.

Some time later, the bus finally reached Ginecea City. Marie wondered how two hours felt like twelve. Although illuminated only by street lamps and the majority of the scenery lay hidden behind the large cones of light, she had never seen anything as imposing as the viaduct stretching before them. The structure was made of granite and shone white. Elegant statues bordered the high parapets on both sides. The road itself was six lanes wide, but at the moment, their vehicle was the only one using it. When they reached the center of the bridge, she tried to gauge how high they were over the river, but darkness engulfed everything beyond the statues.

"Ginecea, the beautiful," the driver announced, her voice matching Marie's admiration, once the bus cleared the bridge. "First Door."

Rising majestically before them sat one of the ancient gates the capital was renowned for. The fact that, despite the name, there was no visible gate or door surprised Marie. The bus rumbled under a high arch opening on the façade of a majestic building that matched the bridge. On the other side of the arch, the city proper started. "Ginecea, the beautiful," she repeated the driver's words.

Pure breeds didn't believe in doing anything halfway. Their capital city was the pinnacle of architectural excellence. Marble, granite, and obsidian had been used lavishly. It was evident they spared no expense when it came to maintenance. Some buildings on either side of the ancient cobblestone road were centuries old but looked brand new. Poles, more metal sculptures resembling plant stems than streetlights, sported big lamps hanging like flower bulbs. As the bus left one neighborhood for the next, Marie saw that the decorations changed, and so did the architecture of the buildings.

The slow procession through Ginecea lasted at least an hour, which Marie spent with her mind shut down and her eyes wide open. She had decided only the present counted since she had nothing left. Once entombed inside the waste plant, she would never leave again. And even if she could go anywhere else, none of the people who had cared for her would want to be in the same room with her. She shook her head in a vain attempt to free her heart from the bitterness those thoughts birthed.

"We've arrived." The driver pulled the bus in an alley just outside the cone of light of the majestic streetlamps. They were engulfed by darkness with the same rapidity as if someone had switched a light off.

The two guards stood, and while one walked the few steps to the door, the other positioned herself behind Marie and Rane. "Let's go." The woman poked at Rane's shoulder with her baton.

The doctor didn't complain. She gave Marie a small smile and then got out of the seat. In a matter of minutes, they were escorted off the bus. Marie furtively looked left and right to take in some of the details, but the tip of a baton on her back convinced her to keep walking. The entrance to the building was on the street, just a few steps from where the bus was parked. A wooden door opened and closed. They exchanged the lashing cold of the night, redolent of metal and stone mixed with exhaust fumes, for the warmth inside the house, which smelled of cleaning agents and baking. Someone fumbled with the switch and the place was day-lit, causing Marie to recoil at the sudden brightness.

"Welcome to the half-house." A pure breed in her sixties, a grandmotherly type with white, curly hair, bright brown eyes, and a soft figure, welcomed them. "I'm Margareta and I'll take care of you tonight."

Marie and Rane presented themselves and then followed the woman through the half-house. Marie had never heard of such thing, but the place was cozy, nothing of the grandeur the rest of the city seemed so fond of. It was also old, the furniture attested to a life of use, and the walls had seen several rounds of painting, but the overall feeling it emanated was of care.

"You'll sleep in the same room, so I can accommodate the guards in the other." Margareta walked slowly, dragging one leg slightly. "I gave you the one with the better view," she whispered to Marie, who was closer to her.

Marie blinked at the statement but managed to attempt a half-smile. She looked at the small hallway with the low ceiling and felt her lungs shrinking. Her shoes clicked loudly on the worn marble tiles covering the floor in a pleasant white-and-black pattern.

"Here." Margareta opened a white door, a faint light-blue hue popping through. "I'll bring some refreshments in a minute."

The guards checked the room from the doorway, seemed satisfied by what they saw, and let Marie and Rane in.

"I'll be right back." Margareta closed the door behind them.

She heard the sound of the key turning inside the lock, a sad reminder of their predicament. She gave a brief glance at the room: two small beds covered with quilts, which had been stitched and repaired to the point their original designs were altered beyond recognition. A big window dominated the wall opposite the door. She walked toward it and made to open the heavy curtain.

"Marie—" Rane came to her side and took Marie's hands in hers. "I never wanted for you to get involved. I'm so sorry Callista wanted to punish me so much that you ended up in the middle of it."

She was taken by surprise by the doctor's apology. "I should've kept my mouth shut." She had been wondering why she talked back to Callista.

"You're not here because of something you said. You were at the wrong place at the wrong time. It's all my fault. I didn't think she would go to such extremes." Rane's eyes were full of tears and the expression on her face showed her pain.

Marie squeezed the doctor's hands back. "I'm so angry. I hate—
"

"You've got a million reasons to hate me. I ruined your life."
Rane lowered her eyes on the floor.

"I hate pure breeds." Marie knew she and the doctor were only
pawns. "What's the story with Callista and you anyway?"

"I was in love with her once and she couldn't stand the idea she
might've felt something for me as well." Rane wiped her tears with
the back of her hand. "In retrospect, it's me who should've never
declared my love for her. I should've known better. I should've
known it would end tragically." She shook her head, then chuckled.
"And I was right, wasn't I? Thanks the Goddess I never thought to
ask my m—the rector to smuggle the meds for me. Otherwise,
Madame Lana would be in this mess too."

Marie's stomach growled. *Get used to that.* Stories of starvation
and other horrors associated with the waste plants came back to her.
The sound of the key turning in the lock brought her attention back
to the present.

After a moment, Margareta appeared, balancing a tray on one
hand, ring of keys dangling in the other. "Here's some food. I'm
sorry I can't let you out to eat in the kitchen, things have happened
in the past." She made an arch with her key-holding hand to
encompass everything she wasn't saying.

Rane accepted the tray from the older woman and put it down
on one of the shelves jutting from the wall right to the door. "I
understand."

Margareta reached inside one of the pockets on the front of her
dress and provided them with plastic utensils. "Again, things
happened in the past."

Marie and Rane took the useless forks and dull knives and
thanked the woman. With no coffee table, nightstand, or desk
available, they resorted to sit on the edges of the two beds, facing
each other. Margareta didn't give any sign she was going to leave;
she settled her frame against the doorjamb and engaged in harmless
chitchat about the weather and other equally uninteresting topics.
While Rane tried to mumble some form of assent once in a while,
Marie lowered her head, started eating and tuned out the

conversation. The food—meatloaf and peas—was simple but tasty and she wasn't in the mood for small talk—until something they said broke through her barrier and snagged her attention.

"I'll tell Lana you were in good spirits." Margareta was collecting the now-empty plate from Rane and moved toward Marie, who promptly raised her own plate to her. "I'll come back with some herbal tea. It will help you relax."

"Thank you." Rane's lips curved up in a sad smile.

Marie had the feeling Margareta's previous statement was more involved than simply offering sleeping aids. As soon as the door closed behind the older woman's back, she turned to the doctor with the question that had kept tugging at her mind since they had left Redfarm. "Who's the rector to you?"

Rane scooted on the bed until her back was against the wall, then gave Marie a long stare, sighed, and shrugged. "Madame Lana is my mother. I guess it's safe to tell you now." Her hands went to her chest, and the envelope hidden under her shirt shifted and became visible for a moment. She immediately flattened it.

Marie's mouth hung open for a few seconds. "Oh…" She had thought the woman in the picture looked familiar, but she would have never associated the smiling face to Lana's austere one.

"As you can imagine, it's not something we like to bandy about."

"Well, of course… but how…?" Marie was at loss for words. Rectors didn't have kids. It wasn't a social rule per se, but propriety demanded a woman in charge of girls to be celibate at best. To have a daughter and employ her in the same establishment the rector directed must be a grave infringement of the rectors' code of conduct.

"She couldn't bear to lose me and forged some papers when I was a toddler." Rane interrupted Marie's history lesson by conversing with a studied calm. "I was raised at Redfarm under her vigilant eyes."

"Have you been living there the whole time?"

"No, when I was of age, I was sent to work at Callista's family-owned medical practice as an apprentice. Callista's mothers saw potential in me, and fathered women need doctors too. As soon as I finished the training, I asked to be sent back to Redfarm where I knew the rector would let me work without interference."

"So, Madame Lana knows of your... ideas?"

"Of course. She's covered for me all these years. How do you think I was able to keep a men's infirmary that rivaled the women's?" The hint of a genuine smile appeared on the doctor's face.

Marie was stunned by the revelation. She had gotten everything wrong about the rector. "I have no idea. I never worked in an infirmary, men's or women's."

"I was so pleased when she sent you to me. Mom has always chosen wisely. She's great at reading people." Rane was visibly relaxing.

Conversely, Marie was utterly confused, a state she disliked greatly because normally led her to tense up. She regretted having asked. She had expected a more plausible, although highly inconvenient love story. "Nobody ever suspected?"

"A few people know, but they are loyal to my mother and would do anything for her." Rane sounded proud.

"I'd never thought the rector would inspire anything but fear." Marie couldn't stop herself. "Forgive me. I mean no disrespect—"

The doctor laughed and raised her hand to stop her. "Don't worry. I grew up having my mother as the rector. I thought the worst things of her at times, but she's a great humanitarian. I wished you had the time to get to know her. You would've been surprised." She raised her knees on the bed and laid her chin on them, the joyous moment gone.

"I'm already surprised." Marie had the good grace not to say she was indeed shocked. What a scandal it would have been if such truth had been discovered.

"You would've loved Redfarm, I know." Deep sadness tinged the doctor's voice again. "I'll never forgive myself for your involvement in this... nightmare."

The door opened before Marie could say anything.

Margareta entered with a big smile and another tray. A minty aroma invaded the small room. "I thought you might want some cookies with your tea and I already baked a coffee cake earlier this morning and I had some left." She laid the tray on the bed where Marie was sitting and then asked if they wanted milk, sugar, or lemon.

"Why are you so nice to us?" Marie answered instead.

"Because it's my mission." Margareta didn't seem offended by her abruptness.

"The half-house thing?" She took a cookie from the white plate on the tray.

"I pledged several years ago to bring a modicum of solace to the fathered women destined to the waste plants." Margareta gently sat on the edge of the bed, careful not to upset the frail balance of the sloshing teapot towering on the tray.

"Why?" Marie asked between bites. The cookie was light and with a citrus aftertaste. She savored the way it dissolved on her tongue.

"Someone dear to me was sentenced to a waste plant and I was unable to say good-bye to her. She left without the comfort of a friendly embrace." The older woman's eyes went to the curtained window, out of focus for the slightest moment, and then her smile reappeared. "Did you have a chance to look at the view?" Without waiting for their answer, she stood up and went to part the heavy curtains.

She revealed a sight straight out of a travel magazine. Both Marie and Rane went to the window.

"Listen to Ginecea." Margareta opened the glass panes and inhaled the cold breeze rushing in from outside. "Sorry for this." She tapped the metal bars forming a grate over the window's frame. "Again, safety reasons."

Before them, on the other side of the river Taber's bank, lay the political center of Ginecea. Ancient spires of white marble mixed with sleek glass and modern iron created a breathtaking landscape.

Marie's eyes filled with tears. She wasn't sure why she was crying, but couldn't stop. The wind froze the tears on her skin, and for a moment, her sight was sharper than usual and she thought that whoever had named Ginecea City "the beautiful" was wrong. She had been wrong before. The pure breed city was majestic, elegant to a fault, and very intimidating. A place that reminded you constantly of your station in life and she instinctively hated it. The placid blue waters of the river Taber reflected the lights from the streets and the clouds from above, creating an ever-moving tableau; a few barges anchored to the pier just under the half-house undulated with a sloshing sound. Marie was reminded of the port in her beloved Trin, but the smell was different. It lacked that salty quality that was typical of marine water. And she hated Ginecea for that too, for bringing back memories of a place she would never see again.

CHAPTER 9

The morning came too soon and neither of them gained an iota of sleep. The city lights illuminating the room to a pale glow, Marie saw Rane turning and tossing on her bed, but she didn't need the conversation that would follow had she said anything. Instead, she breathed slowly and didn't move, her eyes focused somewhere outside the window they had left open. At some point during the night, the cold breeze had mellowed to a gentle rustle, almost pleasant on her skin and certainly useful to cool her troubled thoughts. She watched as the light outside changed from a pale yellow radiance to a whiter, sharper reminder of the day ahead. When the timid knock on the door was followed by the rattling of keys against the wooden panel, she finally closed her eyes to savor darkness if only for a second.

"I brought you breakfast and prepared some lunch you can eat later." Margareta didn't waste time in saluting them; she strode inside with another of her trays and laid it on Rane's bed.

The doctor nodded, maybe a thanks. Marie acknowledged the older woman's presence, but besides having opened her eyes as Margareta had entered the room, she didn't move.

"You think your lives have ended, but it isn't true. People will remember you. I will remember you. Live to the fullest." Margareta stood between the two beds, and when Marie, finally stirred by her speech, raised her head to better look at her, she saw the woman had meant every word. Margareta's eyes were shining with unshed tears, her hands hidden in the pockets of her gown designed for practicality and not beauty.

"How many?" Marie caught the flicker of understanding in Margareta's already mournful expression.

"It's a cruel number. I remember all of your names, faces, ages." The older woman sighed and then went to sit at the edge of Marie's bed. She absentmindedly patted the surface, her expression unfocused. "I can see all of you."

Marie had the feeling Margareta saw only one face and pitied her. Whomever she was remembering was probably gone—she'd been gone the moment she put a foot in a waste plant—but she couldn't forget and that must have been painful. "I don't want you to see me."

"But I will." Margareta locked gaze with her for a moment and a sad smile rearranged her features. "The guards are coming in half an hour. Be ready by then." She stood and left, her gait tired and slow.

"I don't know if I'd want to be in her place." Rane had waited for the door to close and the key to be turned in the lock before speaking. "It must be exhausting living with so many ghosts keeping you company." She leaned over the tray, took one of the two plates, and started eating.

Marie reached for the tray and looked at her breakfast. The plate was laden with colorful morsels that smelled of rich pastries. She had never tried one, but the few times she had been out back in Trin, she had wandered to the bakers' district.

She brought the flakiest of the treats to her lips, tried a small bit, and laughed. At Rane's raised eyebrow, she answered, "I always hoped one day to be able to eat one of these. I never thought it would be like this."

"When I was about your age, I hoped one day Callista would pay some attention to me, although I was only one of the many fathered girls she flirted with and then threw away. I got my wish after all." Rane laughed too, a humorless sound.

"I wish we hadn't stopped here." Marie finished the pastry and then ate everything else on her plate. Although it felt wrong to her that she would be hungry when the situation required a somber attitude, Madame Carla had instructed her not to waste food, even when it was plain and just meant for sustainment.

"I agree with you. This half-house is more to assuage a wealthy pure breed's guilt than to help fathered women to meet their destiny." Rane had already cleared her plate and raised one of the fuming cups from the tray. She drank slowly, her face turned toward the sunrays inundating the room.

"It's easy to forget Margareta is a pure breed." To Marie's eyes, the older woman was nothing if not the opposite of a pure breed. She was gentle, unassuming, caring, all qualities the haughty pure breeds didn't have.

The doctor nodded. "She's a Corelli." She said it as if it explained the whole story. "As in *Margareta Corelli*."

The name was famous, the Corelli family was one of the most influential in Ginecean politics, but other than that, Marie had no clue as to what Rane was referring to. She shrugged and went for her cup of tea and was surprised to find it wasn't tea, or at least it wasn't just tea. Spices, milk, and sugar had been added to the hot beverage.

"Chai," Rane said. "Callista was fond of it and asked Cook to prepare it for her when she was still at her mothers' house." She inhaled the aroma and then finished her cup.

Marie drank hers in small sips, sure she would never savor something as refined as this chai.

"Of course you wouldn't know her story, but Margareta's scandal was on every newspaper's page when I was a kid. She fell in love with a fathered woman who was her maid and made it public, uncaring for decorum and what her family thought of it. She wanted to change the world and her family taught her a lesson." Rane put her now-empty cup and plate back on the tray and then went to the window to look outside, her hands on the bars.

"The fathered woman was sent to a waste plant to die." Marie stacked her plate on top of the other.

Rane turned to face the room. Whatever was outside didn't interest her. "She was sentenced to a waste plant, but never reached it. When the guards came to pick her up, they found both Margareta and the girl lying unconscious on the floor of Margareta's bedroom. They had barricaded themselves inside and then drank poison. Margareta was brought to the nearest hospital and saved." The doctor started stretching, methodically moving her arms and then her neck and torso.

"The girl was left to die." Marie had to say it out loud.

"I remember the other fathered women at Callista's house commenting that it was a blessing. They would've preferred that..." Rane finished her stretching by bending over her feet, effectively hiding her face from scrutiny.

Marie wondered about her words, as she had always done when her friends had commented on that topic. For a moment, her mind went to a few happy afternoons spent with Idra and the other girls, answering what-if kinds of questions. It had been great fun imagining herself in dire situations, but now it was real. It wasn't a game anymore. The answer to that question was the same though. "I don't want to die."

Rane smiled. "Despite my attempts to the contrary, me either."

Marie was strangely relieved to hear that. For all her talk about being fifteen and mature, she knew she needed an adult by her side. The door lock rattled without a warning knock, and the guards entered the room, Margareta at their heels.

"It's time." She spoke from behind the two women, anxiety laced with sadness in her voice.

Rane stepped out of the room before one of the two guards would make her. Marie soon followed. The five of them formed a somber procession from the hallway to the main door. Once on the doorstep, Marie turned to salute Margareta and saw she was silently crying. "Thank you. I will remember you too."

The older woman was startled by her words, but when the meaning of what Marie had just said sank in, she smiled and wiped her tears. "Thank you."

Later, when Ginecea was long lost behind hills, Rane whispered to her, "It was kind of you."

Marie knew right away what she was referring to. "She deserves to know she won't have to pray for my soul as well. As you said, that house is crowded with too many ghosts already. Mine won't be one of them, if I have any say in it."

"Still, you're a kinder person than you want others to believe. I know you hated the half-house as much as I did. You kept staring outside, fury in your eyes." Rane lowered her voice when she heard the guards complaining they were being loud.

"I didn't realize you were watching me." She had thought to be so clever to fake she was sleeping.

"Not the whole time. I stopped when I realized you weren't in the mood for chatting."

Marie started to protest, but Rane stopped her. "It's okay. I didn't want to talk either."

"What's it going to be like? Living in a waste plant?" With her nose against the cold glass, her breath misting up the surface, Marie wondered if the word "living" was the right one. She wasn't ready to die, but wasn't sure being stranded for life in a waste plant was considered living.

"We'll know soon enough." Rane pointed at the window. "Vasura is somewhere over there, behind those mountains."

"How long will it take to get there?" Despite her former desire to reach Vasura as soon as possible, now she would've given anything for another hour back at Margareta's. Fear rode from her stomach to her throat in the form of something unpleasant, panic rising within her at every breath.

"I won't leave you. I'll be with you." Rane took her hand in hers and gently stroked it.

The gesture meant to soothe her fear didn't work. For a fleeting moment, Marie imagined someone else's fingers caressing her, but it was neither Idra nor Verena, and she gasped, not wanting Grant's memory to come along for the ride. She was already miserable; adding a sense of shame to the mix wasn't what she needed. But Grant's face floated before her eyes when she closed them for a reprieve from the unpleasant reality.

The terrain changed several times. After the hills came the lakes, then a river valley, then the placid waters of the blue sea in the faraway distance. Then the hills again, the desert, and mountains peaks as far away as the sea had been. Finally, the bus started climbing toward an imposing plateau surrounded by thick forests resembling a green ocean, the foliage from the majestic trees undulating to the wind as waves.

"I always wanted to travel," Marie said to no one in particular. A nervous laugh would have followed, but she was becoming numb, as she had when the captain had announced she was to be deported to a waste plant.

"Be careful what you wish for…" Rane's voice had a singsong quality.

She turned toward the doctor and saw the same detachment she felt. "Because it could come true. " After that small exchange, she bore the remainder of the geography lesson in silence. Although she sat still the whole time, her eyes stung a little when she realized they were five hours from Trin and understood the doctor's heartache when she had glimpsed her city.

It took several more hours—stars were visible—before the driver left the main road to an unused-looking gravel path. The woman carefully navigated the road, slowing down as she skirted a trench full of rainwater and other hazards on their way. Finally, illuminated by an army of tall street lamps bordering the perimeter, a woman-made edifice came into view. Not a lot to look at in terms of architecture, but big and square. At closer proximity, the building turned out to be an enclosed wall. A big, gray, unforgiving structure. The driver brought the bus to a full stop by a high column that interrupted the monotony of the equally tall wall stretching forever in either direction. Idling the engine, the driver rolled down her window, reached out to push a button on the column, and when a buzz-like sound answered, she asked permission to enter Vasura. Around the perimeter, all the street lamps started pulsating.

"How big is it?" Marie looked at the gray barricade and shivered at the thought of what awaited her on the other side.

Rane shrugged. "I don't know. But my guess is quite big."

Not a sound accompanied their waiting. Minutes passed. The plateau on which the waste plant stood was silent, no animals cooing or wind raffling leaves on the nearby tree. Maybe it was just her imagination, but when a portion of the wall slid sideways to reveal a large courtyard, she could have sworn even the sound from the bus engine had been muted. A moment later, two guards exited a gate on the opposite wall of the courtyard. They were fathered women, no pure breed by the uncultivated look of them.

They both positioned themselves by the bus door and one knocked on the glass panel. "Release them," the guard ordered, her shadow made intermittingly longer by the sharp, pulsating light that increased the hard lines on her tan face and left everything else in the dark.

The driver opened the door and the two guards who had escorted Marie and Rane went to exchange a few words with the fathered women. Marie was too scared at this point to retain the meaning of what they were saying and simply obeyed when she was asked to exit. Once Rane was outside too, the door closed behind them and the bus left. The bag with her meager belongings hanging from her back, she stared at the wall sliding back in place and the lights immediately stopped pulsating.

"To the branding." One of the two fathered women had spoken, but the fog in Marie's mind held fast. She looked to Rane for guidance and saw she looked as lost as Marie felt.

She turned her head forward, but a veil of water altered her vision. Maybe it was raining; her addled brain was slow in deciphering input from the outside. She stumbled a few steps ahead, then stopped when the guards passed through the smaller gate without looking back. She knew deep down resistance was futile—her imprisonment was going to happen with or without her consent, but her legs refused to cross that final threshold. Rane grabbed her by the elbow and gently pushed her along.

"Welcome to Vasura." The guard who hadn't spoken yet smiled at Marie and Rane.

Marie was shocked to see the woman had meant it. That was even more unsettling than a barked command.

"The branding will be over soon. Don't worry." The woman stepped closer to her and laid a hand on her free arm. "I'm sorry, but it's the law. I didn't make it. Every woman sent here has to go through it."

When the guard retracted her arm, the sleeve of her uniform slightly rode up and showed part of her forearm. A string of numbers. Slowly, the word "branding" acquired a whole new meaning. Horror struck her when she finally understood the woman didn't sport a normal tattoo on her arm. She opened her mouth, but not a single syllable came out of it.

"It'll be fast. I assure you of that." The guard was looking at her with concern. "I can provide you with something to lessen the pain if you want." Personal knowledge etched her expression.

Then something snapped inside of her, a fury so intense it took Marie by surprise. "No, I want to feel everything. I want to remember."

Rane looked startled at her words, but then nodded.

"Okay. Then let's get it over with so you can start a new life at Vasura." The woman seemed pleased by Marie's answer and walked ahead toward a small building just a few yards on the right.

Marie looked around. Now that her senses were slowly coming back to her, she started noticing the world behind the second wall. A whole city lay before her eyes. Gray, low buildings dotted the paved roads while bustling activity was undergoing. Even that late at night, people moved around with purpose, mostly on foot, but also on small carts pulled by horses. A second, more careful look revealed a detail that shocked her. A paramount feature of Vasura, it seemed. She blinked, once, twice, then faced Rane to be sure she wasn't hallucinating.

"Yes, I did hear of it... but witnessing it is another thing altogether." Rane's eyes were wide, darting right and left.

Women and *men* were moving around, some of them even working together. And there were kids of both genders playing in the streets.

"It happens every single time," the other guard—the older brunette—commented; she had feigned disinterest since ordering them out of the bus but was now looking at them with mirth in her eyes. "This way." She knocked at the door of the small building and entered without waiting for a response.

Oppressing heat bathed them once inside. It took a moment to get used to the dim light from the dozens of candles scattered on the tiled floor. The effect was hypnotic; the wavering light was enough to look where she put her feet, but not enough to see what was hidden in the darkness. Combined with the warm air, she struggled to inhale. It lulled her into a sudden stupor. The brazier came into view at the end of the hallway they had just crossed. Sudden fear gripped Marie, and with it, a painful sharpness of the mind. Only the expecting look from the brunette steeled her resolve not to make a scene in front of her.

"I'll go first." Marie spoke slowly, trying to hide the panic rising in her chest. She hoped the doctor would understand her silent plea. She needed to finish this quickly.

Rane nodded again. "Sure, go ahead." Her tone was flippant, but she gave Marie a small caress on her back to let her know she understood.

An older woman, her hair cropped so close to her skull she resembled a man, beckoned them to come closer with a gesture of her bony arm. She raised an eyebrow when Marie approached her. "I see," she said after a few seconds of unblinking stare. "Remove your shirt." The woman sat by the brazier and tilted her head in wait.

Marie hesitated; she wasn't wearing an undershirt, just her bra. The idea of undressing before everyone almost undid her prior resolve, tears threatening to spill. Madame Carla had impressed upon her pupils that a fathered girl first and foremost must defend her honor. Showing skin wasn't proper.

"Think of her as a doctor and that you're here to get vaccinated." Rane was behind her, her hand on Marie's arm, gently squeezing it. "Will you hold my hand when it's my turn?"

Marie knew the doctor didn't need her help to get through the ordeal, but was glad for her lie. She tossed her shirt over her head and then covered her chest with it, clutching the cotton.

"Sit on the stool and give me your left arm." The order was given with a tired tone. The old woman must have gone through myriads of brandings. She turned to her right to open a big tome lying on a low table.

Marie sat as told, but before completing the task and raising her arm, she asked, "What's your name?"

The older woman raised her eyes from the book and looked over the brazier. Surprise was soon replaced by interest in her wary gaze. "Why do you want to know? Nobody's ever asked before."

"So you won't forget about me." Marie kept her eyes on her.

The older woman tilted her head to the side, the orange-red coals illuminating the lower part of her face, and her uneven teeth shone unexpectedly white when a grin spread through her face. "They call me Mala."

"Marie." She raised her arm then and watched as Mala chose between several branding tools neatly arranged on a second low table on her left. She then turned to check a board hanging on the wall behind her. The white surface was filled with a string of numbers. The first half was crossed off with a marker. She double-checked the first unused digit and then turned to face Marie. "Ready for the branding irons?" Her lips mouthing the numbers, she leaned over the tome, grabbed a pen from the table and scribbled them on a yellowed page already half full with writing.

"I don't have a choice." Marie looked at the tools. Dipped in the fiery coal, their extremities were slowly changing color until they reached the same shade of orange and red as the coal. There were too many of the branding irons, more than she wanted to count.

"No, you don't. But remember, I don't have a choice either." Mala raised her eyes toward the guards behind Marie. "Hold her still."

"It's for your safety," the gentler guard whispered in her ear.

She braced for the pain she thought she knew was coming, but when the first iron touched her skin, she screamed. By the time the fourth had left its sickly message on her forearm, she could barely breathe, but the torture continued way after she had reached her limit. She didn't faint though. Finally, Mala raised the last iron from her sizzling skin; the familiar smell of seared chicken filled the air, and she felt her stomach contracting. She retched. Someone helped her stand and led her to sit in a corner. There she sat, frozen. The screaming started again, but this time she wasn't the one losing her mind. Soon, too soon, she was hauled up and forced to walk when her legs barely felt like they could support her.

"I'll see you both later." Through the pain and the haziness, Mala's words reached her ears and she recoiled at the thought of having to visit that place again.

Once outside, the cooler temperature felt freezing cold over her drenched body. Her hair hung lifeless and heavy on her shoulders and she wished she didn't have hair at all. The pain propagated from her arm to the rest of her body in sharp, pulsating spikes that made her sweat despite the cold. Not daring to look at the mangled arm, she kept it at an angle, away from her waist.

"The pain will lessen." The fair-skinned guard was still holding her intact arm.

"I know." She wanted to be alone to be free to cry, scream, and curse all the pure breed women to oblivion.

"You'll be free from duty until tomorrow morning. Rest and report to the barracks at six o'clock sharp." The brunette pointed at a low building composed by several cargo containers put together. "Tonight, you'll have your beauty sleep at the novice quarters." She steered them toward another cluster of giant metal boxes. Someone had taken the time to paint the corrugated surfaces in white. As they neared the only visible entrance, Marie saw that a few flowers had been planted around the perimeter. "You'll be taken care of in case there're complications."

A woman was already at the door, waiting for them. She looked in her mid-thirties, muscular, short hair, but not as short as Mala's, and had an olive complexion. "How did it go?" Her lilting accent betrayed her marine origins, but she infused it with a no-nonsense attitude.

"They didn't faint." The gentler guard motioned for Marie and Rane to go inside; her hand squeezed Marie's arm with intention and so she looked at her. "I'm Cata." After introducing herself, she left.

"My name is Zena and I'm a nurse." The woman stood with her back straight, her legs wide open, and her arms crossed behind her back, resembling more a soldier than a nurse. "You must be Marie, and you Rane. Do you need anything?"

Marie stared at the woman, pain blinding her. Rane croaked something about being a doctor.

Zena's expression changed, her eyes looking at Rane with renewed respect. "A doctor—" She reached for Rane's unhurt arm and shook her hand. "About time we got a doctor."

"I'll do my best to help." Rane grimaced and Zena released her hand.

"I'll go get the salve for you." Zena beckoned them inside, keeping the metal screen opened with her booted foot. "It will help you sleep." Her arm outstretched, she pointed at a corridor opening to the antechamber. "Your beds are that way."

Marie heard the doctor and the nurse talking; mostly Zena did the talking while Rane grunted monosyllabic answers. She concentrated on the pain, thinking it would go away. Inadvertently, her branded arm touched her body. She screamed and then sank to the floor, sobbing. *Why me?*

"You didn't do anything to deserve this." Zena was at her side, carefully cradling her to her chest, making sure she wasn't touching Marie's wounded arm. Her voice had softened. "It wasn't your fault." Her big hand stroked Marie's back with a gentleness Marie hadn't expected from the woman.

"No, it's mine." Rane dropped on the floor too, sitting on her knees, her face marked by tears.

Marie realized she had talked out loud, and tried to extricate herself from the nurse's embrace.

Zena relaxed her arms and let her go. "It's okay to be scared. You're in a lot of pain."

"I'm not a crier." She shook her head. "I'm not a coward." But in declaring so, she felt she was being exactly that.

A small smile appeared on the nurse's severe face. "Women double your age faint the moment the first iron touches their skin. You're a young, courageous woman and we need people like you here."

Marie accepted her proffered hand and let the woman help her to stand on wobbly legs. "I feel lightheaded." She actually felt she couldn't walk at all.

"Shock." Rane was trembling too. "Normal."

She leaned on the nurse's strong frame, unable to combat the shaking and the chills that accompanied the searing pain anymore. They passed other women, but none of them stopped the slow procession.

Zena addressed them, asking for the salve and a pack of gauze, and the women scattered around, leaving them alone in a big room with no apparent windows and a claustrophobic, low ceiling. She accompanied Marie to one of the beds placed in two rows facing each other and looked at Rane from over her shoulder. "Doctor, pick one. You're the only visitors tonight." She helped Marie to a bed and then lowered what looked like a hook hanging over the head of the bed. "We'll keep your arm raised, so you don't accidentally sleep on it."

She looked at the woman, vision blurred, and then at the hook. "Okay." Marie started laughing. A terrible sound, interwoven with sobs and muscle spasms. She closed her eyes, hoping to wake back up at the Institute. Fever came, and then chills. Someone applied something pleasant over her arm, a cream with a minty scent. Her eyes watered from the vapors, but it was a nice change from the throbbing pain.

Heat from above like a blanket over her body woke her the next day. She slowly opened her eyes to see her arm had been bandaged and was now resting over a pillow by her side. Sweat covered her from head to toe, her tongue felt like sandpaper inside her mouth, and she could barely swallow. The sound of a chair being dragged closer echoed inside her head as if her skull was an empty room. Her eyes moved looking for the source of the loud noise.

"How do you feel?" Zena was sitting mere inches from her bed.

"Confused." She tried to raise her uninjured arm and it fell on the bed, lifeless.

"We had to drug you. You were thrashing around and the doctor was worried you'd go too deep in shock." Zena looked at Marie as if assessing her for a few seconds and then her face relaxed.

"Thank you." Had her body responded to the command, she would have hugged the woman. "Can I have some water?" Her words sounded like they came from under a pillow and she wasn't sure the nurse had understood, but then she saw her walking out of sight and coming back a few seconds later with a pitcher and a glass. "Thank you."

Zena raised Marie's head, then brought the glass to her mouth and let her swallow a few sips of water. "You okay?" When she saw that Marie was fine, she let her finish the glass. "I'm afraid you'll have to report for duty later in the afternoon."

Marie looked around for Rane, wondering where she was.

"The doctor was called to work first thing in the morning. I managed to convince the field boss you were in no shape to start your shift until later in the afternoon." The nurse put the pitcher and the glass back. Her expression was mournful. "Listen, girl, you must toughen up and open your mind. This place can break people. You'll see things you aren't used to. And you look too frail and young for your own good." Despite her words, her hand fell lightly on Marie's head and patted it with slow strokes.

Marie allowed the intimacy, finding a measure of solace in the stranger's affection. The idea that she shouldn't have felt comforted flickered among the chaos of her confused thoughts, but she needed that more than she needed to preserve her respectability. And then a question emerged—did being respectable mean anything out there? Did she care anymore? Her answer to that question was to lean against Zena's caress. "I can be tough." She wasn't sure what the woman had meant with the open-minded bit.

The woman's chuckle reverberated through her hands. "Of course you can. But I had to say it. It made *me* feel better."

The nurse's words reminded her of the harsh talk-downs Madame Carla gave her pupils when something bad would happen at the Institute. More than once, she had thought the rector had looked more scared for them than anything else. Maybe that was how adults coped with the fear of something happening to their loved ones. She missed the lashing-outs and the seemingly severe punishments. She had missed the Institute long enough. Redfarm hadn't turn out to be the great place she had dreamed of. The feeling she was alone threatened to fill all her thoughts and she drew strength from the notion that a stranger could be worried for her. The sound of Grant's voice came out of nowhere, dispersing that little of peace she had conquered.

A hand squeezed her arm. "Hey, sleepyhead? Are you here?"

The words brought Marie back. "Oh, yes, yes." She shook her head and tried to move sit upright position, but her head swayed.

"We had to give you strong painkillers. Just rest against my arm." Zena helped her up again and then gave her some water. "Your head will clear in a few minutes. I need to apply some salve to your burns. Brace for it. It won't be pleasant." She let her go for a moment and then replaced her support with two pillows she put under her head. "Better?"

Marie nodded, warily looking at the nurse's fingers working on the gauzes on her arm. "It smells terrible." Cooked meat.

"Look the other way." Zena's hands hovered above the last layers of bloody gauzes.

Marie shook her head. "I need to look." But she did brace for the worst. Nevertheless, a gasp escaped her mouth.

"It'll look better once it's healed." The woman raised her left sleeve to reveal her branding. The name "Vasura" was followed by three numbers and then a symbol Marie didn't recognize. "After a while, you'll come to like it and to be proud of it."

She raised her eyes from the branding to Zena, surprised by her last statement. "I don't think that's possible."

"In time, you'll see I'm right. Remember what I said about opening your mind." The nurse applied a thick ointment on Marie's arm. It wasn't as minty as the one she had used the night before.

Marie's nose stung when the acrid scent reached it. "And that smells even worse."

Zena smiled at her childish complaint and then chuckled. "Deal with it. You'll have to clean and take care of yourself coming this afternoon. I'll give you a jar of this salve to take with you."

CHAPTER 10

The end of her stay at the novices' barracks came too soon. In the following hours, Zena brought her three small meals, greased her arm with liberal amounts of the same pungent ointment, and told her to leave it un-bandaged for the time being. Finally, when it was evident there wasn't anything else to be done, she hugged her and Marie hugged her back, her feelings running too wild to deny herself some human warmth.

"I'll walk you to the field manager." Zena helped her, wearing a white shirt and loose pants. "Fortunately, you're too young to end up at the recycling facility. But at eighteen, you'll be asked to work a month a year there. Everybody does it." Her face darkened.

"Is it as terrible as they say?" Recycling was this waste plant's specialty. Vasura was one of the biggest facilities and took care of the proper disposal of Ginecea City's waste. "I heard the stench reaches the high heavens."

The nurse reacted to her words and gave her a piercing stare. "The smell and the toxic vapors can be fatal inside the chamber."

Marie wasn't sure if she had just been chastised for what she had said and didn't try to further the conversation. Besides, she had already heard all that was to hear about waste plant's inner works.

Still, Zena continued, "That's why we keep kids out of it and we have one-month shifts for the adults. It doesn't happen often, but when the smell wafts toward the central hub—"

Marie didn't want to keep talking about the recycling center. She'd have to worry in three years. Now, she had a lot on her plate already. "What's the central hub?"

"It's one of the main places where people gather more often."

"Like a central plaza?"

"Exactly like that. Anyway, what was I saying before you interrupted me?"

"About smells wafting."

"Oh, yes. When it happens, it's terrible." The woman walked to the door and waited for her there. "You'll like the fields."

Marie slid her sandals on and silently followed the nurse outside. Once at the door, she looked back at the oppressive, stifled barrack and was glad she didn't have to stay there a moment longer. The sun shining outside blinded her for a moment, but the breeze blowing her hair out of her face and neck was pleasurable. Day-lit, Vasura was even more imposing than she had thought the night before. Acres and acres of the walled compound lay before her eyes. From the relative height of the barrack's landing, she could see a whole world was contained by the gray barricade. Streets divided Vasura in rectangular spaces occupied by hundreds of colorful containers, not gray buildings as she had mistakenly seen in the dim, nocturnal light.

"I'll give you the tour as we walk to the fields." Zena pointed at buildings as they went and explained to her what she was looking at.

Not an easy task since, apart from the colors, everything looked the same to her. When Marie complained about it, the woman answered by pointing at the blocks of colors and said, "It's actually easier than you think. Everything painted in white is either an infirmary or a hospital. Pink is for cafeterias. Blue for resting places. Green is for the dormitories. Then you have the houses for the families, but they're in a different place, far away from the central hub." Finally, she walked directly toward one of the pink buildings, a cafeteria, and tapped on the corrugated metal wall. "Do you see this?"

Marie couldn't see anything beside the woman's big hand.

Zena frowned, then moved her hand by the side and a drawing was revealed.

A rectangular black frame contained several symbols. "What are they for?" She touched one of the symbols, a triangle with a circle inside.

"This cafeteria belongs to a specific tribe, but everybody can eat there."

Marie let the information sink in. "And the other three symbols?"

"Political orientation, religious affiliation, and type of food served. This cafeteria caters to vegetarians."

"Political orientation and religious affiliation? What are you talking about?" As far as she knew, there was only one of each on Ginecea and she had never had any interest in politics. She wouldn't be eligible to vote until her twenty-first birthday, and even then her decisional power would be minimal. By law, fathered women had to elect a representative for every ten thousand of them. In turn, the elected fathered woman would vote for all of them.

The nurse's lips curved in an enigmatic smile. "Freedom of expression is welcome here."

Marie wondered about that last statement, but then a bright color caught her attention. "What are the purple buildings for?"

"Gambling. But don't even think about that. Minors aren't allowed inside." Zena gave her a stern look.

"Gambling? But what would you gamble with?" As far as she knew, wasted women didn't earn salaries. Or so she had been told countless times at the Institute. *"Don't go complaining about how little you earn as a fathered woman, when there are people who have to work all day long for nothing at all."* It had been one of Madame Carla's favorite refrains.

Zena laughed. "Time out."

"Time out of what?"

"Gamblers try their luck to get out of the recycling month." Zena finally looked away. "But as I told you, *do not* walk close to the purple buildings. Bad people tend to gravitate there and you don't have to get out of anything for another three years." As she finished talking, a worker came out of one those buildings.

"Workers have gambling places too?" Marie was still surprised by seeing men freely walking among the women.

"They're the same places." The nurse was walking faster now.

She had to adjust her pace to keep up with the woman. "What do you mean? And can you slow down?" Already out of breath and unaccustomed to feeling so weak, she paused for a moment and crouched on the ground.

"Have you already forgotten what I said about opening your mind?"

Marie thought Zena sounded like a broken record. She was getting tired of all the warnings the woman was imparting to her. "And?"

"Men and women live together here." The nurse turned and stepped back to her side. "We don't have separate quarters."

"What?" For a moment she forgot about the throbbing pain and her lack of stamina. "You must be kidding."

"No. It's the truth. Once you live in a waste plant, you aren't a fathered woman anymore."

To Marie's ears, the woman's words sounded both blatant and obscure, but she didn't have time to ask her to explain what she meant because a cart came by and they climbed on the running board jutting from it.

"It's a long way to the fields and you aren't in any condition to walk any faster." Zena showed her where to put her hands and then told the driver to go.

The rest of the way, Marie kept her eyes opened and took the sight in. She could see a color pattern in the clothes worn by the people walking by.

"Everything and everybody is color coded at Vasura." Zena seemed to have read her thoughts because she provided the answer without Marie having to ask the question. "It makes life easier for everybody."

The ride lasted for several minutes, and they passed quite a few neighborhoods, some of them better kept than others. Some of the barracks were smaller, and they were normally the better-kept buildings.

Zena pointed at those smaller barracks. "Families."

Marie saw a woman coming out of one of them and then a man followed her outside holding a small boy in his arms. Her eyes widened and she turned toward the nurse who smiled, amused, and mouthed, "Told you to open your mind." Finally, the cart stopped and they jumped down.

"Okay, here we are." Still smiling at Marie's reaction to the unorthodox domestic scene, Zena pointed at a vast expanse of cultivated fields starting from behind a gate and stretching as far as the eye could see. The gate was only decorative since it stood by itself without a fence explaining its presence. The words "Goddess of Vasura's Fields" were painted in neat letters at the top of the arch over the wooden gate.

The inscription sounded like a bad joke, but Marie's ability of feeling offended was dwindling by now. She couldn't become red anytime she came upon something out of the ordinary.

"Let's go." Zena nudged her across the gate and they walked a short distance toward an orange barrack almost hidden by thick vegetation. She walked up the steps leading to a screened door and rapped on the metal. "Valery? I brought you the new recruit. Are you there?"

A hoarse voice responded, "Where would I be if not waiting for you to finally show up?"

Zena entered the barrack with Marie in tow. "How was your day?" She smiled at the woman sitting behind a desk.

Marie couldn't see a lot of the woman's face because the barrack was dark from the vegetation obstructing the two small windows and a white puff of smoke shrouded her. Marie coughed.

"You brought me another delicate violet." Valery stomped the cigarette's butt in the ashtray on the desk.

"She's one tough girl." Zena patted Marie's healthy arm. "As you know, looks can be deceiving."

"We'll see about that." Valery pushed the chair she was sitting on out of the way with a strident sound of wheels dragging on the linoleum floor and then walked to meet Zena. "You can leave her now. You're done with the babysitting duty for today."

"It was easier than usual, actually. So, this is Marie—"

"You're late and I don't care if the new doctor said you weren't able to work. You'll start a double shift, starting now" was the field manager's curt welcome. "See you next time, Zena."

"Try to get on Valery's good side." The nurse winked at Marie and then left with, "She isn't as bad as she looks."

Marie immediately missed her. An imposing middle-aged woman with long, red braids was looking back at her with mild distaste. She was already tired of Vasura. "What do you need me to do?"

"Go with Nora. She'll tell you everything." Valery, who hadn't thought necessary to present herself to Marie, whistled with both fingers in her mouth, her face angled to one of the two windows. A girl Marie's age came running inside. "Nora, she's yours."

"Yes, sirra." The girl, a petite thing, dark, with sleek hair tied in a long ponytail, saluted Valery, waited for the field boss to give her permission to leave and then faced Marie with a genuine smile. "Come with me."

Marie wanted to ask about the "yes, sirra" bit, but refrained. It had sounded archaic and ludicrous, but things were obviously different at Vasura, and Nora's smile was nice enough to stir her thoughts in another direction. Once outside of the smoky place, her lungs cleared of the smelly nicotine and she faced the girl. "Hi, Nora. I'm—"

"Marie. I know! I was so excited someone my age was finally coming." Nora took her hands in hers and then kissed her on both cheeks. "I've been waiting for you for so long! It's so nice you're here." A big hug followed. Her head stood just under Marie's chin.

That startled her more than anything else. "Nice meeting you too." She managed to move away from the girl without appearing too brusque.

Nora must have felt her reluctance though. "I'm sorry, but I hoped you'd be here at the beginning of the shift, and I've almost missed you altogether since mine is ending in half an hour... but I can stay longer to keep you company if you want—"

Marie stopped the rambling with a smile. "I don't want to keep you here longer than necessary."

"Oh, no, it would be my pleasure. Not that I have anything better to do anyway." The girl finally stepped back and gave her some space. "I've some work for you."

"Okay." For some reason, while Zena's affections had felt right, Nora's were upsetting.

"Today, we'll keep it simple. You'll look around to get an idea of what you'll do and then we'll go back to the dormitories." Nora seemed to bounce at every step, a blur of dark hair and orange shirt.

"But the field boss said—" Marie could barely keep the same pace, but, meanwhile, they had walked a good distance and were now standing before another orange barrack.

"Valery said to give you double shift, right?" Nora knocked on the door of the barrack and entered when none answered.

Marie nodded and followed her inside. Unlike the field boss's office, this barrack was airy and bright. It was also full of low tables laden with small pots containing equally small plants in several stages of growth. "Is this a nursery?"

"Yes, and you'll double shift here for the remaining of the day." The girl turned on one of the lights hanging over the tables and illuminated one of the pots.

"Doing what?" She liked the place immensely already.

"We've got some planting to do. There're a few pots that need to be replaced. Stuff like that." Nora waved her small hand in the air in a vague gesture. Then, she threw a big, green apron and a pair of green rubber gloves at Marie. "Be careful not to get soil on your branding."

Marie's eyes went to the girl's naked arm where the letters and the numbers covered the skin of her slender forearm. The girl caught her looking and she turned at the last second.

"I got it only a few months ago and it was so painful." She said it as if talking about getting her ears pierced.

Marie was happy the girl was eager to talk. "Did you come recently too?"

"Oh, no! I was born here. Natives get their brand when they turn fifteen. It's a rite of passage for us and we get our tribe's symbol right away, since we're already part of our parent's tribe."

Nora stated the last part with a matter-of-fact shrug and Marie would've asked more, but the girl started shoving pots under her nose and put her to work. She focused on the small tasks Nora gave her to stop thinking about the pain in her arm. When she raised her head from the table several hours later, she saw it was dark outside and strong illumination had replaced the sun over the fields.

"Bright, steady light. The way I like it. Not those terrible pulsating things…" Nora was looking outside as well.

Marie was going to ask what she was talking about and then remembered how the streetlamps had pulsated when she had arrived, but Nora was talking again. "We force the crops to grow at double speed. This way, Vasurians can't go hungry."

"Vasurians?" Marie had to ask this time.

"What do you prefer to be called from now on, a *Vasurian* or a *wasted woman*?" the girl asked, for once in a serious tone.

"Well, if you put it that way, I'd like to be a Vasurian." And finally, for the first time since she had left Redfarm, Marie felt the moment deserved a true smile.

"Exactly." Nora laughed.

She wasn't ready for a laugh, but the girl's enthusiasm was good to her. Her arm sent her a new wave of pain and she grimaced.

"Is it still very painful?" Nora pointed at the gruesome patch of red, mangled skin and sleek ointment Marie had been trying very hard not to get in contact with anything.

"Yes, very." Her eyes went to the girl's branded arm, the name of the waste plant and the three numbers exposed for everybody to see. "What's this?" Her finger shot for the symbol following the numbers, but stopped before she touched the girl's arm. Her numbers and letters were of the same length as hers. She had noticed earlier. The only difference was the symbol.

"My tribe's symbol, of course." Nora looked at her with big eyes. "I told you."

"Your tribe?" Marie tilted her head to better look at the sign resembling a circle cut in half by a barrette.

"Yes, the tribe I was born in has a 'theta' as its symbol. You'll have one too." The girl turned her forearm to better show it.

"I'll have one?" Suddenly, Mala's words about seeing her again echoed in her mind and she shivered.

"As soon as a tribe decides to adopt you, of course. But don't worry. You'll be part of a tribe in no time. You don't seem a loner at all." The girl smiled in reassurance, misunderstanding Marie's reaction.

"Vasura is divided in tribes?" Slowly, several pieces started clicking into their rightful place.

"Yes." Nora's head bobbed in assent.

"And you were born here." She hesitated, not sure how to ask what she meant to ask without offending her by being crude. But then she realized she had nothing to ask.

Still, when Nora said it, she inwardly gasped at the girl's nonchalance. "Yes, my mom and dad belong to the same tribe. Maybe you'll be accepted in my tribe!" She took Marie's hands in hers and started dancing around in circles.

All the while, Marie's mind churned with all the questions she had but couldn't utter for fear of being indecent. But first and foremost, *Mom and dad? Did she just call a man... dad?* One last circle and her branded arm accidentally made contact with something. Unwanted tears sprung to her eyes.

"I'm so sorry. I didn't mean to hurt you." Nora let go of her immediately, her hands covering her mouth.

"I know. It isn't your fault." She wiped her tears and tried to even her ragged breathing. "Do you think my shift can be cut a little bit shorter?" The desire to be alone was more demanding than the physical pain.

"Yeah, sure. Valery only barks. She isn't going to check on you anyway. Let's go to the communal dormitories." The girl switched off the main light but left on the ones warming some of the pots, then gestured for Marie to follow her outside.

They walked for a good fifteen minutes in the warm night, nocturnal animals crying far away and storms of mosquitoes flying under the lamps.

"It is always so warm here?" Marie finally asked when the silence had become uncomfortable.

Nora, who had said nothing the whole time, smiled broadly, two delightful dimples coloring her face. "It's cold now."

"Oh—" Marie was going to say she liked some heat, but the girl interrupted her.

"Wait! I'm sure you must be hungry."

Her stomach growled and reminded her she hadn't eaten anything in a while.

"Let's go grab something." The girl made a U-turn on her heel and directed her to the opposite direction. "The closest cafeteria is around that block." She pointed her chin ahead where several pink barracks stood in the middle of what looked like a well-manicured garden, complete with benches and a central area with a structure that resembled a fountain.

In a matter of minutes, they went in and out of the cafeteria, which inside just looked like any other cafeterias she had seen. Nora had ordered for her a big sandwich and a bottle of water and slowed her pace to permit Marie to eat on the go.

A few minutes later, dinner already a thing of the past, Nora stopped by a light-blue building and pointed at the place with a grand gesture of her hands. "You'll sleep at the communal dormitory until you're accepted in a tribe, then you'll move there." She saw Marie's hesitation and paused on the stoop before knocking at the door. "Yes?"

Marie bit her bottom lip and looked up at the girl.

"What is it?" Nora's hand hovered a few inches away from the door.

"Is it...? Are there any...?" She blushed.

"Are there any what?"

"Men?" Her voice came out as a choked, unintelligible whisper, but the girl must have understood her because she smiled and shook her head.

"Communal dormitories are never mixed, silly Marie. And they're for the people who have just arrived and don't belong to any tribe, yet." Nora's voice had a singsong quality as if she were talking to a little kid who needed to be explained everything. At the same time, she rapped on the door—which Marie noticed was orange. "We've got private housing for the families. And every tribe has both dormitories for the singles and houses for the couples."

A moment later, two girls, a few years older than Nora and with a much more subdued disposition, came to welcome them.

"Carine and Trisha, this is Marie. Marie, Carine and Trisha." Introductions aside, Nora stormed inside, bringing her along by the hand.

Another petite brunette, Carine, and a slightly taller auburn-haired, Trisha, to remember. Marie was already dizzy. Deep inside, she didn't want to know the girls' names. She gave the place a distracted look, which, despite corrugated metal walls and the small windows dotting them, reminded her too much of her dormitory back at the Institute. Longing and regret washed over her, but she steeled her heart and held back the tears. Nevertheless, they stung.

"I like what you did with the place. Nice shade of lilac," she heard Nora say to the two girls and then went on asking if they had decided to apply for any tribe yet. Marie wasn't interested in knowing their answer, so she looked around to get a feel for her new home. Several layers of paint had been applied to the walls. The latest incarnation showed the previous palette where the lilac had peeled. Beds were oriented infirmary-style, heads to the walls. She counted at least twenty on one side, so there must be around forty women sleeping there. *So much for privacy.* Funny how her brief staying at Redfarm had accustomed her to the luxury of having to share sleeping quarters just with one person. Or maybe she just longed for Verena's placid temper and quiet friendship. She closed her eyes and kept them shut for a long moment.

"Are you okay?" one of the two girls asked, her voice too close to Marie for her liking.

When she was sure she was beyond making a scene, she opened her eyes and looked at the girl. The petite brunette with a worried expression was waiting for her answer. "My arm."

Three sets of eyes zeroed on her offended appendage and that was when the fussing started.

"You should do this—"

"You should do that—"

"No, it's better if you—"

"When it was my turn, I did this and—"

They all talked at the same time. She brought a hand to her right temple and at the same time looked for a bed to sit on. "My head's killing me."

Silence dropped on the room. Then Nora timidly opened her mouth to apologize. Marie waved the girl's worries away. "It's okay. I just need to be by myself for a moment." She hoped the trio would understand and was rewarded by three nods.

"Of course. Come to your bed." The auburn-haired Trisha pointed at a bed at the faraway corner of the room. "We'll find a better spot, but we're full right now."

Marie eyed the shadowy corner and saw that her assigned bed was the last of the row and it stood against the wall and under a window. "No, it's perfect. Thank you." Then the girl's words prompted her to ask, "Where's everybody?"

Trisha's eyes went automatically to the door. "It's dance night. The girls are out having fun."

It's dance night, she repeated in her mind, disbelief coloring her thoughts. She looked at the girls, wasted young women, preparing to go to a dance. Zena's warning to keep her mind opened came back to her loud and clear.

"I heard it's going to be so nice..." Carine played with a lock of her hair, lips turned down in a childlike frown.

From her wishful tone, Marie understood they had drawn the short straw. She smiled at the girls. "No need to stay here on my behalf. I'm fine."

"We thought you needed company... first day at Vasura and all..." Carine couldn't help a glance at her arm. "Sorry."

She attempted a smile. Those girls were trying hard to be nice to her. "I'm very tired and once I take care of cleaning the wound, I'll sleep like a rock." She walked to her new bed and sighed. Yet another place to call her own.

"Are you sure?" This time, Nora was the one asking.

Marie turned on her way to her corner and reassured her with a better version of the smile she had already tried to use. "Yes. See you tomorrow morning?"

The girl didn't seem convinced, but stepped back toward the door. "If you really don't need us..."

She shook her head. "Have fun."

"Tomorrow, then!" Nora went to the door.

"We'll ask the other girls to be quiet when we come back later tonight." Carine followed Nora.

Marie truly smiled at that, but nobody saw her because she was already facing her bed. "That would be great. Thanks." She waited until the door closed and the dormitory was finally silent. Then she went back to the door where she had seen the main switch for the big light illuminating the room too brightly for her throbbing headache. Once the light was turned off and the only glow showing her the way to her corner came from the outside lamps, she let go and cried. Not sobs or anything loud, just a stream of wet tears washing her face. She sat on her new bed and looked outside. The whooshing sound of the leaves brushing the metal wall was hypnotic and she concentrated on that while her eyes traveled to the building in front.

A pale light came from inside the window facing hers. Something moved in and out of sight and startled her. A glimpse of a blond head came into view; it was just a moment and then was gone again. For reasons unknown, that sight calmed her and that gave her the strength to clean her wounds and smother her arm with the pungent salve. Once down, she lay on the bed, eyes on the ceiling, and tried to relax. Her new roommates came back from the festivities while she was still awake. She immediately turned toward the wall and slowed her breathing to feign deep sleep. It worked. Voices behind her immediately dropped to a pleasant whisper.

"I like her so much, but she never looks at me."

"The music wasn't as great as the last dance."

"You think so?"

"I think it was great. They even played our song."

"Why doesn't she look at me?"

"Don't know. You're so pretty."

"Did you see the new recruits?"

"No."

"A whole cargo of workers came yesterday."

"Let's hope the new girl is nice."

"They said she was in a lot of pain."

"Poor thing..."

***

First thing the next morning, Zena dropped by for a brief visit. "How're you holding on?"

"It could be worse, I guess." Still groggy from having slept maybe the whole of sixty minutes and in several naps, Marie was hopelessly trying to put up a good show. She raised her arm to let the nurse examine it. "Is it supposed to look this way?" What she meant was if her limb was going to detach itself anytime soon. The

140

pain was still excruciating and her head was still throbbing, or maybe it was the arm.

"It's redder than it should be, but nothing to be worried about. I'm more concerned about your evident lack of sleep." Zena slowly caressed her head.

As before, Marie sighed at the gesture. She could have fallen asleep to that, but a bouncing Nora appeared behind the nurse's back.

"Raise and shine, girlfriend!" Her biggest smile yet completed the picture. "Time to go eat breakfast and then chop, chop. Valery woke up on the wrong side of the bed."

Marie wondered how someone living in a waste plant could be so cheerful. The she remembered that Nora had been born there and didn't know any better. *Poor thing*, she thought, but then she realized her error. *No, poor me who knows better...* "Give me five minutes."

"Let me help you." Zena took the ointment jar from her hand and methodically removed the previous layer of what now looked like dirty grease. "It's actually not as red as I thought. Healing has already started. When it starts itching, that's a good sign. Your skin is knitting itself."

Marie was glad for the reassurance because the pain in her arm was making her anxious that it would never go away. She had never had in her life anything that had lasted for so long and with such intensity. It scared her not being able to control what was happening to her body. It made her angry that the pain was driving her to tears at the very moment. But she managed not to cry and that gave her a sense of great satisfaction.

"Done. Rane asked about you."

"I wanted to ask you about her. Where is she? And why I haven't been assigned to an infirmary?" Marie had thought about that a lot during the almost sleepless night.

Both Zena and Nora looked at her surprised by her question, but Zena answered her. "She's at the hospital, of course." She paused for a moment. "And why should you be in an infirmary?"

"Because I'm training as a nurse." The reality of her present position dawned on her and she amended, "Until two days ago, I was working with the doctor back at Redfarm." Or was it three days? She wasn't sure of how long had passed since the moment Callista had doomed her out there.

The nurse looked at her with suspicion. "Why didn't you say anything earlier?" Marie didn't have time to say anything back because Zena pointed a finger at her and asked, "Rane will validate your claim, right?"

Marie vigorously nodded. "Yes."

"Well, this is good news." Zena's lips turned up in a smile.

At the same time, the always-cheerful Nora looked anything but pleased by the revelation. "I guess it's great."

Zena gave the girl a look and then faced Marie again. "I'll talk to Valery and I'll arrange your transfer from the agriculture to the medical field."

"But she just arrived!" Nora looked at the nurse with pleading eyes.

Zena dismissed her with a wave of her hand, sticky fingers spreading the strong smell of the ointment under their noses. "She can always visit you." She cleaned the grease on her pants, leaving several handprints on the heavy cotton.

The girl turned her big eyes to Marie. "Will you?"

"Of course." She nodded, sealing the deal with a handshake, which immediately transformed into a vicious hug. Marie couldn't believe something so small could be so strong. Cheeks blushing, she silently implored Zena to help her out.

The woman waved her away. "You go eat something. I'll run to Valery to explain the situation."

They exited the barracks at the same time. Zena went north and they south toward the cafeteria. Not even three steps and Nora enthusiastically greeted a group of girls walking toward them. Marie stood behind, preferring to remain aside. A playful wind made little storms of the confetti lingering from the previous night's activities. She closed her eyes and breathed slowly. The day promised to be warm and humid but now was pleasant, and the hope she could keep working with Rane made her feel light. Scuffled steps brought her back and she caught the end of a group of workers rounding the corner. Before the men disappeared behind the barrack, a set of green eyes zeroed in on her.

"Grant!" Her legs moved of their own initiative and she stood before him, her arms outstretched to hug him, but she realized what she was about to do in time and stepped back, flushed and breathless. "You're here." She looked around, worried the girl was behind her, but Nora was a few steps back and talking to her friends. She moved behind the corner, where nobody could see her and Grant.

He followed and then looked down at her, relief in his eyes. "When did you get here?" His hand reached for her head, but stopped just as she had. "I can't believe you're here."

She stood, her mouth agape. The warmth of the almost-happened caress lingered between them. "I was so worried about you." Her heart started beating at a funny pace. "What are you doing here?" She thought she'd never see him again and now he was here, standing before her. Her eyes darted sideways to see if Nora was coming after her, but Grant's presence was more compelling than her fear of being discovered.

He lowered his head for a moment and then raised his eyes to stare into hers. "Turns out I was lucky."

"What do you mean?" She shifted from one foot to the other.

Grant smiled at her. "I was the third in line."

Memories from the night Callista had sentenced her to Vasura came back. "So you were sent here." She didn't say out loud how glad she was things had worked out that way, but she felt a lightness she hadn't expected to experience.

He tilted his head as if to look at her better and then his gaze paused on her arm and his smile dimmed. She instinctively tried to hide it, but he moved his hand on her shoulder and stopped her. "Is it still painful?"

She felt an electric zing scorching her skin at the contact with his hand. The gesture was too intimate. Heart wildly beating in her throat, she didn't jerk away from his touch, his fingers gently squeezing her skin in a small circular massage. "Zena just told me it's healing well." The twelve numbers branded on his arm got her attention. "Did it take long for the pain to become bearable?"

Grant's lips curved up, not quite a smile. "A few days."

She grinned in response. "Then I'm perfectly on track."

He suddenly stepped back from her, a flicker of fear passing behind his green eyes. Someone moved behind her and she remembered Nora. Her heart, already vexed by so many different emotions, skipped a beat or two. She tried to calm her nerves and turned. "Nora!" She didn't know what to say. *It's not what you think?*

One small movement of Nora's chin pointing at Grant and she blinked in surprise. Had she understood what the girl wanted? Her eyes widened, but before she could ask or do anything, Nora took the situation in her own hands by introducing herself to him. The lines of what was proper and what wasn't were getting blurry. But of one thing she was certain: no proper fathered woman would ever be caught offering her name to a worker just because. That certainly wasn't proper.

Grant looked at the girl as if she had sprouted horns on her head. When Nora reached to shake his hand, he failed to reciprocate the gesture. He looked at Marie, silently asking for guidance, and she shrugged, as conflicted as he was. Mostly, she hoped not to attract any attention by refusing to comply with the girl's eccentricities. Finally, to her relief, Grant outstretched his hand and took Nora's in his, but Marie had to provide his name.

The girl grabbed it and energetically shook it. "Nice meeting you, Grant."

Marie watched as Grant, easily twice in height compared to Nora, returned the greeting with his eyes darting left and right, probably looking for a guard coming to throw him into an isolation chamber for having touched a woman in public.

Nora seemed oblivious to the tension she had created. "Have you been appointed to a field?"

"Yes…?"

"Then you haven't turned eighteen yet." The girl seemed pleased by that. "No recycling duty for pretty boys like you, yet. And which field have you been appointed to?"

His eyes became even wider and he retracted the hand she was holding. He hesitated a moment, probably trying to figure out how to answer. "The apple orchard."

The girl's face lit up. "A friend of mine works there. You'll like it." Then she turned to face Marie. "It isn't far away from Valery's fields."

"Hey, recruit?" A man in his mid-forties, brown hair tied in a long braid and several loops dangling from both his ears, waved at him.

"You should probably go." Nora looked at the man and smiled at him.

Grant turned to face the man and blanched. He made to move, but then spun on his heel and whispered to Marie, "I'm glad you're fine."

She didn't know what to say or do. Nora's presence made everything difficult. "Bye…"

He started walking backward and before turning and disappearing behind the corner, he gave her one last look, but thankfully didn't say anything.

"See ya." Nora waved her hand at him. "He seems like a nice boy."

Marie stared at her in disbelief. "He's a worker." She couldn't help but wonder what was passing through the girl's head.

"Seems quite obvious." Nora's lips formed an amused smile.

Maybe she isn't all there. "Worker as in a *man*…?"

Now, it was the girl's turn to regard her as if she were simple. "And?"

"You just talked to and shook hands with a man!" She lowered her voice at the last second.

Nora laughed. "Oh, that's nothing."

"That's nothing? Are you insane?" She regretted the use of the word almost immediately, but the girl didn't seem to take it personally.

"The look on your face is priceless." Nora laughed some more and then wiped her eyes. "I treat everybody the same."

The statement left Marie almost speechless again. "You do?"

Nora nodded. "I do. Besides, weren't you talking to him when I found you?"

She sighed. There wasn't much she could say to that. "I was sentenced to spend my life here for less."

"I heard the stories about outside." The girl shuddered, then stepped closer to her and laid one hand on her arm. "You'll see things are different here."

She let Nora pat her, too distressed to care. "I can see it already, but how? Why?"

"Vasura is a world apart." And with that, she released her arm and bounced away. "Aren't you hungry?"

CHAPTER 11

They had just finished eating their breakfast, a simple fare of oatmeal and sweetened milk, when Zena entered the cafeteria. Eyes on the crowd, she scanned the big hall until she spotted them. She wasn't alone. A tired-looking Rane was with her.

"Doctor!" Marie felt relieved at seeing Rane's familiar face and waved for them to come sit at their table.

The woman smiled when she saw her and made a beeline toward them. "Ready to start your training again?" Something was wrong. Although she looked genuinely happy to see Marie, her movements were stiff and her voice restrained.

"When can I start?" She stood, tray in hand, ready to go.

"Now?" Rane tried to laugh, but her face didn't respond. Deep lines made her look older and bitter.

"I guess you worked it out with Valery." Nora's shoulders lowered in defeat.

Marie put a hand on Nora's. "I'll come visit you at your place."

"Are you sure?" The girl's eyes shot up.

She touched her heart. "Promise."

"I'll miss you."

"I'll miss you too." Marie surprised herself by meaning it. In the short time she had spent with Nora, she had come to regard her as a possible friend. Another of the girl's uncomfortable, intimate hugs followed, and then she left with the nurse and the doctor.

"Are you okay?" she asked Rane as soon as they were out of the cafeteria, walking toward her new job. Zena was in a hurry and had them at a brisk pace.

Rane paused to catch her breath. "The branding got infected and I'm feeling weak, but nothing that can't be solved."

Zena realized they weren't behind her and walked back to meet them halfway. "Can you work?" She gave the doctor a thorough look.

"That woman needs my help. I'll rest later and now Marie's here to give me a hand. We make a good team, don't we?" She turned to Marie, who nodded.

"Good thing I was assigned to infirmary duties for the next trimester then. I can give the two of you a hand. You don't look well, either of you. And our patient is ready to give birth as we speak." Zena sped up and they followed, trying to keep up with her brisk pace.

Marie wanted to ask what woman they were talking about, but her curiosity was satisfied a few minutes later when they reached the infirmary. At the center of the main hub and not far from the Goddess of Vasura's Fields—even thinking of the name made her feel she had just cursed—there was one of the fields' infirmaries that took care of all the people working there. She soon discovered that women and men had separated infirmaries, which somehow struck her odd, given what she had seen so far of the place. Or maybe, despite what everybody wanted her to believe, things at the waste plant did follow Ginecean society rules after all. Either way, Marie surprised herself again because she was slightly disappointed. As soon as they entered the room, the wailing from a woman in pain assailed her ears. At the same time, Rane and Zena ran to the bed tucked in the corner to attend to the patient.

Soon, the woman's crying became feeble and the doctor started talking to her, even yelling at her. "It's too soon. Don't push! The baby isn't ready yet. Listen to me and breathe."

Marie heard the frantic tone in Rane's encouragements and tried to peek at the woman. She was still crying, semi-hidden by the doctor and the nurse both leaning over her. And then she saw her. "She's pregnant!" Both hands over her mouth, she gasped and recoiled several steps back. She had known of course. But it still shocked her.

"She's giving birth." The nurse didn't turn but went to the other side of the bed to stand at the woman's head.

Marie could feel her face on fire. She had never seen a pregnant woman before. Being in the presence of one giving birth was wrong and she couldn't think beyond that. Not even when the nurse called her to come closer and help massaging the woman's back. Her legs refused to move. She hadn't felt sick at the sight of blood, she hadn't fainted during her branding, but this was too much. She was already at the door when Rane raised her head from her patient and turned to look at her.

"You wanted to be a nurse once." Her voice was low, but her words and their meaning carried to the end of the room where they reached Marie like a slap on her face.

She stepped farther back until she could feel the sunlight kissing her hair. "I can't…"

"We help everybody." The doctor's eyes conveyed her silent judgment.

She felt the full weight of it. "What's happening to her?" Shame and several different other sentiments suffocated her, but she did walk back into the room.

"The baby's in the wrong position and her hips are too narrow," Zena answered instead of the doctor, who was now crouching before the woman's open legs.

Marie wanted to faint right there and then, but felt she had to keep walking toward the bed. It made her feel petty to be judgmental of a donor. It's not that the woman had any say in the process. She should have pitied her instead. Then another thought popped in her mind and she wondered why fathered women were forced to be donors at Vasura. Why would they have them there at all? It's not that they needed to populate the place with fathered women and workers. Probably they received more people than they could afford on regular basis. Then she thought of Nora and what she had said about having a mother and a father. Nothing made sense here.

"Relax and breathe. Follow my voice." Rane had one hand over the woman's outstretched belly and the other had disappeared under her skirts.

Marie couldn't believe how big and round the pregnant stomach looked. She wanted to ask if it was heavy or painful to walk with that weight. But even the simple act of asking was inappropriate.

Fighting years of Madame Carla's teachings, she walked back to the bed, every step heavier and slower than the previous. What happened next was so unexpected that everything else seemed trivial.

Rane crouched lower and told the woman to breathe one more time and stay still. "I'll try to move the baby into position. Now."

Her words were followed by the most terrifying cry Marie had ever heard. She saw the doctor pushing the belly with one hand. After the cry came the screams, one after the other, loud. Finally, Rane murmured something and breathed in relief. "I can see the head." She moved out of the way for a moment and Marie was at the right angle to see exactly what she was looking at.

The sight was so alien to her that for several seconds she couldn't put together the dots. She tilted her head and then finally understood. "Oh my Goddess…" She felt suddenly queasy and almost ran away again.

Zena raised one brow. "Stay where you are. We may need you."

Marie froze on the spot, the urge of losing her breakfast stronger than before. Meanwhile, Rane had given the woman permission to push, whatever it meant, and another frantic scream seared the air inside the infirmary. Then, silence. Something small and wet landed into the doctor's hands, and for a moment, nothing happened. She saw the way the two women looked at each other and understood something was terribly wrong. A soft sound, like a kitten's meow, came from the doctor's cradling arms.

Rane turned, looking for Marie. "Mind her." She'd already returned to the mother's side when Marie realized she had entrusted her with the mewing being. Her left arm useless, she found herself one-handedly carrying what looked like a baby. She was the tiniest thing Marie had ever seen and it was covered in blood and completely wrinkled. The small head moved against her chest and she snuggled the baby closer to her, immediately worried she was cold. "What's happening?" Apart from the small noises coming from the baby, nobody uttered a word. The moment stretched and no answer was given. Without realizing, Marie had started rocking the baby ever so slowly.

"Somebody tell me what's happening." If the screaming and the crying had been terrifying, the silence was oppressive. Rane and Zena were working around the woman, one securing an IV to her limp arm, the other checking her pulse.

"They won't let anything happen to your mom. Don't worry." She said this and other nonsense while cradling the baby, not sure why she felt the need to do so. Her eyes remained glued to the scene unfolding before her, hoping somebody would clue her in.

Finally, a hoarse voice asked, "Where's my baby?"

Marie couldn't help but weep at the question.

Rane turned and beckoned her closer. "It's a girl." She took the baby from Marie's awkward embrace and gently deposited her in her mother's trembling hands.

The woman's eyes lit the moment she saw her baby. "She's so beautiful."

A few hours later, when both mother and baby were officially out of danger and Rane found her way to a stretcher, Marie and Zena walked outside to take a break.

Sitting on the first step, the nurse looked up at Marie, who was leaning against the wall by the door. "What was all that?"

"All that what?" Marie looked down at the woman, bracing for the lesson she knew would come.

"Rane told me you worked with her and tended to men back at Redfarm." Zena let the statement dangle.

"It's true." She sat on the stoop, chin on her knees.

"Which is why I went and asked for your transfer." The nurse kept her head high to meet her gaze. "So what was that? You can save men's lives, but not women's?"

"Yes... no!" Marie opened her mouth, closed it, and opened it again. "She was pregnant."

"And? She didn't deserve to be taken care of?" Zena's tone contained a bitterness that warned Marie to be careful with her next words.

She struggled with it. "Of course she did—"

"But?"

Marie regretted to have come outside. "I was taught that a fathered woman—"

Zena raised one finger to stop her and then slowly looked in every direction. Finally, she locked her gaze with Marie again and shook her head, her mouth stretched in a thin line. "There are no fathered women here."

Marie was momentarily shocked by the harshness of the delivery. Several comebacks played in her mind, but none of them strong enough or smart enough. "She's a donor." The moment she uttered the words, she was ashamed she had even thought about it. She didn't think the woman's eyes could get any colder or her face show more disappointment.

"Donors are forced to get pregnant," Zena explained the obvious and Marie felt even worse. "And that woman is no donor."

"She's not a donor?" She straightened and blinked against the sun's glare.

"Vasura is no semen factory."

Of course. Zena's having some fun at my expense. "But how would she get pregnant?" It's not that it hadn't passed through her mind. "How was the baby conceived if the mother wasn't...?" She couldn't talk about that.

Zena raised one eyebrow, gave her one long, scrutinizing look, and then finally sighed. "I must remember it's not your fault."

She was relieved not to be the recipient of the woman's disgust anymore, but she still felt uncomfortable. "What isn't my fault?"

The nurse's eyes were now focused on some faraway point. "Pure breeds keep us and themselves in such blissful ignorance it's scary." She stood and cleaned some imaginary dust from her pants. "Fathered women don't need the aid of a specialist to get with child. It's easier than you were led to believe." She patted Marie's head and went inside the infirmary.

"How?" The woman was already out of sight, but Marie didn't follow her right away. The sudden memory of Carnia and Grant united in an intimate embrace came back to her. She didn't want to think such thoughts. They made her feel sullied and something else that started in the pit of her stomach and left her angry. She fought against the onslaught of unwanted memories. But there could be only one answer to her question. That mother who had almost lost her life giving birth wasn't a donor. She hadn't *been* chosen. *She had chosen to become pregnant.*

Marie was overwhelmed by the truth. She was also confused. She should have been shocked. And she was, wasn't she? She must be too dazed by everything that had happened in the last few days. Too many changes in her life. Too much physical pain. Too much heartbreak. Her mind could only take so much and her arm was throbbing again. She did the only thing she could do to keep her from going insane: she started walking away from the infirmary to distance herself from what had happened there. At first, she dragged her feet on the unpaved road, kicking pebbles right and left. Then she broke into a run. Warm wind blazing over her sweat, eyes blinded by the internal turmoil, she ran until her lungs begged her to stop. And a split second before she could see where she had run to, Nora called her.

"Hey! Missing me already?" The petite brunette struggled with the weight of two big sacks of soil she clutched to her chest.

Marie saluted her. "Do you need any help with those?"

The girl smiled and shrugged. "No, it's okay. I don't want any dirt to end up on your arm. But he can help me." She pointed at someone behind Marie.

She knew who was approaching before she turned, and her heart gave a little treacherous summersault that told her why she had run to the fields. And that, realization troubled her. *Only because he has the answers I'm looking for,* she lied to herself. Was that the reason why she wanted Nora out of the way? Was she going to ask how kids were born outside of a semen factory? She blushed and she felt her skin flashing to a deep red, but thankfully Nora wasn't looking at her.

The girl's smile had deepened. "Would you, please?"

Grant, his orange suit already dirty and stuck to his body in places, appeared beside them. "Sure…" He must have been surprised by the girl's request. She hadn't commanded him, but requested his help with gentle words. He looked as confused as he had been earlier in the morning.

"Hi, Marie." He wiped the sweat from his forehead with the palm of his hand and then the hand on his shirt. He leaned and took both sacks from Nora. "Where to?"

"To the storage shack." She led the way, and now hands-free, she took Marie by the elbow, as if they were going for a leisurely stroll.

Why not? Marie wasn't in any hurry to get back to the infirmary and the unpleasantness of having to confront Zena again. She adjusted her gait alongside Nora's and they started chatting. The girl started chatting, that is. She mostly listened and Marie nodded once or twice, her senses attuned to Grant silently walking behind them. She would have turned and talked to him instead, but that wasn't done. And he couldn't walk with them, either. Five steps behind as customary, seen—as it was impossible to avoid noticing him, given his size and colors—but not heard. A good worker knew that. And a good fathered woman should've known that too. Maybe the nurse was right. *What's wrong with me? I go all judgmental on somebody I don't even know and then here I am, wishing I could openly talk to a man.* Because it was one thing stealing glimpses of him secretly and by chance but another to desire it could happen at will. *It's wrong.* But was it her fault if her heart and her body were betraying her? *I'm strong. I'll fight this.*

"So how do you like your new job?" Nora was asking.

She had a sense of déjà vu. It hadn't been so long ago she had a similar conversation. She had been shocked, too, that first time. She found it funny how history was repeating itself. "Eventful. I assisted to a girl's birth."

Nora squeezed her elbow in excitement. "Oh, how was it?"

She was surprised, once more, by the girl's attitude and demeanor. No fathered girl would ever ask such question or be remotely interested in knowing how birthing worked. It was improper. But then again, it took only a sideways glance to be reminded of where she was now. "Not what I would've thought." *If I ever thought of something like that.* Which she hadn't once in her life until she had been catapulted in the middle of a birthing. The intake of breath that came from behind them consoled her. He was fazed too by Nora's questions.

The girl continued, "Is the baby cute?"

"Cute isn't the right word." She flinched at the gory memory of the baby landing into Rena's hands.

Nora's eyes went distant, her face showing a smaller version of the smile she often threw around. "My sister was so cute when she was born. She looked like a little doll. I could've hugged her forever."

Marie stopped in her tracks. "You have a sister?" She thought the list of surprises was never going to end. Nobody had sisters. For sure not fathered women. Not even pure breeds. They needed a special dispensation from the Priestess.

The girl's small smile dwindled to nothing. "Had a sister. Rosette died when she was two. A fever and she was gone. Something happened... and medicines were scarce for a period of time. Lots of kids and elders didn't make it. Lots of families lost their loved ones."

Whatever was the next question Marie had for her, it died in her throat. "Oh, I'm sorry."

"It was almost ten years ago." Nora released her hold on Marie's healthy arm and indicated a squat building in front of them. "Let me open it for you." She had turned around to talk to Grant.

At loss for what was expected from him, he nodded and lowered the two sacks on the floor between his open legs. A big tree shaded his face from the harshness of the sun, but she could still see his green eyes broadcasting his questions. He locked gaze with Marie and a flicker of understanding passed between them. They were both strangers in a strange land where nothing made sense. But life would be so much easier for him at Vasura. She wasn't sure about herself.

The shack's door was opened with a big clank and both she and Grant were startled by the sound. "Here," Nora called and they both stepped forward at the same time, only for Grant to stop to ensure the five-feet space between them.

"You'll soon forget about all that silliness." Nora was looking at them, still uncharacteristically serious.

Grant accepted her prediction in proper silence, but Marie couldn't help but comment. "It's a new world, right?" It didn't come out as funny as it had sounded in her head, and it solicited a sideways glance from Nora.

"You've got all your life to see I'm right." She showed Grant where to store the sacks and thanked him again for his help. She must have read something in the way his upper lip slightly arched upward. "You do have a choice."

Marie was going to reply that unless you were born at the Temple and had two loving mothers, you never had a choice. A man didn't even register on the scale. But the brunette was still brooding and she shut her mouth. She saw Grant looking around to see who was listening.

"You can go. Thank you again." Nora seemed deflated. She waved her small hand to release him from his duty to her.

A few women passed by. They didn't stop or even pause to look at the trio, but Marie tensed immediately. Thankfully, Grant slowly lowered his head and left without looking back. "You must stop this nonsense. People will be punished." She hadn't meant to sound mad, but not long ago, she had taken care of workers who had been disciplined and she remembered the scars on Grant's body.

"You won't get punished." Nora closed the shack's door with slow movements.

"It's not me I'm worried about." The words were out before Marie could censure them.

But Nora smiled back at her. "Then there's still hope for you."

Marie had no retort and politely asked to be excused. "I'm sure the doctor is looking for me." Which was probably true.

***

Once she had returned to the infirmary, she had found Rane and Zena busy with the new mother and the baby. Several women were crowding the bed and she saw flowers and small gifts lying around. She had read in some of the glossy magazines secretly passed around at the Institute that it was a pure breed habit to bring presents and floral arrangements to new mothers. Her power to be surprised had reached its limit for the day and she couldn't muster the energy for outrage, confusion, or even mild interest. When a man entered the infirmary and made a beeline toward the bed, she simply headed out.

"Take the rest of the day as well," Rane had called after her, and she was glad the doctor wasn't mad at her for leaving without asking for permission. Maybe her face was saying more than her silence. She wandered through Vasura. She didn't go far, too scared to end up in some of the places she had been warned of. The waste plant was big, and despite—or because of—the color combination, after a while she didn't recognize landmarks anymore. The whites of the infirmaries followed the pinks of the cafeterias, and the blues, and the oranges. She had the feeling that if someone didn't know where she was going, she could easily get lost. The corrugated walls of the barracks had been painted in colorful tones, but the rainbow repeated itself every two blocks. The rectangular frames indicating the buildings' affiliations must have helped, but she hadn't had time to learn what they were for. At first glance, there weren't two symbols alike. Nevertheless, the Vasurians seemed to know exactly where to go. As she had witnessed only two nights ago, people, women and men, were sprinting around, sometimes even crossing paths.

Marie, a mere half an hour into her walking, paused to regroup. There was a small brick wall bordering one of the cafeterias and she sat on it, content to observe the crowd that was unaware she was among them. *Seen but not heard.* She found it funny. The sun set low on the horizon, and she relaxed, basking in the soft afternoon breeze. Before her, people went in and out from one of the barracks. The building was distinctively different from the others by sporting a rainbow of colors instead of one. Curiosity won and she went to check what the rectangular frame said. Inside the black frame was the stylized shape of two embracing figures. On the barrack's landing, leaning lazily against the handrail, stood a woman. She was a beautiful brunette with long, lush hair and a voluptuous figure who reminded her of Verena. The brunette smiled at her and Marie smiled back, longing setting in her heart mixed with the knowledge she would never see her friend again. A familiar voice called her name and she turned. Zena was hurriedly walking toward her from the opposite corner.

"I can't leave you alone for five minutes." The nurse spoke to her but frowned at the Verena lookalike. "Don't you see she's just a child?"

"Hi, Zena. It's always nice to see you." When the nurse gave her a pointed look, the brunette laughed, a melodious sound. "Of course I did. She looked lost. I wasn't going to—"

"That's enough." Zena shook her head, but she didn't look mad. "Bye, Rachele."

"See you soon, Zena." The brunette saluted her with affection.

Zena protectively circled Marie's waist with her arm. "Let's go somewhere else." She led Marie to the brick wall she had sat on earlier.

"What's that place?" Marie had decided she liked Rachele.

Zena sighed. "How old are you again?" She looked at the building where the brunette was sending her kisses. "Let's say that some of us don't have time to build meaningful relationships, but we still long for human contact."

"Oh…" Marie's mouth remained shaped as an "O" for a few second before she managed to close it.

A woman approached Rachele. They exchanged a few words and then went inside the rainbow building. Only a few seconds later, a man exited from the same door accompanied by another man. Marie's eyebrow shot upward and she turned to Zena.

The nurse nodded. "Yep." Then she raised one hand. "No more questions please."

Although very sheltered, Marie wasn't naïve and she flushed a bright shade of red. Several minutes of awkward silence passed before either said anything.

Finally, Zena nudged her. "So, how do you feel?"

Marie rocked on her legs. "Confused, mostly."

"You're young. You'll understand in due time. Vasura is… different."

"Were you born here?" Marie asked. She wanted to understand now.

"No, I wasn't."

"And how old were you when you were sentenced to Vasura?" Marie hoped she hadn't offended the woman.

Zena's eyes stared at somewhere ahead of them, but then her expression softened. "I was not even sixteen when I was sentenced, as you say, to come here to rot and die."

"What did you do to get life at a waste plant?" She realized the question was probably inappropriate. "If I may ask."

The woman shrugged, her eyes fully back on the present. "Oh, it's public knowledge. I didn't want to be some pure breed's whore and she tried to force me. Even drugged, I stabbed the bitch several times. Too bad I didn't kill her." Glee lit her face. "Pardon my language. I've been living here for so long…"

"No worries." Marie wasn't as shocked as the confession required. She had heard of pure breeds who didn't treat the fathered women in their service much better than men. It was one of the reasons why pupils only left the Institute if Madame Carla was sure the pure breed family they were going to work for was a good one. Or in her case, if the rector knew the employer well. "Well, that must've been… terrible, but good for you, I guess."

"Thankfully, I can defend myself. Always have." Zena studied her for a moment before saying, "The doctor told me what happened to the two of you. It sucks."

Marie nodded. "Nothing can be done anyway."

"I want to apologize for earlier. I've been living here for so long that sometimes I forget how it works outside." Zena offered her hand to her.

Marie took it.

"How's your arm?" The woman must have noticed her slight frown when she turned to reciprocate the shake.

Marie moved the arm up and down and remembered she hadn't cleaned the wounds yet today. "Not as bad as it was yesterday."

Zena became the nurse and gave the offended limb a thorough examination. "You're one tough blonde."

She liked the compliment. "Thanks."

"See you tomorrow, kiddo." The woman patted her on the shoulder and walked away.

Marie followed her imposing figure passing through the night crowd like a hot blade through butter until she disappeared around the far left corner where Grant stood, looking intently at her. She shot him a puzzled look and he made sign to join him.

He waited for her to reach him and then walked around the blue barrack. "Hi."

They were shielded from the rest of the place by the waste material, but being out there in the open still made her feel anxious. "Hi."

"I've got something for you." He was carrying something in his right hand, a small jar. "It's a salve we use when we're badly hurt."

She was so startled by his gift she forgot everything else. She opened her hand to accept it, but then hesitated. "Do you have enough for you? In case you need it."

Seemingly surprised by her thoughtful question, Grant smiled and pushed the jar toward her. "I have some left."

She was still reluctant.

His smile deepened. "I'm used to pain. It's okay. I want you to have it."

She couldn't help but return a smile of her own. "Thank you for thinking of me." His fingers brushed hers when leaving the jar in her possession. The intimacy made her gasp, and he removed his hand.

Something passed through his green eyes. "I'm sorry."

They weren't touching anymore, but the air was charged with his presence and she couldn't breathe. "I—"

He stepped back, a grim expression had replaced the smile. "I didn't mean to offend you."

Her hand shot out to stop him and he looked down at her fingers curling up his arm. "You didn't," she blurted out. Then she thought carefully of what she wanted to say next. Finally, what he could have misunderstood as an order to stay became a plea. "Please, don't go." She saw how his face showed all the emotions he went through and felt relieved when she recognized in them some of her own. "I didn't mean to offend *you*."

He relaxed his stance and leaned against the barrack. "I know the man whose baby you helped deliver."

"Do you?" She found a clean spot and sat on a brick. She was forced to look at him at an awkward angle, but her legs didn't seem to want to hold her any longer.

"Yes, he works my same rotations. He couldn't stop blathering about his kid and how he was stuck there while his woman was giving birth." He crossed his legs and sat by her, his right knee close to her leg, almost touching it.

Marie couldn't stop thinking that if she breathed deeper, her body would shift just enough to close that gap and she would be touching him again. But she didn't act on her whim, and if anything, she almost stopped breathing. She nodded. "He came in as I was leaving."

"I couldn't believe the man was allowed to openly talk like that." He adjusted his legs, and as a result, the gap between them widened. "I've never thought it could be possible."

Marie knew what he was talking about and her heart ached. "You could be with Carnia here."

"Yes. We could've been together." He moved again, toward her this time, and they did touch for the briefest moment.

She hated the feeling. She suddenly wished he were a bit farther away. "Too bad she was sent to a semen factory instead of here." The words came out as spiteful as they had sounded in her head, and yet she couldn't keep her mouth shut.

His eyes darkened and his brows shot up. "Carnia is a good person."

She had the good grace to lower her eyes, but it stung. "So I heard." She felt his gaze on her and like the time at Redfarm when he had confronted her, she knew she had appeared petty.

"What did she do to you?"

She kept her eyes glued on the point of her sandals, wiggling her toes to have something to do. Had he already asked her that question? He might have. "I barely knew her."

"So it's because she was with me?" His voice raised one or two octaves too many to be safe, but he didn't seem to notice.

He had startled her with the question, but when she finally looked up, she saw he hadn't meant what she had thought. Her honest answer would have been, "Yes," but he would have thought

Marie simply disliked a man-lover. The answer he heard coming out from her mouth was, "No. I wouldn't dislike her because she was with a man." Which it would have been a lie only a few months ago.

"Then why?" Grant sounded puzzled.

Because she was with a particular man. You. "Because I just don't like her. Do I need a reason?" Had she just stomped her feet, she wouldn't have felt any less childish. And again, she thought the scene was a replay of some act she had already gone through.

"I guess not." He seemed to think about it. "Still, I don't like it when you're mean." His intense gaze kept her under scrutiny. "Because you aren't."

His words made her blush. She had liked that more than any other compliment she had ever received. And that scared her. "I can't be here." Memories of hugs she hadn't shared with him flashed before her eyes and she desperately longed to let everything go and forget who they were and why it wasn't possible for her to feel what she felt. Crutching the small jar to her chest like a shield, she left before he could reply. His call reached her ears and he sounded hurt. At the very last moment, she turned, and he was still staring at her, his green eyes emanating a cold light. She walked a step toward him, but at the same time said, "I can't—"

He raised one hand to stop her. "Don't bother. I thought you were a different person." Then he was gone and she felt as if her heart left with him.

CHAPTER 12

The afternoon was unseasonably warm and Marie and Nora fanned their faces with two pieces of cardboard Nora had shaped into fans. Not very effective, but nothing short of a fall wind would have brought them solace from the torrid heat.

"It's not even spring." Marie had been complaining the whole day about the weather. At this time of the year, she had expected Trin's pleasant warmth, not this unbearable heat. She complained about the weather every time Rane or Zena had asked what was wrong with her. When Nora came to pick her up for the afternoon break, she had wanted to confide in her about her confrontation with Grant. After all, if not open-minded Nora, who else could understand what was happening to her? But then, apparently by mistake, Nora had given her a peck on the lips and Marie had thought better of it.

"Look who's there." Nora pointed her chin toward the end of the little alley where they had hidden for their break. They had found the solitary corner by turning right instead of left at the crossway between the infirmary and the cafeteria. The relative isolation from the busiest parts of the central hub was a plus in their eyes and they had decided the afternoon snack could be skipped altogether. It was too hot to eat anyway.

Marie liked the idea of having a special place all for themselves. First at the Institute and then at Redfarm, occasions to be truly alone were rare. But Vasura was the size of a city, probably a big one, and one could get lost and never found again. Lost in her thoughts, it took her a moment to realize she was looking at Grant. Semi-hidden by the shadow cast by the building to his left, only his eyes were visible, and she was immediately lost in them. After a moment, he gave her a smile but didn't come any closer. He seemed to think about it, his expression showing conflict, but eventually, he walked away without a word, barely a nod. Disappointment ruined her good mood.

She'd had a glimpse of him in the morning just as she exited the cafeteria with Nora. Grant had walked by and their eyes had locked. Among the morning crowd, a sea of people sprinting in every direction at once, they had looked at each other, unable to say a word, the memories from yesterday still too raw. So they had walked from the corner of the cafeteria to the infirmary's steps, sharing the same stretch of street, but not together. She had fought her nerves, wanting to say something, but Nora's presence and several others' prevented her. Once on the stoop, she had turned to talk to him, but he had gone, swallowed by the crowd, his dark-blond head bobbing in the distance. And now, he left again without a word. He didn't want to talk to her. *I shouldn't have insulted his precious Carnia.* But deep inside, she knew that wasn't the problem. She had insulted him and he thought she was like any other man-hater.

"He's probably on some errands." Nora patted Marie's knee. "He's not avoiding you."

The oppressive heat was nothing to the burning in her cheeks. "And why should I care?"

Nora opened her mouth to say something, but Marie stopped her. "And why on Ginecea would you think I'm concerned with anything he is or isn't doing?" She knew she should lower her voice. "He's a man."

Nora, who hadn't closed her mouth yet, gave her one long look and flashed an appeasing smile. "No reason. I just thought that this morning—"

"This morning nothing happened." Which was why she had been upset the whole day. She couldn't stop thinking about him and how to make things right between them. She had been so close to being in his arms and was terrified by the magnitude of her longing. It wasn't right. At Redfarm, she had thought he was in her thoughts because of the things she had witnessed. Nothing more than a strange fascination. But now?

"If you say so."

Marie was desperate to change the subject. "What do you do when summer comes?" She wiped a trickle of sweat running down her front shirt. The temperature had grown several degrees in the last few minutes.

Nora gently raised Marie's hair and blew on her neck. "If no supervisor comes around, normally, we open the pool."

She allowed Nora the intimacy but felt the urge to stop her. She couldn't understand why it upset her so, but it did. Verena had braided her head and caressed her, and even kissed her head from time to time, but she had never felt so uncomfortable. The sensation was pleasant, but it left her confused on where they stood. Undeniably, there was something, but her heart hadn't beaten faster this morning when she had spotted Nora waiting for her on the cafeteria's steps. Nor had she stopped breathing now when Nora's fingers had brushed her neck. "Is there a pool here?"

"Not officially. Not on the layout registered in Ginecea anyway." She nodded with her head a yes, which was at odds with what she said next. "So we don't have a pool."

"I don't understand." It wasn't the first time Nora made a similar comment about Vasura's apparent whimsical layout. Marie had discovered soon enough that the big billboard hanging at the main entry, the one with the detailed map of the waste plant, was a hoax. Apart from the name of the plant and the color-coded legend on the side, there wasn't a single landmark that appeared to have ever been there.

"Once in a while, there's this big gun from Ginecea who's supposed to come and check we're subdued enough." Nora talked with the repetitive quality of someone who had listened to adults' conversations and was now reporting verbatim. "Ginecea barely acknowledges our existence. We're the pure breed's most embarrassing third-removed cousins. We're the women they would've preferred were born as men. Waste plants are left alone, practically forgotten until they decide to take a brief interest in us and destroy with a single visit the peace it has taken us so long to build. The work of years gone in one day."

Marie let her finish, wondering which one of her parents had spoken the incendiary words. "What happens when the pure breeds come?"

Nora absentmindedly caressed her back. "They don't tell us when a supervisor comes, so when she arrives, we tidy up the place so she'll give us a clean bill."

"How do you tidy up the place?" Vasura was huge. It seemed almost impossible to clean up a place so dispersed.

Nora shrugged. "Well, the usual. Women and men separate and we fake that we hate them like we're supposed to, like the pure breeds and fathered women do. Bribes are also common."

"Bribes?" Marie raised an eyebrow. "What bribes can you pay them if you don't have any money here?"

"We don't need money to live here, but we do receive payments for certain services—"

"What kind of services?" Marie's tone must have been slightly panicked, because Nora exploded in a big laugh.

"You should look at yourself." She wiped her eyes, sighed, and then patted Marie's leg. "Don't worry. You won't be asked to do anything untoward to save Vasura. There are a few pharmaceutical companies who seek us to make waste disappear. I'm told it's a lucrative business." She smiled. "Vasura keeps the money for those special, rainy day occasions."

Marie felt better. "And do the bribes work?"

"It did the last time a supervisor was here. It was three years ago. She was out of the way the same night she arrived." Despite the reassuring words, a sad note tinged Nora's voice and expression.

"And what happens if the pure breed is honest?"

"*When* it did happen, women and men paid with their lives." Nora stopped caressing her and brought both hands on her lap. "My dad's father was tortured and then killed just because a supervisor saw him talking to two girls. They were family friends."

Marie wasn't sure if Nora wanted to keep talking about it and silently took her hand in hers.

Nora squeezed her hand. "I was only five years old, so I don't remember a lot. Just a few things and how scared my mom and dad were and how he had to hide somewhere else away from us the whole time the pure breed stayed here. A few days after she arrived, an army followed to help her."

"It must've been terrible…" She couldn't imagine what they had gone through. She had never had a mother. Most likely a young donor who didn't want to deal with a screaming baby had dumped her at the Institute at birth. Not that fathered families were common anyway. But she could understand the heartache of having someone you loved ripped from you.

"Sometimes, I dream of those days. The image of the pulsating lights warning about a pure breed's presence still haunts me. Now, every time I see a flickering light, my whole body shakes. When you arrived and the sentinels activated the alarm, I didn't sleep that night. I kept thinking of my baby sister…"

Marie remembered how peppy Nora had looked the first day they had met and realized how it must have cost her to act that way to make her feel welcome. "I'm so sorry…"

"People still talk of that period as the Massacre." She shuddered. "Mom says having those nightmares is my way of healing. But it was so long ago. I should've been healed already, don't you think?" Nora turned to face her, as if waiting for an answer.

She shook her head slowly. She didn't know of such things, but if a person had lived through something called a massacre and lost a sister because of it, probably a whole lifetime wasn't enough to heal from its memory. "You need more time. Everybody's different."

"Lately, the dreams come more often."

"Maybe it's because you're worried it's going to happen again?" Marie saw how affected Nora was by the talk and felt the urge to hug her, but resisted.

She nodded. "Yes. Everybody says a visit from Ginecea is due soon." Nora started playing with the hem of her right sleeve, undoing the thread at the seam.

"Who says so?"

"I heard my mom talking to a friend. And I saw they're opening some of the barracks at the northern ends of the fields. They're for the men." She pulled at the thread until the sleeve was open up to her elbow, but she didn't notice. "I'm worried."

Marie closed her hand around Nora's nervous fingers and smiled to reassure her.

*　*　*

A few weeks passed. Marie started noticing small changes in the Vasurians' demeanor. At first, it was just a subtle segregation of the genders. Women and men were taking different routes and keeping different hours. One morning, she realized how much she had come to anticipate those five minutes when Grant's schedule and hers coincided. From that first morning, it had been happening every day. It's not that they ever talked—a bustling crowd always surrounded them—but like planets briefly orbiting each other, they walked for all of those five minutes along the same path. From the right corner of the cafeteria where she and Nora ate their breakfast to the left corner of the infirmary where she spent all her day. Every single day. But not today.

"You seem more distracted than usual." Rane smiled at Marie. She was teaching her a new stitch, but it wasn't working.

"I'm always focused when I'm here." She had never liked to be reprimanded, even when the words were as soft-spoken as now.

The doctor sighed, then took the needle from her hands. "We're done." Rane returned it back to the tray laden with all the surgical instruments they were using on a chicken. "You try very hard, yes, but sometimes, like now, you're not really here."

One look at the carcass and she had to agree. She wasn't at her best. "I did bleed this poor fellow to death, didn't I?"

"Yes, you gave it a long, terrible death. Thankfully, it was ready for the soup." She cleaned the instruments with a strong disinfectant. "What is it?"

Marie was looking outside, and not a man was to be seen anywhere. How funny that she had been so shocked at the beginning to see them and so disappointed now *not* to see them. "Is it true that a supervisor is coming?"

Rane looked outside too and she nodded. "I've been told it's been several years already since last visit."

"Yes, three years."

The doctor looked at her with a puzzled expression. "How do you know? Nora?"

"Yes, she's terrified for her parents."

Rane pointed a finger at the window. "I know things are being put in order. I'm sure everything will be fine this time." The door rattled behind them and their heads turned at the same time. Zena had come back from her monthly visit to the fields. They didn't know what she did or whom she met there. Nora and she had speculated about those leaves the nurse took.

"Why the gloom?" Zena asked them.

Rane summarized their conversation and Marie noticed how the nurse imperceptibly blanched and then masked it with a neutral expression when the massacre was mentioned.

"Were you here when it happened?" the doctor asked Zena.

The dark flicker on Zena's face came back and stayed longer this time. She didn't hesitate to answer though. "Yes, I was here." She took one chair by the armrest and went to sit close to the window. "I was in my twenties when the Massacre happened."

"Did you lose anybody?" Marie asked, immediately regretting her question.

But Zena surprised her once more by answering. "I did. We were in love and we were planning on adopting a kid. She was at the wrong place at the wrong time and took a bullet not meant for her."

Rane, who had been warming some water at the little portable stove, came back carrying three steaming cups by the handles. "The soldiers shot on the crowd?"

The nurse's mouth thinned and her eyes went dark. "Yes, they did, but the bullet that killed Bianca was mine."

The nurse's words left both Rane and Marie speechless.

Zena raised her cup to the ceiling. "Cheers to Ginecea's fall. If I'm lucky, I'll still be alive when it happens."

A few minutes of silence passed, no one in the room able to say anything. The nurse finally broke the spell. "At least she's sleeping in her favorite spot..." Her eyes went outside the window, focusing on the direction where the fields were. "I had it easy. You can't imagine what they did to the heterosexual couples."

Marie's mind was already reeling and she was grateful for Zena's decision to keep the details for herself. She didn't want to know. Her stomach had relocated into her throat already. She decided to stir the conversation to a safer ground.

"Why now? Why is everybody convinced the supervisor is coming now? Do they follow a schedule of some sort? Every three to four years or so?"

"No, it can be three years or ten between 'visits.'" The nurse brought the cup to her lips and gasped when the tea proved to be too hot.

Marie had been taking a sip at the same moment and put the cup to rest on the windowsill. "Then why now?"

"We aren't completely isolated from the rest of the planet. Despite what Ginecea thinks, we still receive news from the outside." Zena nursed her scalded lips with the palm of her hand.

"How?" Marie had heard rumors about communication channels that ran parallel to the officials.

"We have people outside who used to know Vasurians in their other lives, when they were still fathered women or workers. They help Vasura keep track by smuggling information. I know you said that once you were a wasted woman, nobody would ever remember you. I was told the same. It's a lie. People who loved you would never forget about you. It isn't easy, but we can still communicate with the rest of the world."

Marie understood now. "So somebody warned Vasura a supervisor is coming."

"Yes, around a month ago, one of our contacts intercepted a mail directed to a newly appointed supervisor." Zena tentatively brought the cup to her lips again, and this time, she could drink from it.

Marie took hers and drank it too. "And?"

"A supervisor is only appointed when needed." The nurse took long sips between words.

She thought it was unfair a supervisor would show up as soon as she had arrived and said so.

"Ginecea is only fair to the pure breeds." The doctor grimly smiled and both Marie and Zena raised their cups to that.

***

Several days passed, the "ginefication"—as the process of tiding up Vasura to the Ginecean standards had been called, in an attempt to make fun of something that terrified everybody—was well on schedule, and as result, everybody's mood was dark. Men were rarely seen at all in the main hub anymore. Members of mixed families had agreed on a temporary separation. Marie had consoled Nora when her father had left to live with the other men. Heartbreaking scenes were seen all over Vasura for almost a week. Marie's own heart had broken at the scene of a little kid sobbing when his father had to leave. The young mother had tried to console her son, but she was too distraught to be of any help. Marie and Nora had played with the kid until the mother had stopped crying and then brought him back to her.

Day after day, she had to confront her own heartache. She looked for Grant every morning, hoping to see him at the corner of the cafeteria, only to be disappointed when he wasn't there. For no apparent reason, work at the infirmary was slower than usual. Any other time, she would have rejoiced at having a relaxed day of work, but with so much time left to nurture idle thoughts, Marie couldn't help but think of him. She wondered what he was doing. How he was feeling. Did ever think of her? Rane and Zena tried to keep her occupied by sending her for errands, but the long walks to fetch clean towels from the laundry or to deliver useless mail didn't help. She almost asked Nora if she would show her where the men were staying. She knew the general direction, but Vasura was too big to wander by herself. Once, while coming back from one of the errands, she thought to have seen a man walking by. She didn't think twice and followed him for a good ten minutes, until the person turned to ask her what she wanted and turned out to be a masculine woman. She laughed and cried at the same time the whole way back to the infirmary.

"We have an unexpected birth today," Rena announced the news one hot morning.

Marie welcomed the idea. Since that very first day of work at the infirmary, they had cured wounds, burns, dehydration, scratches, but nothing more serious. "Do you expect any complication?"

"The mother just entered the last trimester and she looks quite small." The doctor was preparing a corner for the birthing.

"She's a sturdy girl. I know her. I don't think we'll have complications with this one," Zena said, and a moment later, a blonde in early her twenties entered the room accompanied by two older women.

Marie was surprised by the relative calmness the mother emanated. She was in pain, but didn't complain. By contrast, the other two women were so agitated Zena asked Marie if she could prepare an herbal tea for all.

"It's our first grandkid," one of the two explained.

"This is not our first delivery." Rane smiled and the women relaxed.

"I'm sorry." The oldest woman took a seat by the young mother, who had silently taken her place on the bed and was calmly waiting for everybody to settle.

Marie looked at her and was surprised when she winked and said, "You'll see what fuss your mothers make when you'll have your first baby. I'm almost glad my husband had to leave. He was driving me insane with his worries."

She had to turn away from the scene. A deep emotion settled inside her ribcage and she felt her heart wanting to explode. For the first time in her life, Marie longed to have what this woman had, a loving family. In fifteen years, she had never given a second thought to the fact she didn't have one. At the Institute, everybody was like her, unwanted. But Madame Carla and the other girls had always made her feel as if she belonged and she was too young to think about a future with someone. At Redfarm, she had discovered the meaning of the word "lonely," but Verena had been there for her. Now in Vasura, she found this strange world where people were free to fall in love outside of what society ruled. She wasn't the Marie who had left Trin a little more than three months ago. She wanted it all, mothers who were worried for her, a companion who cared for her, and friends to fill the loneliness. A companion. She hadn't immediately thought of a girl. A solitary tear fell down her cheek and she wiped it away. Her eyes went to her bare wrist where once Idra's bracelet had been, and she sobbed in earnest at the loss of something more than a gift. She had left it under her pillow back in her room at Redfarm and never thought about it until now.

"It's going to be okay." Zena's arm circled Marie's shoulders.

She hadn't noticed the woman but was grateful for her words. "One day, soon, it will be okay," Zena added, and Marie realized the nurse had spoken for the two of them.

"Let's help this baby into the world." *Maybe his or her world will be a better place than mine.*

After dinner, instead of going to the dormitory where she knew the other girls were going to talk all night, she went for a walk and ended at the spot where Grant and she had spoken last. She hadn't meant to at the beginning of her stroll. It was hot, and the metal box that was her dormitory already resembled a steam bath without the pleasantness of the balmy scents, and she wasn't looking forward to any conversation about crushes and such. Her legs had brought her there. When she turned the corner and saw a shadow leaning against the metal sheet, she made to turn to avoid company at all cost.

"Marie?"

She heard Grant's voice and spun around, her heart racing. She closed the distance in no time; she didn't even know how she had moved so fast without tripping on the debris lying on the ground and hidden by the darkness surrounding the place. She looked for his eyes and was rewarded by two green lights. The golden and brown speckles were still there as she remembered. She probably couldn't have described the shade of her own eyes, but she knew all the nuances of his by heart. "Hi."

"Hi." He smiled and she did as well. Then, without warning, he leaned forward and took her in his arms.

Marie hadn't expected that. If she had experienced trouble breathing when she had heard his voice, now she stopped altogether. Her mind screamed at her that a man was holding her. Her body reacted by snuggling closer until she was completely embraced by his bigger, taller frame.

Then he whispered to her, "I wanted to see you." And her legs gave out. His arms tightened around her trembling frame and didn't let her fall.

"I wanted to see you too." She had said it. The words that should have never left her mouth were out in the open. "I looked for you all these mornings, and during the day, the only thing I could think was you."

He slowly caressed her back and she shivered. "We've been told to keep to a different area for the time being. But I wanted to see you so much…"

She liked the way she felt in his arms. It was perfect. "I'm sorry I didn't talk to you earlier. You were right to be mad at me."

He put a finger on her lips. "No, it was wrong of me to judge you that way. You didn't make the rules."

She was mesmerized by his voice, soft and warm, by his eyes never leaving hers, by the way his whole body seemed to curl around hers. For once, she felt small and she liked it. "I was scared."

He took her face between both his hands, his fingers caressing the line from her ears to her jaws. "I'd never hurt you."

She closed his eyes, his caress almost hypnotizing her. "I was scared of me, of my feelings for you, of what I wanted."

He stopped caressing her. "And what do you want?"

Heart beating faster and no oxygen left in her lungs, Marie opened her eyes and then looked away, too embarrassed to voice her most hidden desire.

"Look at me." It wasn't an order, but a soft plea and she couldn't help but obey. "What is that you want?"

His lips were so close to hers, she just had to stand on tiptoe to finally know what it felt like to kiss them. She had thought of it non-stop, replacing Carnia with herself anytime the memories came to taunt her.

"Marie…?" He looked away from her, surprise on his face, and she lost some of the courage she had summoned. His eyes still pointing at something behind her, he applied the slightest pressure on her face before releasing her. "I must go."

Tears already clouding her vision, she saw the light pulsating at the corner of her eye, and the disappointment and hurt soon transformed into fear.

Grant stood frozen, the light intermittently illuminating his face. "It's happening."

"Go! You must run!" Marie pushed him away when she saw he wasn't moving.

"But you?"

"I'm going to be fine." She fought the urge of asking him to follow her to her dormitory. She would have preferred to know where he was. "Go!"

CHAPTER 13

Once she saw him disappear, she ran back to the infirmary. Somehow, she knew Rane and Zena would be there.

"The supervisor just arrived." The doctor was shaking, her face pale, her hands around a cup that, from the strong smell wafting from it, didn't contain any calming herbal tea.

Marie, already terrified, looked at Zena for an explanation.

"She saw the new supervisor." The nurse was folding and unfolding cloths. "It's an old acquaintance of hers."

"Who is she?" Marie went to face Rane and she laid one hand over hers to stop the doctor from inhaling the contents of her cup.

Rane stared at Marie's hand as if she couldn't recognize what she was looking at. "Callista. She's the new supervisor and she'll not be bribed."

At hearing the name, she too started shaking. "Are you sure it's her?" It was a stupid question and she knew it.

Rane nodded. "Yes, and she didn't come by herself. She's escorted by an army wearing gold and black."

The room was moving around her. "The Priestess's Army? But why?"

The doctor shook her head this time, her eyes watering. "She'll tear down Vasura and she won't be happy until she's finished."

A sharp knock on the door resonated through the whole barrack. Two soldiers entered and positioned themselves by the door, rifles at ready.

Marie went to Zena, who protectively brought her under her wing. Rena looked like a statue, not trembling anymore, but preternaturally still. Arguing voices reached them, but they didn't have to guess about what was happening for too long. Callista strode inside, immediately followed by three Vasurian guards wearing strained expressions.

"You can't—" One of the Vasurian guards tried to stop Callista, but the pure breed soldiers silently pointed their rifles at her and she raised her arms in sign of peace.

"I work for Ginecea under the order of observing how things are done at this waste plant, if rules of safety are followed, if the hygienic requirements are met, etc., etc. To do my job, I must be free to enter facilities and such without being hindered. Is that clear?" Callista's tone of voice was calm and polite. Her accent was as cultivated as the last time Marie had heard her talking. But the woman was slimmer, she had lost weight, and her eyes were bright. "You can leave now. We don't need your presence to keep things going. Do we, dear Rane?"

The Vasurian guards looked at the doctor, and three sets of eyebrows rose at the same time.

"I said you can leave. Now." Callista's voice rose to high pitch on the last word. For a moment, her cool demeanor was marred by a tinge of heat she couldn't hide fast enough.

"But—"

"Didn't you hear what Major Callista said?" One of the pure breed soldiers moved a step ahead, the point of her rifle touching the woman who had just talked.

"It's okay." Rane tried to smile, but her words were too shaky to be taken seriously. When nobody moved, the rifle was pointed higher to the woman's temple. "Please, leave," Rane said, and the women finally listened. When the door closed behind them, she turned toward Callista. "Congratulations on your promotion. You deserved it, I'm sure."

Callista's eyes darted to the new epaulettes shining on her uniform, a flicker of pride illuminating the hard angles of her face. "As a matter of fact, I did. My effort to clean Ginecea of men-lovers and other abominations was finally noticed."

Marie couldn't help but shiver and Zena brought her closer.

"Aren't you happy to see me?" Callista walked around the doctor, her steps maddening slow, her hands held behind her back.

"I didn't think I was ever going to see you again." Rane trained her eyes on Callista the whole time.

"A nice surprise, don't you think?" The major stopped before the doctor, the tips of her boots almost touching Rane's shoes.

She nodded. "A surprise, yes."

Callista waited a moment and then laughed her trademark humorless, cold laugh. "I always loved the way you play with words and their nuances. You've always said so much with so little. Too bad you were born fathered."

Rane winced. "Why are you here?"

Callista tilted her head and looked at her from that angle, a strange light in her eyes. "To supervise Vasura under Ginecean orders. What else?"

"Then I wouldn't waste time reminiscing with old friends if I were you." The doctor pointed at the door.

"You've always forgotten your station. I remember a time when I found it amusing." Callista took her by the elbow. "I could command you to come with me this very moment and nobody would ever ask what happened to you."

Rane didn't flinch, but Marie wondered how she could stand upright, when she felt her legs had melted into two liquid pools.

"This is the power I have. Do you understand?" Callista squeezed the doctor's arm until she cried. "Do you?"

Rane nodded, tears streaming down her face. "What can I do for you?" Her voice was a hoarse whisper.

Marie hated the pure breed already, but her feelings were growing stronger by the second.

"Good girl. Now we truly understand each other. When I need you, I'll ask for your services." The major strolled out, a pleased smile on her face. The pure breed soldiers followed her outside as efficiently as they had come in.

The door finally closed and the infirmary came alive again. Marie was grateful the major had never looked at her, not even once.

"What was all that about?" Zena went to Rane, her hands on her arms.

"We have history together." Rane gently pushed her away and went to sit on one of the chairs under the window. "She's the reason why Marie and I were sent here."

"She's that...?"

"Yes, she's the former love of my life." Rane turned to look outside and Marie nodded.

"Well, it's clear you're still under her skin." Zena went to refill the doctor's cup from a dark bottle sitting on the counter. "Not for you." She pointed at the bottle and then at Marie, who shrugged. "Here, take some. Pure forgetting nectar. Not diluted." She took a swig herself and then passed it to Rane, who downed the contents of the cup in one single swallow and then coughed.

She kept coughing for a few seconds, then drew a deep breath and leaned against the windowsill where she laid her forehead on the metal. "She followed me to Redfarm. I should've known she would follow me here as well."

Marie's thoughts were focused on Grant's safety and she hoped he had made it to his shelter, out of the pure breeds' way. She had seen the light in the major's eyes and it was clear she was hitching to make someone pay for her frustration.

"She'll leave when her job is done here," Marie said to reassure herself.

The nurse went to pour a cup for her from the same bottle and then came back and sat on the floor between Marie and the doctor. "Yes, but that's the point. A supervisor doesn't have time restrictions."

Marie was starting to wish she could partake of whatever they were drinking; it looked like it was miraculously calming their nerves, while hers were on the verge of exploding. "But from what I heard, they never stay long. Even the Massacre only lasted—"

"Pure breeds only come here because forced to. They're promised higher ranks and fortunes on their return, but they stay only long enough to either discover something they can fine us with or to accept a bribe and leave immediately." Zena drank some more from the cup and then looked at the back of the doctor and sighed. "I have the feeling that for the first time in the history of supervisors, the major volunteered for the job."

A choked laugh escaped from Rane's mouth. "I'm unforgettable."

The nurse's hand reached up to pat Rane's leg. "You're the forbidden fruit."

This time, they both laughed, leaving Marie out of the joke. "Are the men going to be safe?"

Zena's eyes focused on her with a certain difficulty. "They should be. As long as they keep out of the way."

Still leaning with her back to them, Rane tilted her head down to give Marie a look from under her arms and finished the nurse's thought. "And act as the good old slaves they should be in the major's mind..."

"And if she stays for months?" Marie couldn't imagine life anymore with a pure breed army breathing down their necks.

"She could stay for years, but I'm hoping she'll tire of the new game soon. She did tire of me at Redfarm." Rane turned and slowly slid down with her back against the wall and gestured to the nurse to pass her the bottle.

Marie remembered that the last time Callista'd had enough of the doctor, she had sent her here to punish her. What next, considering that sending a fathered woman to a waste plant was a death sentence in the Ginecean culture? What would happen when the major discovered the truth about this place? How things didn't quite happen the way Ginecea thought? She hugged herself. "Yes, we only have to wait."

The same night, Callista sequestered more than twenty dorms to accommodate her army, plus one for her personal quarters. She had the people forcefully ejected from their beds to clean up the barracks to her standards and sent them to fetch accommodations for themselves after dawn.

Marie was among the ones who became homeless overnight and was kept longer than the others to help the army get comfortable in their new places. She had a feeling it wasn't a coincidence. She had scrubbed the floor of her ex-dormitory for hours when one of Callista's minions had declared the place a dump and kicked a bucket full of soapy water upside-down. Her arms aching and the skin on her knees raw, she bit the insult wanting to get out of her mouth and lowered her head.

"Good girl."

She heard the pure breed's leer and saw red. She placed one hand on the sponge, wishing it were a knife. In her mind, she had already stabbed the woman several times.

"Maybe I'll tell you to come to my bed later tonight." The woman stopped beside her.

Even though Marie couldn't see her, she felt the soldier's eyes roaming over her prostrate body and started shaking.

"Shivering in anticipation, I see." The woman laughed. "I'll give you a little taste now, so you've something to look forward today." Her hand descended heavily on Marie's waist to turn her around.

Marie screamed, "Don't touch me!" and tried to escape the woman's hold.

"What are you doing?" Callista's voice echoed behind them and the soldier jumped away from Marie. "You aren't thinking of laying with a wasted woman, are you?"

Marie scuttled away on all fours, the urge of throwing up only made stronger by the loathing she felt for the major. The woman's voice by itself was enough to make her sick.

"Are you, Private?" Callista stepped closer to the soldier.

"No… of course not," the woman stammered and stepped back until the wall stopped her behind her back.

"Good to hear because it would be degrading for a pure breed to touch such filth." Callista's attention zeroed in on Marie, disgust altering her elegant features. "Touching a wasted woman is just one step away from laying with a man."

Marie heard the soldier retching, but she couldn't turn away from the major's stare, her hatred matching hers.

"Sometimes, they tempt you, looking like women when they aren't anymore. Wouldn't you agree, Private? Is that what was happening a moment ago?" Callista moved her head slightly to include the soldier in her monologue.

The woman shook her head and vehemently denied, too scared to realize what her superior had just told her.

"Wasn't this…" Callista threw another disgusted look at Marie, and then continued to talk with the soldier. "This filth enticing you?"

The soldier finally grabbed the meaning of her words. "Yes," she hurried to say. "Yes, she moved seductively to corrupt me. But I was going to discipline her for it."

Marie watched horrified as the major finally smiled and nodded.

"That's what I saw, then. Of course. No soldiers of mine would ever stoop so low. Let it be a punishment then. Publicly. So everybody will know the way I intend to run things here." Callista waited for the woman to drag Marie to her feet. "I saw a lamppost just outside. It will do. But first, we'll summon the rest of them to witness her flogging."

The soldier pushed Marie out of the door and she almost fell down the steps and scuffed the guard's right shoe.

"Look what you've done." The woman spat on the ground at Marie's feet.

"There." Callista pointed at the metal post in the middle of the road.

Marie was tied to it by a piece of crude rope the soldier was careful to tighten until it cut the circulation from her fingers. Marie didn't cry. Her only hope was that Callista would have enough of it soon. But the woman wanted her spectacle and waited for a crowd to form. Marie heard Rane and then Zena call her name, but she closed her eyes, not wanting to see them looking at her. When the private tore away her shirt by ripping it off her back, angry tears rolled from her eyes without her consent. Nora's cries came along with the second or third lash the soldier imparted on her flesh. Callista had been magnanimous of her tender age and had only ordered five lashes. When the fifth arrived, Marie sank on the ground, hating that the woman had showed her mercy and she had to be grateful because she wasn't sure she would have been able to bear more. She heard the major ordering her release and the swift sound of a blade cutting through the rope followed. A moment later, eyes still closed in shame, she tried to cover herself with the shredded remains of her shirt.

She felt people slowly surrounding her. "Sweetie, it's done." Rane crouched beside her. "Let's go to the infirmary where I can take a look at you."

She nodded and tried to stand.

"Let me help you." Zena took her arm by the elbow and gently pulled her up. "Lean on me. I'd carry you, but it would be too painful for you."

Someone pushed her way through the crowd. "Marie—" Nora starting sobbing.

Marie opened her eyes to look at her friend and reached for her hand. But a soldier grabbed Nora and forcefully separated her from Marie.

"This is not a social gathering." The soldier dragged Nora away while she screamed Marie's name.

Marie blinked the tears away, but her friend was gone. Helped by the nurse, she walked to the infirmary in complete silence. An equally silent crowd followed them two steps behind.

Later, Marie was told that Vasurians camped outside the remainder of the night until Rena had come out and informed them of her condition. She stayed inside the next day, mostly lying on her belly while Zena or Nora, who had been able to sneak in, applied the salve Grant had given her so long ago. The little jar was always on her, passing from one pocket to the other, depending on the task ahead. Fortunately, that night, she had hidden it in her pants' pockets. Callista arrived at the hospital later in the afternoon and exchanged a few words with Rane. The doctor was so furious she could barely talk, and the major seemed too pleased by her strong reaction. Marie faked she was sleeping and the pure breed was called outside before she could come to the bed.

The rest of the day passed without incident, and she dozed in and out of a nightmarish slumber that left her more confused than rested. When the moon was high in the sky, she came out of a vivid dream that had made her cry for help and heard a soft commotion happening behind the screen Rane had put by her bed to give her some privacy.

"If you're caught here, there will be hell to pay." Zena's silhouette danced behind the screen.

"Let me see with my eyes that she's okay. I'll go away then, I promise." Grant's dark-blond mane stood over the screen.

"Grant!" Without thinking, she jumped out of the bed and threw away the screen.

Grant's eyes widened at seeing her and he threw open his arms to receive her. Marie felt the pain of his embrace only a second later and couldn't smother the pained cry that followed. Zena pushed him away and was at her side, asking if she was okay.

"I'm okay. Give me a moment." But she was looking at him over Zena's shoulders and she noticed it.

"Are you sure?" the nurse asked, still keeping her body between Marie and Grant.

"Yes, please." She wanted to be alone with him but didn't dare ask.

"I'll be here." Zena stepped out of the way and went to the other corner of the room.

"How are you?" Grant took her hand and brought it to his face.

She didn't know how to answer. It wasn't just the pain. It was the humiliation that still made her weak in the knees a day after. It was the feeling of being powerless and at someone else's complete mercy. Her eyes watered and she wanted nothing but to be hugged by him, to be in the warm embrace of his body. She could stand the pain. One look at the screen, and he understood she wanted him to follow her behind it. Once hidden by the relative privacy of the rice paper wall, she felt more courageous.

"I don't want to hurt you." He shook his head softly when she moved toward him.

"I need this." She didn't stop.

Grant opened his arms again, but this time he carefully put his hands on her shoulders on either side of her head. She leaned into him, her nose pressed against his chest, breathing his scent and listening to his heartbeat. He had run there; she could tell from his still-accelerated heart and the fall and raise of his chest. His hands caressed her head from neck to crown and back in slow motions.

"I didn't know… I would've come earlier," he whispered to her ear and then laid a soft kiss on her forehead.

It felt right. She raised her chin to meet his lips and his heart skipped a beat. Despite the pain, and in spite of everything else, Marie smiled. His lips descended on hers and she forgot herself and where she was. His mouth against hers was soft and warm. A strand of his hair brushed against her face. His fingers were pressing at the base of her head to tilt her face and she let him. When his lips moved sideways, caressing and opening hers, she gasped, the feeling too intense to bear.

"I'm... I don't know..." Grant had stepped back, his lips swollen, his eyes bright, unevenly breathing.

"Is everything all right?" Zena was looking at both of them from over the screen, her eyes taking in the scene.

"Yes." *No!* She wanted to kick herself.

Zena gave her a knowing look and raised her eyebrow. Then she turned to him and shook her head. "Young man, you should leave. It's too dangerous." She saw Marie's disappointment and added, "We might save *you* from Callista's anger if she found him here, but he would be better off dead."

Marie's back throbbed and she was reminded of the courtesy accorded to her. Callista wouldn't be as generous with a worker. If he were lucky, Grant would be whipped within an inch of his life. "Please go and don't come back until things are safe." Mindless of the woman's presence, she took his hands in hers and bought them to her lips. "Soon."

Zena stepped away and turned around. "I'll go see if the coast is clear." She made enough noise to let them know when she was on the side of the room by the window.

Grant's face lit in a small smile. "Marie," he whispered and then bent over her and laid a small peck on the top of her head. "Soon."

"Now!" Zena called, gesturing for him to move. "In a few minutes, it'll be dinnertime and the whole place will be full of soldiers."

Marie grabbed the neck of his shirt and dragged him down for a last kiss. Nothing more than a brush, but enough to send her heart in a mad race once again. "She's right. Go." She accompanied him to the door and watched as he disappeared behind it. A new, different pain permeated her whole being. A different reason to feel tearful. A different reason to feel alive.

"He'll be fine." Zena was still looking outside and she joined her at the window.

"What's happening to me?" She rested her head on the nurse's shoulder. "Why do I feel like I feel?"

"Do you want the long answer or the short one?" Marie felt the quiet laugh in Zena's voice. "The world as we know it could end tomorrow." The woman's head leaned over hers. "You're fifteen, and the heart wants what the heart wants."

Heavens knew she had tried to fight her feelings. "Is it so wrong?"

Zena gently stepped away from Marie and looked at her. "Does it feel wrong to you?"

She sighed, the memory of his lips on hers still altering her breathing rhythm. "No, it doesn't. It has never felt so right."

Zena smiled. "Then follow your heart."

***

Marie wandered through the infirmary the whole night. When she noticed Zena yawning and her eyes closing while she talked to her, she sent her to sleep. She tried to relax and take small naps, but eventually, she had to accept sleep wouldn't come. At dawn, when Callista gave order to blast the siren to give Vasura the good morning, she was awake and still in pain. The private who had gotten her in so much trouble came to announce her break had ended and that every wasted woman had to report for duty in the main hub. The woman almost spit when she said the word "wasted woman." Marie saw the hatred and the disgust in the pure breed's eyes, as if everything had happened the way Callista had everybody believe. As if the private were the victim and not her.

Outside, not even five in the morning, the sunlight timidly appearing, it seemed that the whole female population had been forcefully gathered. Marie looked for Nora. She didn't know what had happened to her after she had seen her last time at the infirmary. Eyes scanning the sea of people, she saw that among the crowd were kids, some as young as two or three years old. Some were boys she had seen playing around. They were now dressed in girls' clothes. Pure breeds corralled the Vasurians the same way they would have done with cattle and made them wait for more than an hour. By the time Callista finally decided to deign everybody with her presence, Marie was on the verge of closing her eyes and sleeping on the street.

The major addressed the crowd with a smile. "I expect your full cooperation during my stay here. Any act not in accordance with my rules will be punished as you have already witnessed. Today, Vasura will have its first census in what appears to have been years. Form two lines, one for the women with kids, the other for the women without kids, and give your name and identification number to my officers."

A murmur rose from the women. Marie didn't understand at first, then saw the mothers clutching their boys and girls closer to them and realized Vasura's lack of official urban planning wasn't the only thing they wanted to keep secret. She saw some of the women with boys try to run toward the lateral alleys. One order by Callista and the soldiers were already dragging away kids by their collars to convince the mothers to cooperate. A rock was thrown at a soldier and two wasted women were hit in retaliation. The cries from the kids calling for their mothers became deafening. Marie could feel their terror and it soon was hers as well. She was frightened beyond reason that the army was going to harm them. Within a moment, panic swelled among the crowd and Vasurians pushed against the army to break the kids free.

"Stop them!" Callista ordered and the army charged against the crowd, rifles ready to shoot.

The Vasurians stepped back at once, a compact, mindless wave trampling everything in its wake. Marie was pushed and almost fell. While straightening up, she saw one of the little boys dressed in girls' clothes aimlessly running around. He was lost under the forest of moving legs and she reached for him before he could be crushed by the stampede. The boy anchored himself to her, his small arms tight around her neck. "Mommy! I want my mommy!" he cried. She shushed him, caressing his head. She swung around, trying to determine where to go, what to do. Shots resonated loud. She ducked, one hand over the boy's head. Several other shots followed. The boy hid his face against her collarbone, his sobs tearing her heart. Someone screamed. She covered the boy's ears. People started running in every direction. The shots were now being fired to kill.

Marie watched as a brunette turned toward her. Their eyes locked in recognition, only a moment before the woman collapsed on the ground, a splash of red expanding on her back. Marie stared in horror at the beautiful hazel eyes now frozen and cold. They belonged to Rachele, the woman who worked at the rainbow barrack. The voluptuous brunette with the sweet smile, who would never smile again. She started hyperventilating and heard her own voice, but she didn't know what she was saying. The kid was clutched to her, frozen. Rachele's eyes remained open, staring at her. Marie's knees hit the ground and she started rocking, automatically caressing the boy's back. She couldn't stop looking at the woman who had been alive only a moment ago. Blood had pooled under Rachele's body and was slowly reaching Marie. She couldn't move. Fingers dug into her right arm. She was upright, but her legs weren't supporting her.

"You, stop this." Someone was ordering her. Friend or foe?

Marie looked sideways. Foe. She was pushed, hard. If it weren't for the boy attached to her like another limb, she would have let the guard push her to the ground. "Mommy," he whispered to her right ear. "Mommy, there, look." He pulled at her earlobe and she turned where he pointed. A woman was running toward them, her face a horror mask. Blood stained her lips and nose.

"Ca—" She started to call her boy.

The soldier who had pushed Marie out of the way turned and pointed her rifle at the running woman. "Stop!"

"Please, don't shoot! She's this kid's mother. They got separated," Marie said, her voice hoarse, every word pulled out with difficulty.

"Is this your daughter?" The soldier swung around and pointed at the boy.

"Yes! Please, let me get to… her." The woman hadn't dared move and was only a few steps from Marie, who was trying to calm the kid with a few soothing words.

The soldier nodded and the woman unfroze. The boy jumped out of Marie's arms and ran into his mother. The yellow skirt he was wearing floated up and down and for a moment revealed the shorts he was wearing underneath. Marie saw the soldier's eyes widening and the mother hurried to smooth the skirt down.

"What was that?" The soldier moved toward the woman and raised the boy's skirt. "Check all the little girls with short hair!" She shouted the instruction one more time to make sure the closest guard repeated it, and soon all the kids were being seized. Meanwhile, she had snatched the boy from his mother's arms.

"What are you going to do to him? Leave him with me." The woman's cries filled the air.

The soldier didn't answer; she moved through the crowd, her rifle in the air and the kid, screaming and kicking to get free, kept flat on her side. The mother followed a step behind, begging and sobbing. The soldier paused enough to turn and hit the woman's head with the rifle's butt. The woman fell on the ground like a heap of discarded clothes and lay motionless. Marie ran to her side and found her pulse. She cried in relief because the woman was alive, but the soldier had disappeared with the boy and soon Marie sobbed in desperation. A repeated tapping sound claimed her attention.

"As I said before, form two lines. Now, all the kids will be checked." Callista's hateful voice echoed over the crowd.

Marie raised her eyes and she saw the major standing on one of the barrack's roofs, safe from the carnage. Beside her, ten soldiers had their rifles trained on the Vasurians below.

Callista raised one hand to stop the murmur her words had instigated. "It doesn't matter to me if you live to see tomorrow. This is a sewage plant. New recruits arrive every month. I can ask to send replacements for all of you. This is how much you're worth to Ginecea."

This is a sewage plant. Sewage plant, the correct words Gineceans used to call a waste plant. Marie closed her eyes and let the tears flow. She felt the air moving around her body as people slowly walked to comply with the major's order. Someone gently laid a hand on her shoulder and a familiar voice whispered, "Stand up."

She opened her eyes to look at Carine. "I can't leave her here." She tilted her head to point at the still woman. "Help me with her."

Carine nodded and they both tried to carry the woman, but she was too heavy for them, so they had to drag her. One soldier noticed what they were doing and ordered them to stop.

"She needs immediate medical assistance." Marie looked the soldier in the eyes, hoping to find some humanity.

The woman, a blonde in her forties, briefly hesitated. Then another soldier came along and her face hardened. "Leave her there. You must get in line."

"A doctor must see her." Marie knew it was pointless to argue with them, but rage and fear were driving her insane and she didn't care anymore if they punished her again.

"There's a doctor there, checking the wounded. Go." The second soldier, an older-looking woman—outranking the first—pointed her rifle behind her to show them the way.

Marie followed the pointer and saw Rane's head emerging over the sea of people. She looked strained, but otherwise she was standing up and shooting orders to someone. Marie, helped by Carine, dragged the unconscious woman all the way to the doctor. "Rane!"

The doctor turned at hearing her voice and her face transformed at seeing her. "I was so worried about you." She let go of whatever she was doing and ran to take Marie in her arms. "I kept looking for you in the crowd." Her eyes roamed over Marie and then widened. "Are you okay? Were you hit?"

"No…" Marie lowered her head to look at what Rane was staring at and saw the red flower under her breasts. Her hands went automatically to touch the spot. "It isn't mine." Two green eyes and a blond mane flickered in and out of her line of sight and she gasped.

Rane whispered to her, "Make him go away. He's going to get himself killed."

Grant was staring at her from behind a brick wall standing just under the roof of the barrack from where Callista was making sure everything went according to her orders. Marie raised her eyes to show him in what danger he was, but he shook his head.

"Please," she mouthed, "Go away." But he didn't move. "I'm fine." She hoped he could understand what she was saying. A soldier walked in front of her and stopped to check what they were doing.

Rane diverted the woman's attention by calling her. "Hey! I can't do anything here. I need help to transport the wounded to the infirmary."

"You need permission." The soldier, a private no more than a few years older than Marie, moved an inch to the right and Marie looked over her shoulder.

Grant wasn't there anymore. Thoughts of him being apprehended by Callista's army invaded her mind and she struggled to breathe. She turned to Rane, unable to stop the sobs tearing her chest, but the doctor warned her not to say anything.

"What's wrong with her?" The soldier gave Marie a good stare.

The doctor pulled her to her side and angled her body so Marie's face was hidden against her body. "Give her a break. She's just a child. Can't you see she's in shock?"

The soldier started to say, "I don't c—" but one of the women standing on the roof with Callista called her. "Escort them to the infirmary," she shouted.

Marie disentangled herself from the doctor's safe embrace and looked up. Callista's eyes were on Rane, a condescending smile on her frigid face. The meaning of her message clear. From now on, they would live or die based solely on her whims.

Rane lowered her head, a solitary tear running a straight, clean line through the soot on her cheek. Callista's smile deepened at the doctor's act of submission. Her lips moved. *"Good girl."* The words as clear as if she had shouted them in their ears. Marie saw how Rane recoiled at the taunting. A slap would have been less painful.

"Don't stand like that." The private poked the doctor in the rib.

Rane blinked once and then turned to fetch some help. "You and you," she summoned two Vasurians who looked relatively in good form apart from a few scratches on their faces and arms. "Look around and see if you can find other people who can help. We need to transport those three women first. The others can wait."

Marie saw four other still figures on the ground. "What about them?" She indicated the two lying side by side in a peaceful pose.

Rane's eyes darted toward the roof and Callista, and she shook her head. "Nothing we can do for them anymore." She pinched the arch of her nose between her fingers and then instructed Marie and Carine on what to do next.

CHAPTER 14

Marie worked at the infirmary the whole day without breaks. The wounded were more than they had expected. Several of them in precarious condition. One woman died later in the afternoon; she had been shot and then trampled by the receding crowd. She had been found only after Callista had declared the census done. By that time, she had lost too much blood.

Nobody had time to grieve over the loss of the human life. People kept entering the infirmary until late at night, when Rane finally had to redirect the less serious cases elsewhere. Around midnight, Mala offered to take care of the infirmary so that Rane, Marie, Carine, who had stayed with them the whole time, and Trisha, who had joined a few hours later, could rest. Nobody knew what had happened to Zena or why she hadn't come back to the infirmary. Marie had looked at the door every few minutes, hoping to see the nurse enter. She kept telling herself that the woman was too strong and that nothing had happened to her. But when she wasn't looking at the door, Rane was. The doctor had the same worried expression on her face, but neither of them uttered a word about Zena.

And so they went to lie on the floor—all the cots were taken—and tried to rest. Marie arranged a thin sheet under her body that did nothing to prevent the cold seeping from the tiles to creep through her bones. The hard surface of the tiles didn't help either. She did sleep though. A fitful slumber filled with nightmares. Sweating while freezing.

Marie's eyes were wide open and staring at the windowpanes at dawn when Callista awakened Vasura again. She and rest of the infirmary's crew and patients who could stand upright walked down the steps in a mournful procession. A few minutes later, an angry but muted crowd had gathered in the main hub as ordered. Dread filled her heart as she realized not a single child roamed the street.

Her eyes darted through the sea of women moving ahead of her and recognized some of the mothers whose kids she had seen a day ago, running and screaming to get back to them. They looked like statues. They moved when asked to, but they weren't there. Marie's eyes went vacant. Callista had started talking, but Marie wasn't listening. A blond mane bobbed for a moment over the wall of heads. She moved through the crowd, leaving Rane and the other two girls behind. They called her. She didn't turn to answer. Despite common sense, she wanted to know if it was him. Heart lodged in her throat, she finally caught up with the blond head, but when the person slightly turned to the right, the nose was wrong, too feminine. Marie breathed once, twice, filling her lungs with air until the oxygen rush made her feel dizzy. A sound between a laugh and a sob escaped her mouth. She was relieved it wasn't Grant, but she still didn't know where he was.

And where is Zena? The thought came unbidden. She turned and looked for the rest of her group, but it was impossible to see anything beyond the person before or after her.

"Starting immediately, wasted women aged fifteen and workers aged twelve will be eligible to work at the recycling facility."

Callista's words reached her ears in a haze. The crowd angrily murmured, but the soldiers placed on the roof made a show of taking aim on them, and silence was restored immediately. It was a sick replay of yesterday's spectacle.

"Male children will be brought to the nursery and raised as appropriate for their sex."

A woman standing by her side started crying, at first soft sobs, and then she collapsed on the ground and wailed. She wasn't the only one. Several images flooded Marie's mind, but the boy screaming for his mother, his little hands stretched ahead of him while the soldier took him away, kept playing in a loop. She couldn't stop herself from seeing the terrified eyes and the small fingers grasping at the air. Where was he now?

"We have analyzed the data from the census and realized this sewage plant isn't utilizing its human resources as it should. There is a waste"—Callista found it humorous and sneered— "of resources, which is easy to fix by creating new shifts. Every woman fifteen and older must report to the new placement center. As of now."

Callista left the roof, but the soldiers remained to ensure their colleagues on the ground properly corralled the crowd. While the younger girls were ordered to stay behind, the conscripted women walked along the line created by the army. Rifles at hand, Callista's thugs directed them toward the place where only yesterday the purple barracks had stood. Now the low buildings were a matte black, paint still drying on the corrugated walls, the acrylic color evaporating under the first rays of sun.

Marie waited in line for her turn. She wished the doctor and the girls were with her. She had never minded being alone, but not now and not here where everything she laid her eyes upon reminded her of pain and death. Any time a blonde walked past her, her heart skipped a beat. Callista hadn't said what she meant to do in regard to the men. Finally, it was her turn to be swallowed whole inside the black hole. She entered the ex-casino and walked to the table at the end of the room. She had no idea how the place had looked a mere twenty-four hours ago, but she was sure it wasn't like this. Besides the table and the chair occupied by a middle-aged soldier, there was nothing else.

"Stop there, by the line." The pure breed pointed with a pen at a piece of tape on the floor, just three or four feet from the table, then went back to her task.

Marie stopped where told and patiently waited for instructions.

"What's your number?" the woman asked. She didn't raise her head from the piece of paper she was filling with lines of numbers.

Marie was started by the question.

The woman tilted her head up and looked at her from over the rim of her glasses, then her eyes pointed at Marie's branded arm. "What's your number, wasted girl?"

Marie looked down at the numbers and letters that had just started to look like they belonged on her arm and recited, "Vasura, three, five, nineteen, and sixty-nine."

The woman gave her an annoyed stare. "Symbol?"

"No symbol." Marie caught herself before adding, *"Unfortunately."*

"Just arrived." The pure breed scribbled a note. "You still remember civilization."

Marie didn't think she was expecting a comment to her statement. Otherwise, she would have liked to say that she got it backward. Vasura was anything but uncivilized.

The woman lowered the pen on the notebook and gave her the onceover. "Do you have any skill at all?"

She looked back and didn't lower her eyes. "I've been training as a nurse."

Eyebrows raised in disbelief, the woman took the pen and lowered it on the paper, but didn't write anything. "Under a doctor?"

"Yes, under Doctor Rane at Redfarm and then here as well." She was proud of having answered without making any sarcastic retort.

"Doctor Rane, you say?" A flicker of recognition passed through the woman's eyes.

Marie had a bad feeling.

"Well, then it's better if you keep working with her at the infirmary then." The woman took something from a basket she had under the table and beckoned her to come close. "You must report every night to the infirmary registry. Now go to work." She removed from a small bow a stamp. "Give me your hand."

Marie reached out and the woman grabbed her wrist and stamped it. "Exit is that way." She indicated a door a few feet from the table.

Marie hadn't noticed it. The woman called someone, and the door was opened from the outside and a younger soldier kept it open for Marie to pass through. Once outside, the soldier asked Marie to show her wrist.

"Infirmary duty." The woman, another young pure breed sporting the usual patrician features and lack of uniqueness, extended her arm to show Marie to follow her.

Marie gave her a brief glance—confirming her notion that pure breeds all looked alike, beautifully uninteresting with their perfect noses and slim bodies. Conversely, the clipped Ginecean accent was anything but monotonous; it grated on her nerves, making it unpleasantly unforgettable.

The soldier didn't bear Marie's silent assessment well and her right hand twitched over the baton hanging from a hoop in her holster just to the right of a shiny gun. "Would you mind?"

Without wasting her breath, she raised her hands and walked down the stairs, three steps that only yesterday had been purple and now were crying black paint through the cracks in the planks. Once on the paved ground, she left black prints behind and found it appropriate. She walked slowly to the infirmary, her thoughts as bleak as the black paint that seemed to never dry under her shoes. The soldier was just a step behind her the whole time.

"Marie, thank the Goddess they didn't send you somewhere else." Rane was at the door, face transformed by the fear, her eyes red.

Marie went inside and looked around. "Zena?" She couldn't stand not knowing anymore.

The doctor shook her head, tears wetting her tired face. "I asked around. Nobody has seen her since yesterday. I went to the morgue… She isn't there."

The morgue. Marie hadn't thought of that. "She's well. I know she's well. She's hiding somewhere." She wanted to believe her words and so she repeated them in her mind as well. "She's strong. Nobody can harm her." Bullets could kill her. An infected wound could kill her. She could lie in a ditch, unconscious. Several scenarios, one worse than the other, kept popping before her eyes, until she was sick with worries and her stomach hurt. And then, the carousel of hopeless thoughts started anew, just the object of her worries changed. Now Grant was lying unconscious somewhere. Finally, she hadn't seen Nora since she had snuck in at the infirmary. "We must go look for them."

Rane tilted her head and looked over her shoulders to the door behind Marie.

"I wouldn't try that," someone said.

She turned and saw Patrician Beauty, the soldier who had escorted her from the ex-casino to the infirmary. She had forgotten about her.

The woman stood before the open door, legs wide, one hand resting on the holster. She shook her head at Marie and her mouth morphed into a grin. "I'll be here the whole day."

***

Even without Door Holder—as the day progressed, the soldier was called several different names—preventing Marie from running outside to look for her friends, she couldn't have left the infirmary. Carine and Trisha hadn't come back. They must have been appointed to some other task. It was just the doctor and herself. A steady stream of Vasurians came throughout the day. Some looking for a comforting word more than anything else. Other nursing wounds of unknown nature. Nobody dared answer questions in front of Callista's woman. She was relieved to see the majority of their patients were adults. Some of them were known faces. Marie rejoiced at seeing the woman she had helped giving birth during her first day of work at Vasura. The new mother had sprained an ankle when she had fallen on the ground. The reason why she had fallen wasn't clear, but she was carrying the baby with her when it had happened. Marie didn't pry, but the grayish-white powder all over the woman's back could mean she was hauling bags of cement when she lost her balance and tried to save her baby from hitting the ground.

"Do you know where they've taken the older kids?" Marie leaned closer to her while massaging some ointment on her damaged ankle.

Nadia—Marie had discovered her name only now—looked at the soldier and then slightly relaxed. "They rounded up the kids, separated the boys from the girls—" She couldn't finish. Her eyes misted and she lowered them to her baby girl clutched to her chest, the small head bobbing under the scarf she was using to breastfeed her daughter in relative privacy.

Marie smiled at the sight of a small foot, the perfect minuscule toes curling as the baby fed and made satisfied suction sounds. Then, darkness claimed her thoughts again. "What about the baby boys?"

Nadia caressed her baby with slow strokes over the scarf. "I don't know."

Marie wasn't sure what the Ginecean protocol with baby boys was. It was one of those topics a good fathered woman would never talk about in company. But it was said that donors who became pregnant hated their baby boys and didn't want anything to do with them. There were rumors about places where women went to terminate their pregnancies. Donors who couldn't tolerate the idea of having to wait nine months to discover their babies' gender. She had never thought twice about those rumors, but she had never been in proximity to newborns before. Now, only looking at the perfection of the small fingers, something stirred inside of her. Not because she had rid herself of all the prejudices against donors and pregnant fathered women. No, it wasn't that. She had just realized a man couldn't help his gender, the same way she hadn't decided to be a fathered woman. It was sheer injustice to condemn a human being from her or his first breath.

"You can sleep here tonight." Rane had approached them and was looking at the baby girl with longing.

Nadia thanked her and then added, "I don't want to go back home. It feels empty without him."

The doctor crouched beside the mother and asked if she could hold the baby for a moment.

Nadia tiredly smiled and opened her arms. "Please, I need a moment of rest."

Marie knew she was lying; she had seen how strong her hold on her daughter was. It had been nice of Nadia to give Rane a moment with the baby and she mouthed a thank you to her. Nadia made a gesture that meant it was nothing at all.

Someone tapped on her shoulder and then called, "Marie?"

She turned to face a girl named Roxanne who had come to the infirmary earlier on for a possible concussion. "Are you feeling dizzy or nauseous?" She had asked the girl to tell her if any of those symptoms occurred.

"Yes." Her voice unnecessary loud, Roxanne bit her bottom lip and looked over their heads toward where the soldier was, as everybody had been doing the whole day.

Marie immediately focused on her. "Both?"

The girl leaned toward her and stumbled.

Marie reached out and stabilized Roxanne. "Dizzy, then."

At the same time, the girl thrust a folded piece of paper in her hand. "I'll sit now."

She stared at Roxanne and silently asked what it was. "Yes, good idea." Her fingers curled around the paper.

Roxanne mouthed something, a name.

Marie brought the paper to her heart. She turned toward the doctor who was still holding the baby. "Rane, can you manage by yourself for a moment?" She pointed at the bathroom in the back of the infirmary.

"Sure." Rane's eyes went to Marie's fisted hand.

Marie saw the soldier's head following her from one end of the room to the other. She closed the bathroom door behind her and cursed there wasn't any key to lock it. She sat on the floor with her back firmly against it, in case the woman decided to check on her, and finally opened her hand. It was a note. From Grant. She read it and then she read it again. Only a handful of words, but they made all the difference in the world.

I'm fine. You're in my thoughts. Grant.

She brought the paper to her lips and kissed it. Grant's longhand was neat. *Neater than mine,* and she found herself laughing on the bathroom's floor.

A firm knock on the door. "May I see what's so funny?" The soldier didn't give her time to answer.

The door hit her back with a slam and she cried. "One moment!" Hastily hiding Grant's note inside her bra, she stood and moved out of the way. Just in time.

"What were you doing there?" The Tormentor—she had just earned another name—gave a good look at the bathroom and then came back to her with an accusing gaze.

"What one normally does in a bathroom..." Marie shrugged.

"You think you're smart?" The Idiot—Marie was having a blast at calling her names in her head—beckoned her outside. "Next time you want to use the bathroom, you ask *me* for permission. Understood?"

"Loud and clear." Marie refrained from raising her hand to her temple in a martial salute. The woman didn't seem the humorous type. "May I go back to my patients now?"

The soldier nodded but didn't look convinced she hadn't done anything wrong. Marie knew she should have flushed the note down the toilet, but having the folded piece of paper pressing against her heart made her feel better. She walked slowly through the patients' beds, checking on their conditions, until she was back at Roxanne's side. "Where is he?" She spoke so low she wasn't sure the girl had heard her.

"The pavilion," Roxanne whispered equally low. "The pure breeds have imprisoned all the adult workers there."

She didn't know where this pavilion was. She had never strayed far away from the main hub. Now she regretted it.

The girl must have read her mind because she added, "It's at the northern end of the fields. Maybe two hours' walk from here. It's heavily guarded."

Two hours from here. Roxanne had walked two hours with a possible concussion. "How did he give you the note?"

Roxanne lowered her voice to barely audible murmur. "While I was walking by, someone shouted. The guards went to check what was going on, and he threw it at me, saying to look for you."

"Thank you." She would have hugged the girl for having taken such a risk, but the soldier was hovering nearby. She pressed her hand over her heart and thanked her again. She didn't ask her to take a note to him. She wanted to. But she understood she couldn't ask Roxanne anything. She had done a lot for her already.

Later, when all the patients were resting or trying to and she had dutifully reported to the infirmary registry, escorted by the guard, she went to sleep on her new makeshift bed, a slightly more comfortable replica of the previous night's accommodation. This time, she put a worn blanket on the tiles and she laid on it, pillowing her head on the balled-up sheet. In her mind, she read Grant's note until her mind couldn't recognize one word from the other. Finally, she relaxed and succumbed to a much-needed sleep. Her last thoughts were about his smile and how beautiful his handwriting was.

When the siren announced dawn for the third day in a row, she opened her eyes, and for the first time since she had landed in Vasura, she wished she could go back to her dreams. The next twenty-four hours were a repetition of the day before. But the fourth, fifth, and sixth mornings all followed a different pattern. Every day started a half hour earlier than the previous one. A week later, the waste plant was awake in the wee hours of the night. Callista never failed to address the crowd from the safety of the roof while she waited for the raised stage she had commissioned to be completed. She announced all the new changes she had made to better Vasura's productivity. She never said where she had taken the boys or what was happening to the men. Public floggings became part of the daily routine. Every night, before the recorded bells called the curfew, women were tied to the pole in the main hub, sentenced, and punished. The reasons for the public humiliation and pain were laughable. People soon lost heart.

Meanwhile, Marie feared for Grant and at the same time hoped to receive a new note from him. Neither Nora nor Zena had showed up to the infirmary. A week after Callista's tyranny had begun, reality had started to resemble a nightmare Marie woke up from only when she went to sleep. She learned a lot in those seven days. Women arrived at all hours because Rane's infirmary was one of three still open. In her eagerness to optimize Vasura's resources, Callista repurposed and reconfigured the majority of the buildings. The result was that a crowd formed before the infirmary and sick people were made to wait. Every morning, a new soldier appeared at the door and was replaced at dinnertime by the night shift. Marie and Rane took turns to eat their three allotted meals. Food wasn't as plentiful as before and the quality of the fare had suffered. Still, Marie barely noticed what she ate. During her meals in the cafeteria, her eyes scanned the equally silent crowd, looking for her friends, then got her hand stamped so she wouldn't be able to re-enter for another meal. The faces she came upon were different, eyes of different colors, but always sad, already defeated. Ginecea had sent another contingent to support the major's efforts to civilize them. Other dormitories were seized to accommodate what now amounted to a true army. Vasura had been invaded.

The first day of the third week, she was gulping down her breakfast, some porridge and a glass of milk, when Nora entered the cafeteria. She dropped the bowl on the table and ran to hug her. "How're you? What happened? Why?" She wanted to cry in happiness.

Nora reciprocated the hug with some enthusiasm of her own.

Marie spun her diminutive friend around. "Oh, but I missed you!"

"Missed you too." Nora wasn't as effusive as she was used to.

"Are you okay?"

She made a smile that wasn't a smile. "I was one of the lucky ones who got assigned to work at the recycling facility. I finished my turn last night."

Marie released her and stepped back. "Was it…?" In her surprise and joy to finally see her friend, she hadn't looked at her. She was the portrait of a tired, older Nora, with dark circles under her eyes and limp hair. An unpleasant tanginess wafted from her, although she didn't look dirty. Her hair was still wet from a shower.

Nora raised her right eyebrow. "Was like I expected it to be?"

Something in the way she said it prevented Marie from asking more. "It's so nice to talk to you again. I thought of you the whole time. I was so scared I wasn't going to see you again."

The small brunette's mouth dimpled in a smile. "Were you really?"

She recognized the tease and smiled back. "Yes, silly. I missed my chatty, exuberant friend."

Nora immediately covered her disappointment, but Marie had seen her friend's eyes cloud for the briefest moment. "I'm so glad to see you, really."

"Me too. Instead of going home, I went here looking for you as soon I was told I had half a day before starting the next job." The girl's hand reached out to caress Marie's cheek.

She let her. "So where are they sending you now?" She knew Nora already had a destination. Callista was nothing but organized and she wouldn't give vacation days for no good reason. She hoped Nora had been assigned if not to the infirmary at least some place near. Only Rane's heartfelt recommendation and the general scarcity of medical staff had insured Marie remained working with her. But the doctor had asked for Trisha and Carine as well and their transfer had been denied.

"North—"

"Where Grant is." She hadn't thought. The words had tumbled out.

Nora's eyes darkened. "No, Grant is at the recycling center. The pure breeds punished him—"

"Why?" A hollow feeling spread through Marie.

Two guards entered the cafeteria, causing the already-soft conversations to die out. Nora made sure the pure breeds weren't too close but still lowered her voice. "They caught him trying to send out a note…"

Marie gasped and put a hand over her mouth. One of the two guards looked her way for a moment but was distracted by a sudden noise coming from outside.

Nora tilted her head and then her eyes widened. "Oh… it was you he was sending the note to, wasn't he?"

Marie nodded, her hand automatically pressing against the folded piece of paper she was still hiding in her bra. His words, close to her heart, seemed to burn against her skin. For a moment, she irrationally feared the guards could see through her clothes and pressed harder until her friend gave her a warning look. She made an effort to relax her hand and compose her face into a neutral mask. "Tell me, please."

"They wanted to make an example out of him. After beating him up, he was sent straight to work at the very core of the recycling facility… the inner chamber." Nora paused.

"What?" The hollowness she had felt a moment earlier was replaced by piercing fear. She had seen Grant after a beating. The marks from the lashes were etched on his body. Old and new punishments had left a permanent map on his skin.

"The place where he works now… it isn't safe." Nora fidgeted with the hem of her shirt.

"Of course it isn't." Something on her friend's face told her there was more.

"He's been inside the main chamber the whole time." She hesitated, but after a look from Marie, she said, "He breathes toxins all day long and the guards didn't even provide him with a hazard suit or a proper mask." She reached for Marie's hand and softly applied pressure. "There's a reason why people work only one month a year at the recycling center. It's harmful."

Everybody knew that. Of course, there was this rumor about wasted women, but Marie had always thought it was an exaggeration meant to scare young and impressionable fathered women. It was funny how, once she arrived at Vasura, she had all but forgotten that wasted women were called such because they wasted away working at the recycling center. She hadn't remembered when Zena had given her the tour that first day after the branding. Or maybe she had conveniently removed the inconvenient knowledge. "How long has he been working there?" The little breakfast she had eaten was now churning her stomach.

"Ten full days."

Ten days aren't terrible, are they? "He has twenty days left." She would ask Rane which product she could smuggle to help him detoxify his system faster. There must have been something she could give him. She was going to ask the doctor right away. He was young and strong. He would be sick for a week or two. That's what she had heard. She regretted not having asked Zena more when she'd had the opportunity.

The girl shook her head. "He's been permanently transferred. He isn't going to get out of there alive."

All of a sudden, the room was too cold. "For having sent a note?" She couldn't believe the magnitude of the punishment compared to the infraction. All the talks about what a death by waste poisoning meant came back to her. Image after image... her mind didn't skimp in details. Before, the subjects of those scary talks were generic people, normally culpable of having done something hideous. Now, when she closed her eyes, Grant was wasting away and dying, driven mad by the pain.

"For having sent a note to a woman and kept her name secret." Nora lowered her voice and then added in a whisper, "You would be there with him now if he hadn't."

Her extremities freezing, she had to sit for a moment. She had been sent to a waste plant for no more than what Grant had done, so Callista's particular brand of justice shouldn't have surprised her. But she didn't want to believe the major would send him to die of such a horrible, slow death. She couldn't believe Ginecea could give a single person so much power over a multitude. Blind rage filled her lungs and drowned her heart. She had never felt anything akin to the feeling she was experiencing. It was frightening and she didn't have a name for it, but it made her shake and sweat. She tasted a sour aftertaste in her mouth. "I need to see him."

"It's not possible." Nora was looking at the door where the soldiers were ordering everybody out. Breakfast was over already.

"I'll find a way." Living how Callista had decided for all of them wasn't living. She had never been so sure about anything in her life, but she wasn't going to simply lower her head and obey a mad woman. Ginecea had stopped ordering her about.

They exited the cafeteria and hugged. Nora brushed her lips before walking away to reach a group of girls guarded by three pure breeds.

"See you soon," Marie said when she was too distant to hear her words. Once out, they had sounded hollow. Something one would say knowing it's a lie. Eyes burning, she watched as her small friend disappeared behind the soldiers' bulk. Under the women's clipped orders, the group moved as one and soon disappeared at the end of the road where a motorized cart was waiting for them. Her heart heavy with rage and longing, she tried to make out the brunette among the indistinguishable dots climbing on the vehicle. The two feelings fought against each other for dominance, and when the cart rounded the corner and disappeared from her sight, she cried.

She blindly walked to the infirmary and went directly to the bathroom where she sat with her back blocking the door, as she had done every day since Grant's note had arrived. She pulled the piece of paper out and read it, even though there were only a few words and she had them memorized the first time. She couldn't admit to herself that she had seen Nora for the last time. She didn't know why the thought had entered her mind, but it was there and had taken roots in her heart and didn't want to go away. Finally, it filled her completely, and what had been reasonable doubt became certainty. Her head split, her stomach heaved, and she felt sick to her stomach. Once all her breakfast was out of her system, she still felt she must rid of the poison circulating through her body.

A knock rapped lightly on the door. "Marie, are you okay?" It was Rane.

"I'll be out in a minute. The new menu didn't sit well with my stomach." As if on cue, a powerful cramp seized her midsection and she rushed to the toilet. Despite having thought she had already gotten rid of her morning meal and probably the previous dinner as well, she embraced the cold ceramic and let the pain take control of her body.

"May I come in to help you?"

Sitting between the sink and the toilet, silently crying, she barely heard the doctor's words. "I'll be fine in a moment." But that was a lie. She was sure she would never be fine again. "Give me just a minute."

"Okay."

The sound of receding steps reached her addled mind, and she lowered her head between her knees and gave free rein to all the dark, twisted thoughts demanding release. She couldn't keep them at bay. Once her despair reached the point where emotional pain became physical, she screamed until her vocal chords burned, hands fisted by her knees, eyes blind. Later, when she exited the bathroom, carefully closing the door behind her, a silent crowd welcomed her back. Every eye focused on her, but nobody said a word. Rane didn't ask how she was feeling; she only looked at her like everyone else and then nodded.

"I'm sorry," she said, walking toward the doctor. There was no time to explain the reasons behind her next action, but by the time Rane raised her eyebrow in puzzlement, Marie had already grabbed one of the chisels lying on the tray by her side and was launching herself at the soldier just outside the door. It took a moment for the woman to realize what was happening. A misplaced sense of euphoria possessed Marie's heart at the notion a pure breed had underestimated her, and she jabbed the chisel, not caring where it would hit, as long as it hit the woman hard enough. Blood spurted from the soldier, showering her in a red rain. She lowered her hand again, but the woman had raised her gun. An inch to the right and she would've been dead, but she had moved out of the way at the last moment. The bullet embedded in the doorjamb instead of her head. The soldier's eyes widened in surprise at seeing her still standing and untouched. The blood loss taking its toll, she slowly slumped against the landing's railing and fell on the wooden deck. Marie waited for the woman's eyes to dim and then kicked her out of the way. The soldier tumbled down the stairs and onto the ground just outside the infirmary where everybody could see her. She steadied her breath and followed the woman outside, standing a few feet by the heaving body, covered in blood, chisel still clutched in her right hand.

The shot had warned Callista's army that something was amiss. Marie could see several soldiers rushing toward them. It would take them only a blink to realize what had just happened. A smile spread across her lips.

And then Rane was outside, horror in her eyes. She must have seen her smile. "What are you doing? Don't stand there! Run!"

She hoped there was time to say all the words that needed to be said. "It's okay."

"Marie, run away. I'll stop them." The doctor was crying. "I'll find a way…"

I'll find a way… Hadn't she said the exact same words? Rane's tears would have broken Marie's heart, but there wasn't anything left to break. "Go inside. Don't get caught helping me. Vasurians need you—" She hadn't time to finish the sentence. Soldiers were already surrounding her and pushing away Rane. Marie slashed at them to make it clear she was the only threat and prayed Rane wouldn't pay because of her. She looked at the doctor one more time. "I'm sorry." Something hit Marie's head just as she saw Rane being forcefully thrown back into the infirmary.

CHAPTER 15

The public flogging came as expected as soon as she came to. Or maybe she was made to come to in order to be flogged. It didn't matter as long as things went the way she had hastily sketched in her head. Callista was furiously pacing on the roof, and the whole of Vasura but the men had been summoned for the spectacle. This time, the major wouldn't show mercy. Marie was counting on that. She hoped carving lashes on her back wouldn't be enough to satiate the woman's anger. She was hoping that dying under the whip wasn't punishment enough in Callista's eyes—that only a slow and painful death would do. And so she bore the whip way beyond the pain of the first five lashes. Gratefully, she fainted, and when her eyes closed against her will for the second time that day, the only sound she heard was her cry standing out in a silence so thick it was deafening.

She woke and found herself still chained to the pole, her hands higher than her shoulders, the sick smell of dry blood filling her nose, making her gag. She wasn't alone. The muted crowd was still there. Callista had ordered them to wait out there? Had they waited for her to open her eyes? No, Callista had wanted Vasura to witness how she dealt with the likes of her. Her lips were bloodied too. Had she bitten them when the pain had become unbearable? The act of trying to ease the pull from her stretched arms almost made her faint again.

"Vasura, look closely," Callista said from behind her.

The woman had left the safety of the roof and was standing a few feet from her. Marie couldn't help but shudder at the sound of the major's reinforced boots echoing closer and closer, until one hand grabbed her hair and forced her to look up.

"This is how I was repaid for being soft," Callista whispered to Marie, her fresh, minty breath caressing her face.

She gagged again. The woman went on talking to the crowd. At length. Finally, what had sounded like a repetition of words took shape into what was the grand finale of Callista's speech. The change in pitch and the dramatic pause had told Marie so and she listened. *Say it.*

"I hereby condemn this criminal to life at the recycling center. She'll end her days inside the inner chamber, surrounded by garbage as she deserves."

Marie breathed in relief and started crying tears of joy.

"You should have thought of the consequences of your actions more carefully." Callista released her hair.

Her face hidden from the woman's scrutiny, Marie laughed a laugh easy to mistake with the earlier sobs. Her shoulders shook for a while. Someone freed her wrists and she was carried away without any care for her wounded back. A soldier took her wrists and tied them once more, this time to the back of a cart, and she was paraded around the place, walking on unsteady legs, barely keeping up with the moving vehicle. She slipped and fell more times than she could count, but each time, she found the strength to get up, a smile on her face for everybody to see. The last time she rose back up from a stumble, knees bleeding and arms shaking for the effort of not letting go, the Vasurians cheered her. Callista's shouts resonated over the encouragements, warning them of repercussion if they didn't stop. The cheers were followed by feet stomping. Shots were fired. A wall of soldiers came between the cart and the crowd. Marie wasn't allowed to see what was happening to her people as she was hauled on the cart already leaving at full speed. The noise of the engine covered the chanting, the shooting, and the cries, but she could hear them in her mind.

She wasn't awake for most of the ride. The three soldiers escorting her were better human beings than she would have given them credit for. One of them brought her some water laced with a substance that made her blissfully unaware of pain. In her confused state, she thought she heard the women saying things that would have granted them a place next to her in the inner chamber. A salve was spread on her wounds. She recognized the smell, and for a moment, she thought Grant was there, then realized it was just the salve. More water that wasn't water was poured in her mouth. Peaceful nothingness followed.

"Here we are," someone said and coughed.

Marie made an effort to open her eyes and keep them open. They had reached the core of Vasura, its recycling center, a distinctive four-story building made of rusted metal pipes and peeled paint. A big tower jutted from the side, at least two stories higher than the rest of the facility. A dark column rose out of it, reaching the sky and forming a thick cloud formation covering the sun. The smell was nothing she could ever describe in words. Death and bonfires. Something sweet and rotten. The hint of a flowery perfume corrupted by decay and sickness. Her throat contracted and her stomach heaved, but by now, there was nothing left and that made the cramps more painful to bear. All around her, the soldiers repeatedly vomited before they were able to don the heavy masks lying on the cart's floor. She hadn't noticed them before. A mask descended on her face as well and she could have cried for the kindness shown to her. She knew they didn't have to. As far as they were concerned, she was already dead.

At the base of the structure, a door opened and several figures covered from head to toe with dark, heavy-looking suits exited in a military formation, flanking both sides of the door, rifles aimed at them. One of the suited figures broke the symmetry and came to welcome them. Once within hearing distance, the woman shouted through the helmet she was wearing. "Why didn't you put on the masks immediately?" She didn't have to add the word "idiots." It was clear what she thought of them.

A few answers were muttered regarding the fact nobody knew it stunk so much.

"The new recruit?" the woman asked, now a few steps from the cart, her whole body turned toward Marie.

Marie came forth and climbed down the vehicle, helped by gentle hands. Once on the ground, she turned to thank them and saw their eyes behind the masks. Tears had splattered on the glass. The woman from the recycling center took her arm and dismissed the others with a mere nod. "This way." The woman pointed back at the building, as if there were any doubt where they were headed. Or if she had any freedom to decide to go with her or not. The other suited figures hadn't lowered their arms the whole time; the only difference, now the rifles were pointed at her head.

Still partially drugged, she fought the urge of easing their worries by saying she had volunteered to come. But the pain from her wounds was coming back, and although the mask shielded the worst of the stench, what reached her nose was enough to make her breathe in shallow mouthfuls of air. The exercise left her dizzy in a few steps.

"You'll get used to it." The woman dragged her by the arm she was still holding. Her gesture wasn't mean, but still caused Marie pain. "What the...?"

Marie saw the woman walk around her and then curse.

"What did they do you?"

The woman was taller than Marie by a whole head and she couldn't see her face, but by her tone, she reckoned her wounds must be hideous. She didn't bother responding.

"I have orders to take you to the inner chamber, but—" The woman stopped a few yards from the door, causing a few of the suited women by the wall to nervously step forward. "She needs medical assistance first." She accompanied her words with one raised hand and they went back to their positions.

She needed to see Grant first, but she lowered her head and endured the walk that followed the woman's decision. Instead of entering the building by the door the suits were still guarding, the woman took a different path that wound around the whole length of the recycling center. Respectful of Marie's condition, she slowly made her way to what looked like a gash between two columns of pipes and instead turned out to be the entry to a metal staircase that led down. Yellow illumination scarcely lit their descent. Marie wondered how the woman could see anything at all with her helmet.

Soon, unbearable heat rose from downstairs and met them in waves. Her broken skin reacted to the surge in temperature and she choked back a scream. She wasn't sure why she even bothered. Maybe the need to prove she was better than them. Maybe stupidity. She stepped out of the staircase soaked in sweat and longing for the spiked water the pure breed had served her. The landing was darker than the stairs, but it took only a moment for her eyes to adjust to the dimness. Behind her, the whole squad of suits had followed in silent fashion. They unnerved her, looking more like visions from nightmares than women. They all walked to the opposite wall where light passed under a door, illuminating its frame. They waited for the door to open, and a few seconds later, only Marie and her chaperone were allowed entry.

Marie blinked at the sudden brightness of the place, and she realized they were in an antechamber, waiting for another door to open, this one sturdy looking and armored. The woman spun the wheel at its center with some effort. The hissing sound announced it was opening, but they had to wait a few seconds before its thick wall left enough space for them to pass through. As soon as they were inside the small chamber, the woman pushed the door closed. A distinctive pop in her ears told Marie the place was pressurized. They waited some more and then finally the door before them opened with another long hiss. As soon as they were on the other side, the woman took her helmet off, revealing a cascade of red curls, soft-brown eyes, a big nose, and generous lips.

"We've a wounded girl," she called to someone and then looked at Marie and pointed at her face. "You can remove it now."

It took a moment for her to realize she didn't need the mask anymore. The stench lingered in the air, but it didn't belong to the place. It wafted in waves from their clothes.

"Name's Corinthia." The redhead pointed at herself. Then her eyes went on Marie's branded arm. "I only have your numbers."

"Marie." She looked around to get a feeling for the place. It wasn't just an infirmary as she had thought. It was a cavernous space opening into hallways and alcoves. Pipes lined the ceiling and they stood on a concrete floor. Lamps hanging down the pipes gave the unsettling feeling of a festive place. There were people, lots of people. A woman had heard Corinthia's shout and was hurrying their way. She was rail thin with sleek back hair that reached the front pockets of the gray scrubs she wore over a lighter version of her chaperone's dark suit.

When the woman reached them, Corinthia didn't waste time in preambles. "Marie was whipped."

213

The woman walked around Marie and then gasped. "For the Goddess's sake!"

"What kinda beast would punish a child so savagely?" Corinthia's face reflected her words.

Marie felt comforted by her demeanor.

"Fortunately, the cuts were immediately covered with a salve." The newcomer was removing what was left of Marie's shirt.

She flinched and automatically stepped back, her hands crossed over her chest for modesty, and she felt trapped in a déjà vu loop.

"I'm sorry, but I need to take a good look at your back." She patted Marie's arm. "I'm Luna. Let's go back to the clinic where I can clean you up."

"The clinic?" Marie didn't understand where she was.

"This is a dangerous place and we've a clinic to cure people exposed to toxins and radiation." Luna had started walking and turned to answer her.

"Radiation? What radiation?" Toxins she understood. The stench itself was enough to kill a person; she could only imagine how dangerous the waste could be to the skin. But radiation? No rumors about waste plants had ever mentioned radiation.

Corinthia bit her bottom lip, exchanged a look with Luna, then shrugged. "Well, it's a long story, but the recycling center uses power that creates radiation as a byproduct. But don't you worry about that now."

"I'll patch you up good and then you'll rest a while." Luna and Corinthia exchanged another look. "She can't show up at the inner chamber like that."

"What I thought." Corinthia sounded relieved. "You'll spend the rest of the day here and then we'll find an accommodation for you."

Marie didn't utter a word. She was wary of the unexpected welcome and the pain now spreading through her body. The effect of whatever the pure breeds had given her was unfortunately gone. The two women ahead of her didn't realize she wasn't following. Not because she had decided not to, but because her body refused to.

"She must be in more pain than I thought." Corinthia's voice sounded muffled.

Marie watched as they looked at her, worried expressions on their faces, and then she closed her eyes. A prick on her arm roused her enough to open her eyes again, but only for a moment because a sense of warmth spread through her and with it, a sense of peace. She had the strange feeling of floating and her mind went back to one of the few times Madame Carla had allowed a field trip to the beach. She and Idra had escaped the adults' vigilance and dove into the crystalline waters of the Great Blue Ocean before someone could stop them. She was hovering now as she had done then. And it was beautiful. The experience lasted long enough for her to slip into unconsciousness with a smile on her face.

"Marie?"

She loved that voice.

"Marie? Are you waking up?"

No, I'm not.

"Is there something wrong with her?"

"No, she was in so much pain her body shut down."

"But is she going to be fine?"

"Yes. Give her time. She was mercilessly whipped who knows how many times. If it weren't for the salve and narcotics someone gave her while she was being transported here, she'd be in way worse shape."

"I didn't even realize the seriousness of her situation when she arrived. She was walking by herself…"

"Why would they do something like that to her?"

"I asked. She stabbed a pure breed, apparently for no reason. It seems she snapped and tried to kill the soldier."

"What? Why would she do something like that?"

"Who knows…?"

"Still, she's a girl!"

"If not even a girl is safe…"

"Even knowing she deserved a punishment, it still was barbaric what they did to her—"

"Callista went too far. She should've been judged in a trial."

"I want to kill that woman—"

"Get in line."

Marie was too tired to keep listening and so she went to sleep again.

"Marie? You're scaring me. You should be awake by now."

That voice she liked so much.

"Marie? Please, wake up."

She heard the pleading and tried to open her eyes, but they were so heavy and she wanted to rest some more. She hadn't rested in years.

"You must do something! This isn't normal."

"You saw the extent of the damage on her back."

"Yes, but—"

"Give her time."

She had already heard that, but her head felt full of cotton and sleeping was easier than trying to understand what those voices wanted from her.

"Marie?"

Someone interlaced their fingers with hers. Her name was repeated several times. Her hand was raised to someone's lips and a soft kiss was laid on it.

"Look at me."

Soft lips brushed hers.

"Look at me."

The kiss deepened.

"Look at me."

Grant's voice was as soft the caresses on her face. Happiness radiated from the inside of her chest and soon filled all of her. She felt the blood pumping through her veins and her heart beat loud. Her eyes opened and he was there. No awakening had ever been so sweet.

"Hi."

"Hi," she tried to say but wasn't sure she had.

His bright green eyes widened, joy suffused his face, and that told her everything she needed to know. "You scared me to death."

"I'm here." She had succeeded. The pain and humiliation hadn't been for nothing. Then, the realization that she would have done it again hit her. And it was like being hit by a freight train.

He squeezed her hand and then turned to face someone. Marie saw his head had been shaved. His dark-blond mane was gone; his tan skin was marred by bruises in various stages of healing. She heard the approaching steps a moment later.

"Didn't I tell you to leave her alone?" A curtain was drawn to the side and Luna walked into her line of sight, and as she progressed toward her, Marie saw she was in a small room, no bigger than a cubicle. Everything was white. There was only space for the bed she was lying on and the chair Grant must have used until a moment ago.

"I couldn't." Grant smiled at the woman.

Marie couldn't help but notice he hadn't broken contact. Her hand was still firmly in his. She needed that. She wanted him by her side.

Luna smiled back at him and laid a hand on his shoulder in a familiar gesture. Her eyes went on their united hands lying on the coverlet, then up to Marie's face. "Hi, there." She bent over her to take her free wrist in her hand. "Welcome back. How do you feel?"

She wasn't sure.

"We made you sleep for a while. You weren't in good shape and your body needed time to heal." Luna sat on the bed and briefly checked her eyes. "You're coming out of it just fine." She stood up and patted Marie's legs. "You should go to bed," she said to Grant.

He shook his head. "Not now." The hold on Marie's hand tightened a bit.

She wasn't ready to let him go yet either and was glad for his answer.

"Okay, but promise you'll go to sleep soon."

"I will." The smile on his face dimpled and his eyes brightened.

"You're terrible at lying." Luna left with a chuckle.

Marie waited for them to be alone and then looked at the curtain. Grant understood her request and closed it. "Grant—" She didn't know what was going to say. Her mind was a chaos of questions that were soon forgotten when his eyes locked with hers and he smiled.

She waited for him to sit on the chair and take her hand again. Silently, she looked at him, her eyes lingering on his scalp. In her dreams, she always passed her fingers through his hair. Still, he was handsome. Lips chapped and a long cut running from his left eyebrow down to his cheekbone, he was breathtaking.

He saw her looking at his mouth and his green eyes darkened. Then he left the chair and went to lie on the bed with her. Silence and shallow breaths. The length of his body along hers. Arms touching arms, legs touching legs. But only for a moment, as if he were deciding what to do. Then he turned to the side, propping his head on his bent arm.

His gaze on her was hypnotic. "Grant..." She couldn't stop looking at how red his lips had become.

Something stirred behind those green eyes and he leaned over her, only to stop a few inches from her mouth. He didn't touch her, but she felt all the oxygen contained in her lungs rushing out. Dizziness came and she welcomed it. She liked that feeling when he was close. When his lips lowered over hers one more time, she stopped breathing altogether, her heart frantically trying to escape her ribcage. He finally kissed her and tears escaped her eyes. His mouth looked for hers, at first tentatively, but her hands reached around his neck and she lowered the rest of him over her. She didn't care that he was pushing her back against the bed. The pain was nothing compared to the ecstasy she felt at having him so close.

"You kept sleeping and I—"

She heard the words whispered in her mouth and felt the tremor in his body. He had straightened his arms and was now separated from her by a few inches. She didn't like it and tried to pull him down, but he resisted her effort and the seriousness in his face made her desist.

"You weren't waking, and at first, Luna didn't let me stay, but I couldn't stay away. I had to see you. I had to talk to you." He took her hand still circling his neck and kissed it.

Marie tilted her head to better look at him. "I thought of you. Always. Since the first time I saw you at Redfarm." Her thoughts had taken several forms, but she could now admit he had been in her mind from the beginning. She wasn't sure when he had taken possession of her heart. She had tried to resist, but it had happened over time.

Grant's mouth relaxed into a smile. "It was night and I was outside in the backyard. I saw you looking down from your window, and I hoped I could get a closer glimpse of you. I was hauling a beam to build that blasted gazebo when you walked down the stairs…"

Marie couldn't believe he remembered. She wasn't even sure he had seen her. Her mouth opened and then closed, unable to say anything but happy beyond reason. He had seen *her*.

"I thought of you, even then."

The way he said it, she understood he felt guilty for that. Joy spread through her.

She must have been easy to read, because he smiled at her and then nudged her nose with his. "I looked for you when I shouldn't have."

"But you were angry at me all the time!" She saw him back then, defending Carnia and looking at her with disdain.

Grant hid his face between her neck and shoulders, his lips brushing the spot under her ear. "I was angry at me."

She shivered at his kiss, half of her mind gone. "Why?" Talking didn't come easy when her body seemed to have ideas of its own of what she should be doing instead.

"Because I wanted to see you, and Carnia needed me." He was still whispering to her throat, which eased the pain she felt when he mentioned her name. But, even dulled, it was more than enough.

It was irrational, but her heart ached when he said it, and only the kiss that followed stopped her spirited retort from ruining the moment.

"I've wanted to do this since the first time I saw you." He gently pushed against her mouth until she parted her lips for him.

Marie knew what was coming but wasn't ready to feel so lightheaded. He explored her slowly, and after a moment, she found herself breathing through him, glad he had moved and was now over her. Her hands roamed over his back and then up to his scalp, where she passed her fingers through his stubble. The sound of people walking by startled both of them. Grant was on the chair before the curtain opened to show Corinthia's amused face, followed soon after by Luna's.

"I see you're awake and feeling much better." Corinthia winked at her and walked the two steps to the bed.

"She does have a dedicated nurse." Luna carried a tray on her hand. "Are you hungry yet?" She looked around for a place to put the tray.

Grant reached out, offering his arms for the task.

"Thank you." Luna gave him the tray and then turned to face Marie. "Have some breakfast, and then, if you want, we can talk."

"We imagine you have a few questions about this place, about us." Corinthia stood by the curtain, her back outside the actual perimeter of the small room.

Marie nodded. She had just remembered she did have questions. Under the two women's gentle scrutiny, Grant helped her eat the sweetened porridge and drink some of the tea. There was easiness in the way his fingers brushed hers that made her blush. It felt intimate and they weren't alone. Then, and it came as a surprise, she realized she hadn't felt ashamed a man was touching her, only conscious they were exchanging affections before other people. But neither Corinthia nor Luna seemed offended by the display.

He must have felt her embarrassment though. "You've some porridge on your chin... there." His finger stopped before touching her face to clean the spot and simply hovered to indicate where it was. "Yes, there."

Marie was mesmerized by his voice, his eyes, his lips he tended to bite a lot when he talked. Questions could wait, couldn't they?

Luna waited until the last spoonful of porridge disappeared in her mouth. "Do you want to know anything in particular?"

Marie inwardly sighed. Maybe she could speed up the process. He squeezed the hand she had let trail by his side and she faced him, since the first question was about him. "What happened to you? Nora told me you'd been sentenced to the inner chamber to..." She couldn't say it. She had stabbed a pure breed for the chance of being sent here to see him one more time. In her thoughts, she had seen him dying, emaciated, and wasted by the toxins. The mere thought still caused her pain.

Grant held her hand to his mouth and kissed it. "I was. I still am."

"I don't understand." She looked at the women who nodded.

"It's true. Per the major's orders, he's working in the inner chamber right now." Corinthia walked a step closer to the bed. "We had to keep him there while the pure breeds were around. They've never actually stayed longer than a few hours to check on the recycling facility. Usually, we send people inside the chamber only to get them out as soon as the coast is clear. This time, we had to leave him inside longer than was safe."

Marie wasn't following. There were so many things she didn't know, but Luna continued before she could ask anything. "Ginecea doesn't care about the conditions fathered women have to work in here—do you think the pure breeds mind if men die operating the machines in the inner chamber? Vasura is no different than one of their maximum-security facilities. People sent here aren't expected to live long."

"Men aren't expected to live at all." Grant's eyes became colder, but a moment later, he looked down at their intertwined hands and made a visible effort to relax his features. "Here, we're useless. They don't need us to father women, since the workforce is constantly replenished, and our arms can be easily replaced by women labor."

"So why send you here at all?" Marie had wondered about that.

Luna gave her an enigmatic smile and answered, "Believe it or not, pure breeds believe themselves to be highly civilized. They would never dispose of the slaves—"She made an apologetic face meant for Grant. "Sorry, that's how Ginecea still thinks of you."

Grant raised his free hand to accept the apology. "No offense taken. I don't care what they call me. I've never thought of myself as a worker. I'm a man."

"Anyway, even among pure breeds, there are good souls—" This time, Luna had to stop for Marie, who had snorted out loud.

"Pure breeds are a selfish, useless race." She couldn't help the acid coating her words.

"Well, there're also pure breeds who cared for you when you were brought here," Corinthia timidly added.

"Yes, after leaving me like this!" The wounds on her back must have awoken as she said the words because stabbing pain shot through her and she gasped. She was mad at Corinthia to even suggest that giving her drugged water would be enough to excuse the soldiers who had escorted her there. "They watched as I was whipped and did nothing." With her teeth clenched, the last sentence was no more than a rattle.

Without saying a word, Luna reached inside one of the pockets in her gray scrubs and procured a syringe. "Something to ease the pain?"

Marie nodded and Luna swiftly held her forearm and injected the medicine. A sudden sensation of cold was followed by warmth and numbness. She relaxed on the bed once again.

A long moment of silence ensued, then Corinthia cleared her voice and said, "*They* didn't do anything, but there are others risking their lives to give you medical assistance." Her eyes went to Luna and she smiled at her. One of those smiles that has inner meanings.

Luna lowered her eyes and Marie thought she saw her blush. "You're a pure breed?" She gave the woman a better look and she found the telltale signs of refined ancestry. "Of course you are." No fathered woman would have that bearing. Now that she knew, every single feature in her face gave her away. "I truly was out of it if I didn't realize it earlier."

"You're looking at me differently." Luna moved away from the bed.

Marie appreciated the gesture. "I can't help it." She regretted having said that immediately. As far as she knew, the woman had only been kind to her. "Thank you for what you're doing for me."

"I understand your rage. I do." Luna was now by Corinthia's side. They weren't touching, but the way they stood close to each other betrayed their familiarity.

"Do you?" Marie could see Luna was different, but how could a pure breed know what was passing through her head?

"I was the last supervisor before Callista—"

Marie interrupted the woman. "You were the one who accepted the bribe and was out of Vasura after a few hours?"

Luna and Corinthia both smiled a similar smile and then Corinthia said, "I did try to give you money to get rid of you, didn't I?"

An amused light shone in Luna's eyes. "You did."

Marie watched as the women exchanged a look so intense she had to avert her eyes, only to end up staring at Grant and blush anyway at his stare. "So you decided to stay, I gather."

Luna beamed. "Yes, I decided to stay, or to be precise, I decided to come back."

"But how? Did your family accept… that?" Marie lamely looked at some point between the two women.

Luna waved her hand in the air. "Long story short, I have no family and nobody knows I'm here. As Ginecea is concerned, after reporting that everything was fine at Vasura, I retired to an isolated farm left to me by my parents."

"What about friends?"

"I was always a loner. A long time ago, I lost track of the few friends I had in college. It was rather simple for me to disappear." Luna's knuckles brushed Corinthia's hand.

Marie thought it was sad that nobody missed this woman, pure breed or not, but she looked happier for it. "And what are you doing here… *here*?" She looked around, her eyes encompassing the small room, but meaning the whole place.

"Here, I'm trying to make a difference."

Grant stirred beside her and Marie turned toward him. "She's a doctor and an expert in radiation," he explained. "Thanks to her, the whole recycling center is safer now. Before, people suffered permanent damage after working here because nobody knew anything about safety procedures and maximum time of exposure. Even the structure has been modified under her surveillance."

She couldn't believe a pure breed had done something for the betterment of fathered women and even men. But Grant was talking to her, looking in good health, when she had prepared herself to mourn his imminent death. And she wasn't anywhere close to the inner chamber. "So who works inside the inner chamber?"

"We all take turns of a few hours every month, but we go inside heavily shielded," Corinthia answered.

"What about him? Did he stay ten days as I was told?" She also remembered the bit about him not wearing any protection.

"Oh, no. We only let the soldiers think he was inside the whole time, but we had him in and out every few hours. Still, we had to keep the charade going longer than we were comfortable."

"But this friend of mine—"

"Nora," Grant supplied.

"Yes, her. She told me you were there for ten days without protection and I thought you were dying and—" She had to fight the urge to caress his face and make sure he was okay and her eyes weren't betraying her.

"We try not to let our secrets out. People who come here for their shift normally leave without being the wiser of what we do. Your friend didn't need to know, but instead, her words will corroborate what Callista, and through her, Ginecea, need to know," Corinthia explained.

Grant applied pressure on Marie's hand and commanded her attention. "Did you do what you did to be sent here?" His eyes were stormy.

Marie didn't answer right away.

Grant took both of her hands in his, his expression so serious she had to avert her gaze. "Marie?" He released one of her hands to raise her chin with a soft caress and force her to look at him. "Did you try to kill that woman, hoping you would be sent here?"

Her prolonged silence was answer enough for him. "You did it... for me?" His voice lowered on the last two words and then he shook his head, his eyes big and liquid. "You shouldn't have."

The last sentence cut a deep gash in Marie's heart. Not the words. Anybody would have said that, should have said that to her. Especially him. No, it was the tone. "I thought you were dying. I had to see you. I had to tell you..." She hadn't forgotten they weren't alone and sighed in frustration. "Things."

Grant shook his head one more time. Sadness in his eyes, he muttered something under his breath she didn't catch, and then out loud, "I'm leaving. Tonight."

She might have heard something else. "You're leaving?"

Grant nodded and bit his already-chapped bottom lip. "You shouldn't have risked your life for me. Anything could've gone wrong. Callista could've let you die under the whip. She could've court-martialed you and shot you on the spot."

She felt the sting of tears, but she didn't let them out. "But I'm here. It worked."

He raised one hand. "Yes, it worked, and if it weren't for Luna and Corinthia, you would've died of radiation exposure in less than ten days. It was senseless." He suddenly stood and stormed out, leaving her with a hole right in the middle of her ribcage.

CHAPTER 16

Marie didn't look down, but if the tearing pain in her heart was of any indication, she was bleeding from it. She still managed not to cry before the two women. "It worked," she repeated instead.

"Sweetie, I'm sorry to say it, but he's right. You gambled with your life without knowing what would happen." Corinthia walked to the bed and sat on the edge.

She looked ahead in the direction he had disappeared. "I had to see him."

"Oh, I can understand that..." Luna smiled softly.

Marie heard the "but" that was left unsaid. "Why's he so angry at me?"

"Because he got scared for you and he's mostly angry at himself." Luna took the place Grant had just vacated. "He was supposed to leave three days ago when you arrived."

Corinthia walked closer to the bed's edge and stopped behind Luna. "But he hasn't left your side."

"He wanted to see you before leaving tonight and was going crazy because you weren't waking up, but he can't stay any longer." Luna patted Marie's arm.

Marie looked first at Luna and then at Corinthia. "Where is he going?"

Corinthia lowered one hand on Luna's shoulder. "Where it's safe for a man."

"Is there such a place outside of Vasura?" Or what Vasura had been before Callista had destroyed its peace. Marie wanted to scream.

Corinthia waited for Luna to raise her eyes to her and nod, before answering, "We've a network of helpful contacts outside of Vasura—"

"You mean the farms?"

Luna squeezed Corinthia's hand and continued for her. "No, we have contacts within the men's community as well…"

Marie was truly confused. "Your contacts are workers? But what can they do for you?"

Luna seemed to think of her answer for a moment. "Well, they aren't workers."

At the assumption that Luna was trying to explain to her they had help from sementals, Marie almost didn't hear the woman's next words.

"They live outside in the desert. They're free men."

At which Marie snorted. "Sorry, but for a moment I thought you were serious." Then the expression on both Luna's and Corinthia's faces made her rectify her previous statement. "You are serious."

Corinthia nodded. "Two days north of Vasura, deep in the desert, men have been building a city for more than two decades."

"How do you know this *city* even exists?" Marie wanted to know how it was possible that Ginecea hadn't found them and squashed them under its heels, but questions were crowding her mind and this one won the race for supremacy over the others.

Corinthia left her spot behind Luna and sat on the edge of the bed. "During the Massacre ten years ago, when the mass executions started, a few men and women managed to escape from Vasura and went into hiding in the desert."

"They thought they could survive in the desert?"

Luna raised an eyebrow, but her words were gentle. "Desperation makes you act without thinking."

Marie blushed at the remark.

"And it beats waiting to be killed lined up against a wall." Corinthia's eyes went far away. "You don't know what it was like back then. I still have nightmares. I would've left too. Anything was better than the horror we had to witness."

But Marie knew. She could still hear the kids screaming for their mothers. If she closed her eyes, she could see Rachele falling on the ground, dying without a reason. "Why didn't you?"

A grin appeared on Corinthia's face. "I was wounded. The night I should've left, I got shot in my right leg and brought to the infirmary where I was sedated by a good-meaning doctor who thought she was doing me a favor. I punched her in the face as soon as I woke the next morning." She tilted her head to give Luna a sideways glance and her lips turned up in a smile. "It turns out, the doctor did me a favor by not allowing me to leave." Some silent conversation happened between the two of them. Then Corinthia focused her attention on Marie once again. "Anyway, to answer your question on how we know the city exists, some of the people who escaped—unfortunately, not everybody made it—found an outpost of free men. Months later, they contacted Vasura to let their families and friends know they were alive. Since then, a communication bridge has been established with the City of Men—"

"That's what it's called?"

"Yes, that is what they called it," Luna answered.

"So, all this time, you helped men escaping to the City of Men?" Marie still couldn't believe a whole outpost of ex-workers could go undetected for so long.

"Actually, no."

It was Marie's turn to raise her eyebrow in puzzlement.

"Apart from that group of men and women, nobody has left Vasura in ten years."

"But if there was a chance to be free, why wouldn't the men take it?"

"Because, as you rightly said just a few minutes ago, Vasura is the only place on Ginecea where a man can be relatively free to do whatever he wants, even live with a woman and have kids. Pure breeds regard waste plants with such disdain we're left alone and without any supervision for long stretches of time. This is a safe haven—"

"Until Callistas happen."

"Yes, until Callistas happen..."

"But we still can do something. We can still resist and save lives without her being the wiser."

"You're smuggling out all the men she has sent to die in the inner chamber..."

"She knows they can't survive the radiation—"

"Callista knows about the radiation?"

"Of course she does. Ginecea replaced the coal plant with a nuclear one because it was cheaper to process the waste that way. We had been sent here to die anyway. No need to make the place safer for its workers. We deserved a short and horrible existence." Corinthia breathed and then added, "But I'm digressing. Supervisors are warned not to go near the recycling center proper because of the radiation."

Luna nodded. "It's true. I knew before I came here, but I wanted to take a look myself and was shocked when I found the conditions people were forced to work in. It wasn't humane. It made me rethink everything I believed was true about pure breeds. I was ashamed to be one of them."

A long silence followed Luna's words. Corinthia covered one of her hands with hers. Marie longed for Grant. "So you'll declare Grant dead and he'll be free to start a new life outside of Ginecea's rules." A sour-sweet feeling possessed her.

"He officially died a few days ago, but again, he refused to leave before you woke."

"It's imperative he leaves tonight." Corinthia said the words, but they were both looking at her.

"You think I'd ask him to stay? I'd never do anything to put him in any danger." She realized she had raised her voice, but their expressions said they doubted that and she was offended. She was also angry because deep inside she knew they were right. She wanted Grant with her and felt guilty. "I want him alive." And that too was true. "When is he going to leave?"

"As soon as it gets dark. Tonight, it's new moon and it'll be safe for him to cross the wall." Luna looked at her wristwatch. "Later, we'll talk about your future, but I must go and take care of a few details to ensure nothing goes wrong." She stood with a sigh.

"Sure…" Marie sat upright and looked at Luna exiting the room.

"Is there anything else you want to know?" Corinthia asked from the curtain. She was leaving too.

She had several questions, but the immediate future was more important at the moment. "Where is he?" She swung her legs off the side of the bed and then looked for her shoes, but they weren't on the floor.

"Do you think it's okay if she goes to talk to him?" Corinthia turned to Luna, out of Marie's sight, but evidently still close. "She just woke."

Luna retraced her steps and spoke directly to Marie. "You should take it easy... but yes, of course."

"Then, since the doctor is okay with it, I'll get you a change of clothes and a pair of sandals." Corinthia hurriedly left.

Luna stayed behind, an uncertain expression on her face. "Love can be painful. Especially at your age." She gave Marie a soft caress on her arm. "I wish I could give you a pill for this... but there's none."

Corinthia's voice reached them from a few steps away. "I couldn't find your size, but hopefully this is close enough." She entered the room, her arms outstretched, carrying a pile of folded clothes and a pair of sandals on top of it. "He's pacing outside."

Marie felt her heart aching at the knowledge he was just a few steps away and hadn't come back to talk to her. Luna left and Corinthia waited for her outside to give her some privacy.

"Ready?" Corinthia asked when she came out of the room wearing her clean, although loose, clothes and a somber expression.

"I need this." She answered the unasked question.

"I understand." Corinthia led her for a short walk through a white hallway on which other small rooms opened. They all looked like the one Marie had occupied. "Out there." She showed an opaque glass door.

"Thanks." Marie could see a nervous figure walking back and forth behind it. She breathed in and out, tried unsuccessfully to steady her hands, and then walked to the door and lowered the handle.

"Be strong."

She heard Corinthia's words at the same time she saw Grant walking away from her.

The door closed behind her and he turned, startled by the sound. It was immediately clear he hadn't expected to see her. "What are you doing up? You should be in bed. You shouldn't be walking around."

It was unfair that he made her want to cry when she only wanted to lose herself in his arms. "I came to see you."

He looked at her for a moment and his expression softened, his eyes reflecting an inner turmoil. "I can't stay."

She shook her head. "I'm not asking you to."

"I don't want to leave." Two steps and he was towering over her, but he didn't touch her. He just stood there, a few inches away, slightly shaking.

She felt the full impact of his green eyes on her and longed to reach out and circle her arms around his back. "I need to know you're alive."

He stepped closer, still not touching her, his eyes still locked with hers, keeping her enthralled. "Come with me."

She experienced a sudden rush of blood from her extremities to her head and froze.

"Come with me. I don't want to lose you." He finally closed the gap and took her in his arms, his mouth looking for hers.

"Grant—" She had so much to say, but in the end, she only wanted him.

"Come with me. I promise I'll take care of you," he whispered between kisses. "I know you could still have a life here. But nobody will make you feel loved as I will. Please, tell me yes."

Marie's mind was blissfully vacant, blood ringing in her ears, but one thing she knew: he was right. Nobody would make her feel like he did. "Yes."

"Yes?" Grant broke contact with her lips for a moment. "Yes? You said yes?"

She nodded and burrowed herself in his embrace to hide against his chest. He raised her face to his and kissed her again.

His eyes were bright. "I'll make you happy."

"I know you will."

"Let's go tell Corinthia. We must prepare—"

"*We* must prepare for what?" Corinthia was eyeing the two of them suspiciously. "This is not what I think it is, right?"

"Marie is coming with me." Grant took Marie under his wing.

Marie looked the woman in the eyes and nodded.

"You can't be serious." Corinthia turned to Grant. "She's fifteen and you're seventeen—"

"I'm going with him. I was sentenced to the inner chamber. I'm dead anyway." Marie shrugged.

"Yes, I know. *We* know and that's why Luna and I have found a safe place for you as well."

"Where?" Grant asked before she could.

"There's this pure breed, Milady, who's helping fathered women build a new life in a place called the Village. Milady just accepted your friend Zena, and she has already agreed to take Marie." Corinthia passed one hand through her red curls.

"Zena?" Marie couldn't help but yell. "Zena was here?"

"Yes, she left a day before you arrived, and I was going to mention her to you—" Corinthia tried to finish her sentence, but Marie didn't let her.

"What happened to her? She disappeared, and we were worried sick she'd been killed. Why didn't she come back to us?"

Corinthia raised her hand to stop the avalanche of questions. "Zena was sent here not long after Callista arrived. She was at the end of her shift when she tried to save a woman who had just arrived from a beating. The guard Zena stopped sentenced her to the inner chamber just as Grant had been. She wanted to let you and the doctor know she was alive, but it was too dangerous, and we promised her we would find a way to get the message to you."

"But she's fine." Marie felt a weight lifting from her chest.

"Yes, I promise you. Zena is fine. We're expecting to hear from her soon." Corinthia paused and then stepped closer to Marie and took her hands while Grant stepped to the side. "Now, let's get back to what is best for you." She sighed. "What you're planning to do is madness. I'm sorry, but it's the truth."

Marie felt Grant going still and tilted her head to look at him, but he had his face trained on the woman.

"Marie, you must understand that the City of Men, even if takes women as well, it is a city built and intended for men." Corinthia spoke slowly.

Marie looked at Grant again, but he didn't return the gaze. If anything, his body had gone stiller. "Grant?" He stepped away from her.

Corinthia walked a step closer to him, leaving Marie behind, the third corner of their misshaped triangle. "You know that."

Grant moved the weight of his body from one leg to the other. His complexion grew paler, and his brows furrowed when he said, "I'd do anything to keep you safe..." He finally looked at her. "But Corinthia could be right."

The woman acknowledged his words with a sigh of relief. "The Village is a safer place for a young girl. She'll have a good life there. Out of the reach of Ginecea but still closer to normality than she would have anywhere else. And she already knows somebody there."

Marie thought about it for a moment. A place where she would be safe. A place where she could have a family with a Nora or an Idra or even a Verena. A place where she could have a safer future than the one Grant had offered. Her heart broke at the idea of a life without him. She walked to him, took his hand, and brought it forth to show it to Corinthia. "I'll go with Grant."

"What?" both Corinthia and Grant said at the same time, both showing incredulous expressions on their faces.

Eyes wide and words broken, he whispered, "You don't have to." He took her hand in his, brought it to his lips, and brushed them across her knuckles. "I want you to have a beautiful life."

Corinthia stepped closer to her. "Please, listen to him."

Marie gave her a smile, then turned to Grant. "I don't want to live without you."

Corinthia didn't look convinced. "You're too young to make such a decision. You could die out there. He's barely an adult—"

"I won't change my mind. I'll follow him to the end of the world and back." At her words, Grant squeezed her hand and she felt his ragged breathing and how he was trying to stay calm. "Can you help me prepare what I need for the travel?"

The woman moved from one foot to the other, a troubled expression on her face. "Marie, please, reconsider your decision. You might think this is what you want, but you don't know."

"I'll leave with him tonight. With or without your help. I'd rather have it though."

Corinthia sighed. "Follow me."

***

Marie endured Luna's attempt at swaying her from her decision, but eventually the two women had to accept there wasn't anything they could say to change her mind and promised to send word to Rane to tell her what had happened to her and Zena.

"On the second day of the hike, there should be someone waiting for you. The City of Men sends scouts every day looking for men on the run. Keep north and they'll find you. You've enough food and water for five days. Never stop, keep walking—"Luna couldn't finish.

"We'll send you a note when we arrive." Marie had said it as a joke, but the light in the women's faces told her they would be counting on that.

"Walk during the night and rest a few hours during the day. Drink a few sips of water once in a while. Keep a steady pace…" Luna and Corinthia took turns giving them advice until it was time to go. At midnight, clouds obscured their normal view of the night sky. A steady drizzle accompanying them, she and Grant left Vasura behind. It was almost anticlimactic how easy it was to step outside of the waste plant. Corinthia and Luna walked them to the wall and opened a small gate hidden from sight by ivy. Embraces, a few more words of motherly warnings, and loving thanks were exchanged, then one small step through the gate and they weren't Vasurians anymore. The brand on Marie's arm seemed to ache.

If only Ginecea knew how easy it was to escape the waste plant, it would have understood how much Vasurians loved it there. Once the sound of the gate closing behind them finalized their new reality, a few tears escaped her eyes before she could stop the flow. Grant took her in his arms and rocked her slowly for a long while.

Then he stirred. His eyes went to the sky and then back to her. "We've got some road to cover before sunup." He took her under his shoulder and they started walking hip to hip.

The night was pitch black, but he somehow knew which direction was north, and after the first moment of silence, they started talking to pass the time. Grant had taken her heavy backpack as soon as they were out of Vasura and so she had only to focus on walking while listening to his warm voice. Her body was still sore, but Luna had given her enough painkillers to keep the worst of the pain at bay. She also had some for the trip. The first light of the day arrived and he called for a break. They had walked for more than five hours and she was exhausted.

"I'll stay awake. You need to sleep." He unrolled a slim mat and then sat on the ground by it. "I'll be your cushion." He helped her down and eased her head on his lap, his fingers playing with her hair. "The second time I saw you and I could get a good look at you, your head was illuminated from behind by the stairwell light. It looked like your face was framed by a halo. Your eyes and your mouth were set out by your fair skin and I thought you weren't real."

Marie shivered under his touch and brought her knees to her chest. He misunderstood her reaction and searched for a sweater in his backpack.

"Better?" He tucked her in it as if it were a blanket, his hands resting on her shoulders. "When I'm around you, I always worry about hurting you."

She wanted to say that he had hurt her back at Redfarm, but the pain he had inflicted had never been physical. Instead, she pulled his hand down, leaned her face against it, and closed her eyes, happy to be lulled by his voice. She had gone too close to losing him to waste time rehashing the past.

But he wasn't of the same opinion. "Remember when you caught me stealing from the cellars?"

She smiled against his hand. "I could never forget."

"I'd been thinking of you the whole time, and when I saw you there, I thought I was hallucinating. My heart started beating so fast and I wanted to talk to you, but you looked terrified and then I was worried you were going to scream and give me away. It was terrible." He laughed.

Marie propped her head on her bent arm to look at him but kept the hold on his hand. "I was paralyzed. I'd never been so close to a man in my whole life—" She felt his body stiffen and softly added, "It's the way I was raised."

His fingers found her hair again and he combed through it in slow movement. "I know, but it hurt so much whenever I was near you. The only thing I wanted to do was kiss you and hold you in my arms, and you looked at me in fear."

She was surprised by his confession. He was so different from her and looked so much stronger than her. She had assumed his strength was also psychological. "It wasn't fear."

He stopped caressing her. "What was it, then?" His unblinking eyes were a dark green in the pale light of the new day.

"It was desire of something I couldn't have." He bit his bottom lip at her words and she lost focus for a moment. "You weren't mine and couldn't be. I dreamed it was just me and you and nothing more. I wished for the whole universe to disappear."

Grant tilted his head right and left and came back to her to slowly smile. "It worked."

"It did." She pulled him down to her and kissed him.

Without breaking contact with her lips, he gently turned her sideways, easily maneuvering her until she was lying on him. "You're so light. You barely weigh anything." His hands roamed along her sides, careful not to apply any pressure on her back. "Sleep." His voice was a warm puff against her ear. "I won't let you fly away."

She felt the aftermath of his smile on her skin and shivered once again, raised her head, and then looked for his eyes. "I've never been so happy in my life." She laughed because it was a feeling so powerful she could hardly bear it. "I want to scream it for everybody to know."

He hooked one hand around her neck and lowered her face to his, keeping her mouth so close to his, but not touching, his whole body trembling, his voice but a broken whisper. "I would've found you."

She couldn't breathe, couldn't say anything.

"Had it taken my whole life, I would've found you again."

Marie couldn't contain her tears and turned her face, not wanting him to see her like that.

He wiped the wetness from her cheeks. "I saw you hiding it before, but you aren't less strong for showing you're human." Murmuring sweet nonsenses, he left a trail of small kisses on her eyes, nose, lips, and jaws. He cuddled her until she relaxed against him and fatigue finally claimed them both.

***

The desert proved to be selective about forms of life. Marie had seen pictures of the Desertica Region, but she hadn't been prepared for the absence of visual clues to determine which way was which. If it weren't for the fact they knew where the sun rose and fell, they could have walked in any direction without knowing where they were going. Dunes and small shrubs, that was all there was to look at. Three days and three nights passed. Although they walked at night and were careful to cover their faces during their daily slumber, they still got sunburned from the times they moved around and removed their covers. On the dawn of the fourth day, Marie started worrying. By that night, she was almost ready to voice her fear that they were stranded in the middle of nowhere. The fifth morning, when they started drinking from the second to the last bottle of water, even Grant started to look on edge. And maybe was just her imagination, but he started to look thinner.

"They're here, somewhere, looking for us." He had been staring at the vast expanse of nothingness for the last hour. His eyes darting left and right, squinting at the horizon.

She didn't dare saying anything.

He looked at her and then shook his head. "I know I kept north. They must be close."

She took him by the arm. "I know you did. We're in the right place." She wasn't sure of anything, but confessing it wasn't going to help. "Let's rest for a few hours and then we'll keep going until we find those men or they find us."

He looked at the bottle and then gave it to her. "Your lips are chapped. You need to drink some more water."

"I'm fine." She refused the bottle and pushed it back to him. His lips were so dry he had drawn blood last time he had bit on them.

"Dehydration sets in before you realize it." He leaned to give her lips a soft brush. "I know what I'm talking about."

She accepted the water and took a small sip. "You too." Crossing her legs, she sat on the mat he had already unrolled. They had used only one for the two of them. She had slept furled by his side and even on him for the four previous days. When she had tried to move to give him some respite, he had said, *"I can't bear the thought of not touching you in my dreams."* She had smiled at that and her heart had beaten at double speed for a while. They should have taken turns at staying awake, but it hadn't worked out well. She couldn't rest if he wasn't, and they soon found that their heartbeats synched and helped them relax, which in turn led them to fall asleep at the same time. She knew it wasn't smart, but out there it was easy to forget they weren't, in fact, alone in the universe.

Grant sank on the thin mat by her side and reached out to caress her face. "When we're there..." His eyes went to some faraway place where the alleged City of Men should have been according to Corinthia's calculations, and his expression clouded for the briefest moment. "I won't let anybody touch you."

She hadn't realized he was worried about that. "We've got to get there first," she mused.

They rested, but not as much as they should have. An underlying tension was present. Finally, they decided to start walking. Night came and then it was dawn again. The last sip of water was drunk. The last bite of bread eaten. They kept walking until their legs hurt so much they had to stop. They hugged each other and didn't bother with the mat. Another cloudless night kept them company.

"I want you to know I'd do it again," Marie whispered to him, her eyes unfocused and her mind foggy.

"Marie..." Grant stroked her back ever so gently.

She slipped in and out of consciousness, memories and images mixing, past and present chasing after each other. "Again and again and again."

***

"Hurry, bring me some water and a blanket."

"Are they alive?"

"I don't know…"

"My Heavens, they're nothing but kids—"

"Did we get to them in time?"

"I can a feel a pulse on the boy."

"What about her?'

I'm alive.

"She's such a small thing."

"All skin and bones."

"Is she breathing?"

"Yes, I can see her chest moving now."

CHAPTER 17

Feeling cold, Marie reached out from under the blanket, her fingers searching for the familiar warmth of his side. Her hand traveled on the smooth surface until her arm was stretched and her fingers fell over the edge. She patted the empty space, the smile turning up the corners of her lips slowly fading. "Grant?" When there was no answer, her eyes shot open, a few confused memories of fragmented conversations coming back to her.

Sitting upright, she looked around at her surroundings. She was in a room about the size of the one she had shared with Verena. Too big to contain only the one narrow bed she was sitting on, the nightstand on which someone had left a tray with some food and a pitcher of water, and a worn-looking chair. On the wall opposite the bed, a rectangular window opened on a sight she wasn't able to categorize at first. Bright light inundated the room, but she wasn't looking at the desert. She left the bed and tiptoed on bare feet to the window. Before her eyes lay a city the likes of which she had never seen.

She leaned over the windowsill and peeked outside, her head going up and down to take in the whole picture. She was inside a gigantic funnel made of red rock. A natural conic formation, which had been excavated inside to make space for human dwellings. At its base, several stories below her window, there were plazas and what looked like gardens. The whole place looked still in the construction stages: some of the structures were finished; others were being built. She looked up and saw that the funnel ended in a big opening from where the light came in.

A knock made her jump. She swung around and saw the door to the right of the bed. "Yes?" she automatically said.

"Can we come in?" an adult male voice asked.

She looked down at herself, and besides not wearing shoes, she still had her dusty clothes on.

"Yes."

The handle was lowered and two men entered. One was older, maybe in his forties or fifties, difficult to judge since he had some gray hair, but he also carried the bearing of a younger man. The other was definitely younger, in his late twenties, as lean in physique as the older. It was always hard to guess a man's age.

"How do you feel?" the older man asked. His voice was warm and his dark-brown eyes gentle.

"Fine, where's Grant?" Marie had retracted to the window, her eyes darting between the two men and the open door.

The older man walked a step closer to her. "Your friend needs to rest some more—"

Panic swelled in her chest. "Where is he? Why isn't he here with me?"

The older man raised his hands in the air, a gentle smile tugging at his mouth. "Don't worry. We took him to the infirmary. He was severely dehydrated."

"Do you want to see him?" the younger man asked.

"May I?" Marie was already heading to the door.

"Of course you can. But wouldn't you like to eat something first?" He looked at the untouched tray.

"It can wait." She only wanted to see him and make sure he was fine.

The two men seemed pleased by her reaction. The younger showed her the way with a flourish of his hand. "After you." He waited for her to pass them and then added, "We weren't sure you were out there of your own will."

For some reason, she felt the urge of defending Grant's honor. "Of course I was!"

The older man smiled. "Later, I'd love to hear your story, Marie."

She stopped in her tracks and stared at him. "How do you know my name?"

His smile widened. "Your friend—Grant you said his name was—right?"

She nodded.

"Grant called your name several times in his sleep." He gave another warm look and then waved his hand in the air as if he were forgetting something. "This is Lucas—"

The younger guy tipped his head in salute.

"And everybody knows me as the Priest." The older man said his name as if it were an amusing joke.

She wondered about the title. As far as she knew, there were no such things as priests on Ginecea. She didn't even know there was a male version of the word priestess.

"Life has a sense of humor sometimes that is difficult to understand." The Priest seemed to have read her mind.

Meanwhile, they had reached the end of a landing that ended in a low parapet overlooking the hustle below. "Welcome to the City of Men." Lucas's eyes swept from side to side and she followed his gaze to take in the incredible sight.

"How long have you been building it?" She couldn't help but be impressed.

"Almost thirty years." The Priest leaned out from the parapet and waved at a group of men working below. They were excavating a new house from the look of it. "There're still so many things to do."

She thought that whatever they had done was nothing short of a miracle already.

"But I don't think you're interested in the city tour." The Priest turned to face the corridor that ran the length of the parapet and disappeared behind an arch. "Your friend is this way." He walked under the arch and gestured for her to follow them through another long corridor at the end of which stood a door.

Marie walked behind the two men, looking at the activities taking place downstairs. "Are there only men living here?" She had been looking for a woman for the last five minutes and didn't see one.

She saw Lucas exchanging a glance with the older man who nodded. He tilted his head over his right shoulder to peek at her. "Women don't live inside the city."

"They don't?"

Lucas shook his head.

"But why?" She was confused.

"Unfortunately, even in the middle of the desert, Ginecea still rules our hearts." The Priest sighed.

"Some of the men aren't comfortable around women, and so the women prefer to live outside the city proper," Lucas explained.

"But, I'm here." She looked around, suddenly nervous.

"Nobody would dare lay a hand on you. You're under the Priest's protection." Lucas smiled at her.

Marie didn't feel reassured. "What about the other women?"

Lucas frowned, but the Priest seemed to have understood her question. "Any person who asks asylum is welcome here. Men, women, and kids are all under my protection."

"Do you have kids?" She gave a brief glance downstairs to confirm what she already knew. There were only male adults around.

"We have men and women living together." Lucas smiled.

She saw he didn't mean to be crude, but she still blushed. Certain habits are difficult to forget. "Of course." They were at end of the corridor.

"We have several mixed families." The Priest paused before the door. "But they prefer to live separate from us." He knocked on it.

She shrugged. "Why?" After spending time at Vasura, she wasn't as shocked to hear that they had mixed families as she should have been and didn't understand why they would keep by themselves when they could have stayed there.

Both men turned to look at her in puzzlement.

"They are men and women who have kids—" It was clear Lucas tried to be as gentle as possible while breaking the truth to her.

"I know what you meant by mixed." It was her turn to smile.

"And it doesn't sound strange to you?" the Priest casually asked, but the light in his eyes betrayed his interest in her answer.

She felt she was being judged, but it didn't matter. "Not anymore."

Lucas's mouth opened, but someone screamed from the other side of the door.

"What did you do to her?" a hoarse voice distorted by the walls demanded.

Lucas sprung the door open. "What's…?"

The Priest raised one hand to stop Marie from entering the room. "Wait here." He followed Lucas inside.

Scuffling noises reached her ears. One or more chairs were thrown around by the sound of it. "Take me to her! Now!"

Marie recognized Grant's voice and stormed inside without thinking. Several people turned to look at her. The scene she witnessed would have been comic if it weren't for the fact that Grant was fighting three men who seemed to be trying to prevent him from harming himself, and Grant looked like he could barely stand. As soon as he saw her, he fell on the floor like a sack of potatoes. A stark naked sack of potatoes. "Grant…" Her first instinct took her by his side in two strides, but then her eyes went to his private parts and she choked back a cry.

A long, awkward moment passed before any of the people reacted. Lucas finally came to their rescue by removing a linen sheet from a bed and draping it around Grant, who wearily thanked him and then asked Marie if she was okay.

"I'm fine. What about you?" She couldn't help but see him naked although he was entirely covered by the white sheet. She'd had only a brief peek before averting her eyes, but one thing was clear: he was quite different from her.

"Now, I am too. I was worried they had done something to you." He had lowered his voice on the second statement, but Lucas shook his head and the Priest sighed. "She's a fathered girl." He looked at them in defiance.

Although she was sure at least Lucas wanted to reply to Grant, he didn't. Instead, he waited for the Priest to answer. "Nothing will happen to her while she's here. I promise."

Grant bit his bottom lip, gave her a sideways look, and ate back whatever he had thought of saying. "Thank you."

The Priest nodded. "Now that the misunderstanding has been cleared, can I ask you, both of you, what your intentions are?"

Grant's eyes widened, his hands clutching at the sheet. "We have nowhere to go."

The Priest looked at Marie. "Is it true for you too?"

She felt an unfamiliar sting to her heart. "Ginecea sentenced us both to death." She hadn't realized until now how painful it was to face reality. She had been busy running for her life with no time to reminisce, but she truly was dead to the world. It wasn't a pleasant feeling.

"Are you looking for asylum?" Lucas turned from her to Grant.

She looked at Grant.

He reached out and took her hand in his. "Only if she's welcome too and only if we can live together."

The Priest was waiting for her to say the words.

She didn't have to think about her answer. "I'll only stay with him."

"You look too young to live together," Lucas commented, one eyebrow raised.

"If we're not welcome here, we'll leave." Grant threw an arm over her shoulders and lifted himself upright.

"We'll find a place right for us." Marie looked at the door, but the Priest stopped her.

"I would never send anybody away. Especially two children." He smiled and then reached them and cupped their united hands in his. "I declare you citizens of the City of Men." He gave both of them a paternal embrace.

"They're barely older than Randal," Lucas muttered under his breath.

"Your son is a toddler." The Priest turned to him and chuckled.

Lucas gave them another look and then waved his hand in their direction, as if the gesture were self-explanatory. "Exactly my point."

The Priest dismissed him with one of his quiet smiles and said to Grant, "I see that you've recovered sooner than we expected."

The three men Grant had been hitting with the chairs, which lay upside down on the floor, nodded their consent for him to leave the infirmary. "He's all yours," one of them said, relief evident in his voice.

"What about some clothes?" Lucas gave Grant a thorough look, the corner of his lip turning up in an amused smile.

"There's a change of clothes ready for him." The man who had talked earlier pointed toward one of the linen cabinets on the opposite wall.

"Then it's settled. Thank you." The Priest helped the three men straightening up the chairs, while Grant hastily donned a shirt and a pair of pants from behind the sheet Lucas held for him as a screen.

"Are we decent?" the Priest asked Grant but winked at Marie. "If you feel like it, we could show you the city and then let you decide where you want to stay." After Marie and Grant nodded, he motioned for them to follow him outside.

Only a step out on the corridor and her stomach growled. She pressed both hands on her belly to silence it. Without looking at her, Grant complained about being too hungry to be able to do anything.

"I could use some breakfast myself. How about you, Lucas?" The Priest took the lead and guided them out of the first corridor, but instead of entering the arch, he opened a door she hadn't noticed before, focused as she was on the sight below.

They walked through a short hallway that resembled a nursery by the number of potted plants dotting the floor and hanging from the walls. "One of my pet projects." The Priest caressed a succulent leaf jutting out from one of the vases near the door. "We need to change the acidity of the soil," he commented, but it sounded like a note to himself.

The hallway opened to a staircase that wound up for several floors. Marie didn't mind the hike, but given her dislike for small, crowded spaces—although the stairwell was lit by sconces and decorated with more plants and even an attempt at a partial mural of a seascape—she was glad when they reached the landing that opened on the open space that constituted the inner part of the city.

"Sorry, more stairs to climb." The Priest showed her the next stairwell.

Rounding the corner, her eyes went to an elaborate metal cage opening onto the landing suspended by a sturdy-looking cable.

"We're working on it, but the elevator isn't ready yet." The Priest looked at the contraption with proud eyes.

"I won't ever step inside that thing," Lucas commented, passing by. "And it takes too much manpower to operate it anyway."

Marie would have preferred riding the elevator, even if it meant being suspended in midair for several minutes. Anything was better than climbing stairs that were becoming narrower and narrower as they went up. The hike seemed to take forever.

Lucas's words partially echoed her thoughts. "Still can't understand why you chose to live up here. What's wrong with the ground floor?"

"Nothing wrong with that. I just like to be close to the sky."

The Priest's wistful tone made her think there was a whole story behind that sentence, but they were finally stopping before a door at the end of what was hopefully the last landing, and she was happy for the light. The older man didn't knock, but lowered the handle and entered.

Before following him inside, she took a good look at the view from the parapet and felt immediately dizzy. She raised her eyes and saw they were close to the very top of the city. From downstairs, she hadn't realized how big the opening on the city's ceiling was. The circular hole was so large she had an unobstructed view of the sky above. She didn't have a way to compare its size with anything else, but the opening was probably as vast as several stadiums combined.

Standing by her, Grant too was contemplating the structure. "Is it natural?"

Lucas, already on the other side of the door, stepped back and looked up. "Yes. An unexpected gift from Mother Nature."

"Coming in?" the Priest called.

Lucas led them in first and then closed the door behind. "To the kitchen."

They walked through a small corridor on which three doors opened, and they found the older man in the last room. "Have a seat."

Marie and Grant sat at the table, nothing more than a beam on four legs. She noticed the look and hastily thrown-together feel the place emanated. "Have you been here for long?"

"No, he just moved a few days ago," Lucas answered.

The Priest had his back to them, busy at what looked like a rudimentary stove. "The moving wasn't so bad."

"For you it wasn't. I was the one hauling all your stuff." Lucas sat on the last vacant stool, saw it was rickety, and stood up again to check one of its three legs.

"You wanted to help." The older man's shoulders moved as if he were trying to quit laughing without Lucas being the wiser. It didn't work.

The younger man turned his eyes to the ceiling. "I really don't understand why you would prefer to live here alone when you could be closer to the people who care about you."

The Priest tinkered some more with the stove and then moved out of the way to reveal a teapot and a pan. "You worry too much about me." His hands full, he walked to the table, balancing the fuming teapot, the pan containing scrambled eggs, and a knit bag hanging from his left little finger. "Your sister's tea-scones."

"Can't believe it. Lorena cooks my favorites for you and not for me." Lucas took the knit bag from him and arranged the contents on a plate, handling the scones with care.

The smell of baked goods invaded the small room and Marie's stomach made a sound so loud everybody laughed, herself included. Lucas handed her one of the scones, while the Priest fetched cups for the tea. She ate in silence. "I've never tasted anything as good as those scones," she said when the last crumb disappeared inside her mouth, which elicited a second round of laughs.

"I'll tell my sister, but I won't specify you were starved and severely dehydrated." Lucas reached for the pan and served her a heaving portion of scrambled eggs. "Catch of the day. Gift of our chicken coop."

"Where are we going to stay?" Grant abruptly asked, playing with the food on his plate. He had stood silently beside her the whole time, seemingly lost in his thoughts. "Not here, right?"

The Priest removed a cloth satchel from the teapot and wrung it with a teaspoon, then slowly poured the tea for everybody. "One day, the City of Men will be a place safe for everybody. We're working hard to reach that, but we aren't there yet."

Marie sipped her tea, her heart heavy. She liked it there. "So?"

The Priest drank from his cup and then answered, "Two friends of mine have built a safe place for mixed couples and they have a teenage daughter—"

Lucas smacked his forehead. "The Sanctuary, of course. Excellent idea."

The Priest gave him a look.

"What is this Sanctuary?" Grant laid a hand on hers under the table.

"What I said, a place where heterosexual couples can live." The Priest put his cup on the table. "Have second and third helpings and then we'll go meet Arias and Guen."

"Yes, let's go." Lucas put away his plate and stood.

Marie and Grant exchanged a glance and then they silently agreed to get it over with. She took his hand and they followed the two men out of the Priest's apartment. Going down seemed faster, mostly because she knew they would eventually reach larger spaces and she already knew the way.

"I can't believe they've managed to build all of this without Ginecea being the wiser," Grant whispered when they stopped on a landing to give the Priest time to greet some men.

"I think pure breeds want to believe what they want to believe, and as they treat Vasura as if it doesn't exist, they could never envision men were capable of building an entire city under their noses. Therefore, they would never look for it." Marie had been thinking about it since she had exited her room.

"Even though—" Grant looked first down and then up, encompassing the city in its entire length.

"You'll see in a moment that it isn't easy to spot the city from the outside." Lucas smiled at them from their right side.

Marie hadn't noticed the man was walking so close to them.

"Hopefully, you'll get to see it today..." Lucas commented, his eyes on the older man, who was deep in conversation with a new set of men who had supplanted the first.

Soon it was evident that his fear was funded. If at the beginning they had descended through several layers of the city without a hitch, the lower they went, the more people were interested in exchanging words with the Priest. An hour later, Lucas proposed to escort Marie and Grant by himself. The Priest nodded to him and saluted them with a nod of his head while answering somebody else's question at the same time.

"It's always like that?" Grant asked, finally leaving the landing they had been waiting on for the last forty-five minutes.

"It's normally worse. He barely sleeps at all." Lucas looked back at the other man and Marie noticed the affection in his eyes and the softness of his tone when he talked about the Priest.

"Have you known him long?" she asked.

Lucas smiled. "All my life."

Grant frowned at the man's answer.

"I was born here," Lucas explained. "My mom and dad still live in the Caves."

"What are the Caves?" Marie was starting to compare the City of Men to Vasura in terms of social complexity.

"When this settlement was established, heterosexual families were the target of severe harassment. My father and my mother, along with other couples expecting kids, looked for an alternative to the city and found a system of caves big enough to host them. They've created a self-sufficient community." Lucas led the way downstairs without further complications. He nodded once or twice to men who saluted him, but never stopped to talk to them.

"They have no interaction with the city?" Grant asked.

Marie's eyes went to a mural that, from the vibrant colors, was created by the same artist who had started the one she had seen before. It was another marine scene.

"The Priest makes sure they aren't severed from the city. He wants cohabitation, not division." Lucas followed her eyes and said, "That's a kids' project. The Priest teaches classes and that's one of last year's community projects to bring all the citizens together. Regardless of where they live." He passed a finger over an octopus' tentacle.

Marie liked the drawings even more. "But we aren't going to the Caves… why?"

"The Caves are for families with kids—" Lucas started, but Grant interrupted him.

"The place where the Priest is sending us, the Sanctuary, hosts heterosexual families as well. I don't understand."

"It's true. The Sanctuary was created by Guen and Arias when they discovered they were expecting their daughter. They used to live in the city…" Lucas paused to wave at someone. "Actually, they're the ones who helped build the city."

Marie found the children's signatures on the bottom of the mural. "I still don't understand why they decided to live by themselves and not join the Caves."

"It's the other way around. They built the Sanctuary first. The other families looked for a different solution."

"Why?" Both Marie and Grant asked at the same time.

"Because as the Priest said, Ginecea's preconceptions managed to follow us even in the middle of nowhere." Lucas saw someone walking toward him and muttered, "I'll build some hidden passageways into this city yet…" Then he left before the man could reach him. After that, the conversation died. He doubled his pace and Marie and Grant had to run to keep up with him.

Finally, they reached the ground level and she was surprised, once more, by the dimensions of the city. From upstairs, she had seen the plazas and the gardens and the shops, but hadn't realized how big everything was.

"Thirty years in the making and still so many things to do." Lucas echoed the Priest's words and they sounded funny in his mouth.

Marie would have loved to spend some time with Grant sitting on one of the benches dotting the gardens. From upstairs, she had seen several secluded spots. Lucas was in a hurry though and dragged them away from the recreational grounds to enter another dim hallway that ended in a small room where a man stood guard.

"Taking them to the Sanctuary," Lucas announced after briefly saluting the man, who gave Marie and then Grant a thorough look.

"Another one of them—" the man said, keeping his eyes on Grant. "A women-lover." He spat on the ground. "As if we need those here."

Marie shivered. She hadn't liked the man's tone from the beginning, but then he had gone too far with the insults. Grant's hand stiffened around her fingers. She squeezed back, trying to silently tell him to let it go, not to confront the man.

Lucas seemed equally annoyed by the man's comments but only shook his head slightly. "Let's go."

"What a waste," were the man's last words as a gate was opened and they left the City of Men behind.

Lucas waited until the gate fully closed behind them, probably more to compose himself than for fear of being heard from the inside, and then said, "Don't ever respond to such provocations. Those people enjoy making you lose your temper and can't wait to beat you up."

"It isn't easy." Grant looked back at the gate.

"That idiot isn't worth your anger." Lucas patted his shoulder. "Last hike of the day for you."

After that exchange, they walked on a path that wound up in a serpentine motion and led them to higher ground. Marie welcomed the outdoor exercise. The smell from the desert was a balm for her nerves. The man's cruel words and attitude had unnerved her and she had to breathe in and out for several minutes before she could talk again. When they reached the top of a plateau, Lucas made them turn and look at the valley below.

He smiled and she wondered what he was looking at, then she understood his previous statement about the city not being so easy to spot from the outside.

"Isn't our city beautiful?" Lucas asked, his eyes bright.

Marie nodded in agreement while Grant whispered, "I've never seen anything as beautiful."

She could barely believe her eyes, but from up there, it was almost impossible to make out the city from the rocky formation lying at the bottom of the plateau. It only took a slight tilt of the head to look at the red rocks from a different angle and discern the layers that composed the city. The structure resembled a multilevel cake where the ceilings of the buildings underneath composed the floors of the next layer. She sat on a flat rock and stood there silent for a few minutes, unable to peel her eyes away from the sight. A thought, almost a prayer, formed in her mind. *Goddess, never let Ginecea here.*

Lucas gave them a few minutes and then called them. "The Sanctuary is less than an hour from here, but the sun is getting closer to the zenith and it isn't safe to stay outside without proper clothes and water." He muttered something else about having lost enough time in social greetings, but it wasn't meant for their ears and Marie tuned him out. Her worries lifted with every step.

Hand in hand with Grant, she bathed in the sun. She had always loved to be in the outdoors and never had the chance. The uncertainty about her future a heavy weight on her heart, she had decided to live by the moment and enjoy anything life was throwing at her. From the moment she had left the Institute months ago, nothing had happened the way she had expected. She was quite sure she wasn't the same Marie who had left the safety of the place where she had been raised to pursue a job she hadn't even known she would like. She had always dreamed of a different life from the one she had been served since birth. A smile curved her lips before she could suppress it, and then she realized she didn't want to.

"What is it?"

She opened her eyes to see Grant looking at her, his big green eyes staring at her in wonder. With Lucas a few steps ahead of them, she laughed and then pulled Grant to her, looking for his lips.

"This is the first day of my new life. Forever." She laughed at her words, joy bubbling inside her heart and making her feel light. "And I want to spend it with you."

A cry resounded over their heads and Marie looked up. An eagle soared in the sky, wings spread, riding the thermals. Its silhouette projected against the sun. Grant picked her up, and while swirling her around, his lips searched for hers.

"I love you." He kissed her.

"I love you." She closed her eyes, returned the kiss, and smiled, feeling as free as the eagle flying high above them. "I will always love you."

Dear Reader, if you liked this book, please consider writing a review. As an indie author, I rely solely on word of mouth to promote my stories. Just a few words from you will ensure my work is discovered by other readers.

Monica

Backstory and Acknowledgments

The core of this novel was written during Nanowrimo 2012, and since then it has changed title several times. The original idea was to depict what happened between the last two chapters in *The Priest*, but the character of Marie, a young fathered woman, demanded a different story. So, while I was writing this book, titles changed to reflect the overall atmosphere of the novel. *The City of Men* became *Journey to the City of Men*, and finally I surrendered to the evidence that I was never going to center Marie's story around the City of Men's wars, and I decided that the best title would be *Marie's Journey*.

The Team

I wrote *Marie's Journey* and I take full responsibility for it
Amy Eye edited it
Cassie McCown proofread it
Alessandro Fiorini created the amazing cover
Roberto Ruggeri formatted it
You, the reader, hopefully liked Marie's story as much as I did writing it

Bio

Monica La Porta is an Italian who landed in Seattle several years ago. Despite popular feelings about the Northwest weather, she finds the mist and the rain the perfect conditions to write. Being a strong advocate of universal acceptance and against violence in any form and shape, she is also glad to have landed precisely in Washington State. She is the author of The Ginecean Chronicles, a dystopian/science fiction series set on the planet Ginecea where women rule over a race of enslaved men and heterosexual love is considered a sin. She has published *The Priest, Pax in the Land of Women*, and *Prince at War*. She is currently editing the fourth in the Ginecean series. She also wrote and illustrated a children's book about the power of imagination, *The Prince's Day Out*. Her latest published short, *Linda of the Night*, is a fairytale love story celebrating inner beauty. Stop by her blog to read about her miniatures, sculptures, paintings, and her beloved beagle, Nero. Sometimes, she also posts about her writing.

Monica La Porta's blog: http://www.monicalaporta.com

The Ginecean Chronicles Facebook page:
http://www.facebook.com/ginecea

The Prince's Day Out Facebook page:
http://www.facebook.com/ThePrincesDayOut

Goodreads Author page:
http://www.goodreads.com/author/show/5757332.Monica_La_Porta

Twitter: http://twitter.com/momilp

OTHER BOOKS BY MONICA LA PORTA

To keep up to date with Monica's new releases and promotions scan the QR code with your smartphone or mobile device.

The Priest – Book One of the Ginecean Chronicles
Mauricio is a slave. Like any man born on Ginecea, he is but a number to the pure breed women who rule over him with cruel hands. Imprisoned inside the Temple since birth, Mauricio has never been outside, never felt the warmth of the sun on his skin. He lives a life devoid of hopes and desires. Then one day, he hears Rosie sing. He risks everything for one look at her and his life is changed forever. An impossible friendship blossoms into affection deemed sinful and perverted in a society where the only rightful union is between women. Love is born where only hate has roots and leads Mauricio to uncover a truth that could destroy Ginecea.

Pax in the Land of Women – Book Two of the Ginecean Chronicles
Love doesn't obey preordained rules. Sometimes, social status and gender mean nothing. The purest of affections can be born between two people living in different worlds. In a society where women rule over an enslaved race of men and love between a woman and man is considered a perversion, Pax's and Prince's union is destined for a tragic end. Coming from an existence of privilege, Pax has never endured harshness. She has never had any reason to doubt the rules Ginecea was built on. Everything changes when she is sent to

spend her summer on a desolate farm and is exposed to the ongoing brutalities against defenseless men. A wrong turn leads her to witness Prince's thrashing at the hands of the guards. One look from him and Pax's perfect life is shattered, the memory of his dark eyes haunting her night and day. As a pure breed, born to one of the most prestigious family in Ginecea, she would have never thought it possible to fall in love with a man. Marked as a sinner, Pax abjures her ancestry to save Prince's life. She hopes they can disappear into the desert, but social prejudice and political schemes give them no respite. The Priestess, the ruler of all Ginecea, has other plans for Pax Layan and her family. Second in The Ginecean Chronicles, Pax in the Land of Women is a dystopian tale set on the planet Ginecea.

Prince at War – Book Three of the Ginecean Chronicles

The City of Men has been destroyed. The pure breeds want him dead. Prince is still running for his life. This time, he's not alone. Pax and the rest of the survivors count on him to keep them alive in the unforgiving desert. Pursued by the heartless Priestess and the President of Ginecea, Prince and Pax fight to find a haven for their unborn child. He knows the two women won't stop at anything to achieve their goal. But he can't fathom the true reasons behind their motives. Ginecea wants the heads of anyone who helped the fugitive men and nobody is safe. Not even the fathered women, slaughtered by a Priestess crazed by hate. The world is in an uproar and Pax and Prince stand in the eye of the storm. Prince at War is the third book in The Ginecean Chronicles, a series set in the dystopian world of Ginecea where women rule over enslaved men, and heterosexual love is the ultimate sin.

Elios – Elios and Gaia Series

He had no name until she gave him one. Elios has existed for eons, yet he has never lived. As a Solean Observer, his latest assignment is to study human nature. When Earth reaches its final days, he will be the one judging whether humanity's memory deserves to be preserved. This is not his first mission, and he is confident that he will make Lex, his Ancestor Guide, proud once again. Then, in Athens, Elios locks eyes with Gaia, and for the first time in his long life, he develops feelings he doesn't have a name for. An impulse stronger than any he has ever felt will drive him to follow Gaia first to Rome, where she lives, and then across the ocean to the United States when she goes to study abroad. In Seattle, unable to fight his sentiments any longer, Elios finally approaches Gaia. What starts as an innocent desire to talk to her just once, soon becomes a fire Elios can't quench. And yet, bound by his oath as an Observer, he can't have any physical contact with her. Struggling between his duties to Solo, the planet that gave him birth, and Gaia, who has become the only reason for his existence, Elios must decide. But fate, in the form of an archeological finding discovered inside an Etruscan tomb, decides for him and Gaia, separating them. Although Elios is a companion novel to Gaia, they can be read in either order. They are both stand-alone stories from different points of view. You met Gaia and Elios in her book; now hear his story.

Gaia – Elios and Gaia Series
While vacationing in Greece, Gaia locks eyes with a stranger, twice. Two years later, back in Rome, she should be enjoying college life; instead, the memories of his lapis lazuli eyes and Mona Lisa smile still haunt her. Gaia longs to meet him again and unwittingly sabotages her romantic life by refusing to move on. Only her anthropological studies about the mysterious Etruscans make her feel alive. A chance to breathe new air is presented to her when she wins a full scholarship to study abroad at the University of Washington. In rainy Seattle, Gaia finally meets the man of her dreams, but he proves to be... otherworldly. Meanwhile, in her field of studies, what starts as an interesting archeological finding about a six-fingered human image, soon evolves into the discovery of the millennium, but not where Earth is concerned. Although Gaia is a companion novel of Elios, you can read these in either order. They are both stand-alone stories from different points of view. You met Gaia and Elios in his book; now hear her story.

The Prince's Day Out
Once upon a time, in a faraway land, there was a young prince who lived confined to his bedroom. Accompanied by his sister, he

traveled to the most incredible places thanks to his imagination. Follow the Prince and the Princess's fantastic journey through a magic kingdom where seagulls transport cities and ships sail on pearl necklaces instead of waves. Twelve whimsical drawings illustrate the story.

Linda of the Night

Linda was born with hair the color of the mature grain and eyes of the lightest shade of blue. Tall and willowy, she's the ugliest girl alive. Kept inside her house by her parents for fear of being ridiculed for her hideous appearance, Linda dreams of being like the dark-haired, curvaceous girls who live just outside her walls. One night, she dares the inconceivable and leaves the safety of her home. For the first time alone, Linda walks for hours until she is lost— only to find her destiny in the arms of a mysterious stranger.